MISTLETOE MADNESS

A SWEET, SMALL TOWN, CHRISTMAS ROMANCE
(SANTA'S SECRET HELPERS, BOOK 2)

LEEANNA MORGAN

ABOUT THIS BOOK

This Christmas, something magical is happening in Sapphire Bay.

Kylie loves everything about Christmas. The lights, the carols, the snow-covered streets and, most of all, the smiles on the faces of everyone she meets. Well, almost everyone. When her friends ask her to organize the biggest fundraising Christmas party Sapphire Bay has ever seen, the florist inside of her is itching to get started. But that means talking to Ben Thompson, the closest thing to the Christmas Grinch she's ever met.

Ben owns the only Christmas tree farm in Sapphire Bay, but that doesn't mean he's full of the Christmas spirit. He came to Montana searching for peace and quiet. But pesky Kylie Bryant, with her addiction to all things Christmassy, is driving him insane.

When Kylie helps him save his business, everything about her begins to make sense. She's getting under Ben's skin and making him feel alive. But a letter from his lawyer changes everything. Will a secret from his past tear them apart or will they finally get everything they've ever wanted?

Mistletoe Madness is the second book in the Santa's Secret Helpers series and can easily be read as a standalone. Each of Leeanna's series are linked so you can find out what happens to your favorite characters in other books. For news of my latest releases, please visit leeannamorgan.com and sign up for my newsletter. Happy reading!

Other Novels by Leeanna Morgan:

Montana Brides:
Book 1: Forever Dreams (Gracie and Trent)
Book 2: Forever in Love (Amy and Nathan)
Book 3: Forever After (Nicky and Sam)
Book 4: Forever Wishes (Erin and Jake)
Book 5: Forever Santa (A Montana Brides Christmas Novella)
Book 6: Forever Cowboy (Emily and Alex)
Book 7: Forever Together (Kate and Dan)
Book 8: Forever and a Day (Sarah and Jordan)
Montana Brides Boxed Set: Books 1-3
Montana Brides Boxed Set: Books 4-6

The Bridesmaids Club:
Book 1: All of Me (Tess and Logan)
Book 2: Loving You (Annie and Dylan)
Book 3: Head Over Heels (Sally and Todd)
Book 4: Sweet on You (Molly and Jacob)
The Bridesmaids Club: Books 1-3

Emerald Lake Billionaires:

Book 1: Sealed with a Kiss (Rachel and John)
Book 2: Playing for Keeps (Sophie and Ryan)
Book 3: Crazy Love (Holly and Daniel)
Book 4: One And Only (Elizabeth and Blake)
Emerald Lake Billionaires: Books 1-3

The Protectors:
Book 1: Safe Haven (Hayley and Tank)
Book 2: Just Breathe (Kelly and Tanner)
Book 3: Always (Mallory and Grant)
Book 4: The Promise (Ashley and Matthew)
The Protectors Boxed Set: Books 1-3

Montana Promises:
Book 1: Coming Home (Mia and Stan)
Book 2: The Gift (Hannah and Brett)
Book 3: The Wish (Claire and Jason)
Book 4: Country Love (Becky and Sean)
Montana Promises Boxed Set: Books 1-3

Sapphire Bay:
Book 1: Falling For You (Natalie and Gabe)
Book 2: Once In A Lifetime (Sam and Caleb)
Book 3: A Christmas Wish (Megan and William)
Book 4: Before Today (Brooke and Levi)
Book 5: The Sweetest Thing (Cassie and Noah)
Book 6: Sweet Surrender (Willow and Zac)
Sapphire Bay Boxed Set: Books 1-3
Sapphire Bay Boxed Set: Books 4-6

Santa's Secret Helpers:
Book 1: Christmas On Main Street (Emma and Jack)
Book 2: Mistletoe Madness (Kylie and Ben)
Book 3: Silver Bells (Bailey and Steven)

Book 4: The Santa Express (Shelley and John)
Book 5: Endless Love (The Jones Family)
Santa's Secret Helpers Boxed Set: Books 1-3

Return To Sapphire Bay:
Book 1: The Lakeside Inn (Penny and Wyatt)
Book 2: Summer At Lakeside (Diana and Ethan)
Book 3: A Lakeside Thanksgiving (Barbara and Theo)
Book 4: Christmas At Lakeside (Katie and Peter)
Return to Sapphire Bay Boxed Set (Books 1-3)

The Cottages on Anchor Lane:
Book 1: The Flower Cottage (Paris and Richard)
Book 2: The Starlight Café (Andrea and David)
Book 3: The Cozy Quilt Shop (Shona and Joseph)
Book 4: A Stitch in Time (Jackie and Aidan)

CHAPTER 1

*K*ylie hurried across the parking lot and stepped inside The Welcome Center. With a quick wave at the receptionist, she headed toward Pastor John's office.

She was late. Again.

It wasn't as if this was one of the fundraising group's usual catch-up meetings. She had an emergency and only her friends could help her.

With a quick knock, she opened the office door. John, Emma, and Bailey sat around the desk with spreadsheets, laptops, and cups of coffee in front of them.

"Sorry I'm late."

"Don't worry." Emma's smile did nothing to calm Kylie's nerves. "Bailey was telling us about the Christmas carol competition."

For the last three months, they'd been organizing events to raise money for Sapphire Bay's tiny home village. As well as adding some early Christmas cheer to the community, the events were bringing more tourists to the small Montana town. Last weekend they'd held the Main Street Santa Claus

Parade and the Night Market. Both events were a huge success—which made her news even harder to share.

Pastor John handed her a cup of coffee. "Have a seat. You looked stressed."

"I am." Kylie took off her jacket and sat beside Emma. "I'm sorry I called an emergency meeting, but I didn't know what else to do."

Bailey leaned forward. "What's happened?"

"We can't use the community center for the Christmas party. The water pipes burst and no one can use any of the rooms for at least four weeks."

Emma's eyes widened. "When did that happen?"

"Last night. I've called all the venues that can seat two hundred guests, but they're booked for weddings and other events."

Kylie loved living in the small town but, sometimes, when you needed something at the last minute, your choices were severely limited. Like now. If she were still living in San Francisco, she could have easily found a hotel or conference facility. But this wasn't California. This was a small town on the edge of Flathead Lake.

"Have you asked the McGraw's?" Emma asked. "Jack and I were looking at wedding venues last weekend and their barn is amazing."

"It's booked. I even called the Cozy Inn, but their conference room is too small." Kylie pulled a list out of her bag. "These are the places I've tried. If you can think of another venue, I'd really appreciate it."

John studied the sheet of paper. "Do the caterers need a commercial kitchen?"

"Probably not. They have a mobile kitchen they can use to keep the food hot. Have you thought of somewhere we could use?"

"Maybe. I'd have to talk to the foreman, but what about

the old steamboat museum? We'd have to move the half-finished tiny homes into the yard, and our tools and supplies would need to be stored somewhere else, but it could work."

The old steamboat museum was on the outskirts of town. When John was looking for somewhere to build relocatable tiny homes, he saw the abandoned building's potential. With its incredibly high ceilings, arched windows, and large foyer, it could also be a stunning venue for a Christmas party.

Emma tapped her pen against her chin. "It could work. The kitchen is too small, but if the catering company can bring a mobile kitchen, it won't matter."

Bailey frowned. "The main hall is enormous. Do we have the time and the budget to make it look amazing?"

"Maybe not." Kylie pulled another file from her bag. "The flood damaged most of the decorations we were going to use. Renting more decorations will be expensive. And with our limited budget, buying new ones isn't an option, either."

Emma wrote something down on a piece of paper. "I'm heading into town tonight to speak to the Business Association about last weekend's events. I'll ask them if they know anyone who could help."

"That would be great."

"What about Ben? Has he decided to donate the Christmas trees?"

Kylie sighed. "Not yet, but he's still happy to provide the mistletoe." Of all the people who lived in Sapphire Bay, Ben was the hardest to figure out. "He's stopped answering my phone calls. I don't know what his problem is. Anyone would think he doesn't like Christmas."

"We all have issues we're dealing with," John said softly. "If you tell him about the community center, he might be more willing to help."

"I don't think that will make a difference." Over the last few weeks, she'd tried everything she could think of to show

Ben how important the trees were to their events. She'd even resorted to bribery. But no amount of gingerbread men, Christmas cookies, or shortbread made a difference. For someone who owned a Christmas tree farm, he was the most "unchristmassy" person she knew.

"As a last resort, we could use the artificial trees on Main Street," Emma suggested. "The store owners won't mind if they aren't there for a few days."

Kylie shook her head. "The whole point of having our events start a few months before Christmas was to encourage tourists to come here. If we take away the trees, Main Street won't look the same."

"Kylie's right," Bailey said. "Try Ben one more time. You never know—he might change his mind when he hears what's happened."

Kylie looked around the table. "Regardless of what he says, I don't think we have any choice but to use the old museum. The profit we make from the Christmas party will pay for at least one tiny home. I don't want to give that up."

"I agree," Emma said. "Apart from not being able to build another tiny home, we'll have two hundred disappointed ticket holders calling us."

"I'll talk to the foreman at the museum," Kylie said quickly before John could offer. He already worked long hours in the church and didn't need the added pressure of organizing the venue for the party. "If there are any issues, I'll send everyone an email."

"Are you sure?" John asked. "I don't mind—"

"I'm sure."

When Emma asked about the music for the party, Kylie had good news. "Willow can perform with her band. Her wedding is the following weekend, so the timing is perfect."

Bailey rubbed Kylie's arm. "At least that's one less thing to organize. If you need someone to help in your flower shop, I have Wednesdays available."

"And our youth employment program is always looking for job opportunities," John said. "There are a couple of students who would be more than capable of helping in your store."

"Thank you." Kylie appreciated her friends' support. Juggling the Christmas events, their Christmas wish program, and her business was becoming more difficult.

If one more thing went wrong, Ben wouldn't be the only person in Sapphire Bay who wasn't looking forward to Christmas.

ON HIS WAY THROUGH TOWN, Ben stopped at the traffic lights and glanced at Blooming Lovely, the flower shop Kylie Bryant owned. His eyes narrowed as he took in the fairy lights decorating the front window, the Christmas tree standing outside, and the baskets of red and white flowers filling the veranda with color.

Blooming Lovely wasn't the only store to break out the tinsel and bring the holiday season forward three months. The sleepy little Montana town had caught a serious case of "Christmasitis". And, judging by the amount of traffic on the road, it was increasing the number of people coming into town.

He just hoped the Christmas program raised enough money to build more tiny homes. He knew better than most how hard it was to start over, especially for the most vulnerable in a community.

Two years ago, he'd arrived in Sapphire Bay to begin a new life. Unlike most of the people who came here, he had savings and skills he could put to good use. Even so, he wondered what he'd been thinking. What did a builder know about growing Christmas trees?

His family and friends thought he was crazy. He'd never owned a garden. Even the indoor plants his mom insisted on bringing him wilted on the windowsill. But through sheer stubbornness, his business was making a small profit. It wouldn't make him rich, but it kept food in the pantry and gave him an excuse to work outside.

The traffic lights turned green and he joined the vehicles cruising down Main Street.

He hoped Kylie wasn't anywhere near The Welcome Center. The tree he'd loaded into the back of his truck might give her the wrong impression. If she saw it, she'd think all her prayers had been answered, but this was a special gift for the church. One tree he could donate. Twenty was out of the question.

He might not be an expert at growing Christmas trees, but he knew about budgeting. The modest salary he earned would disappear if twenty of his best trees ended up decorating a party—even if it was for a good cause. He had bills to pay and a mortgage that would keep him in Montana for a few more years.

Turning right, he headed toward the church. The sooner he saw Pastor John, the sooner he could return to the farm. And the sooner he would be away from the Christmas cheer that made his stomach churn.

JOHN STRODE across the parking lot toward Ben. "You made it here in good time."

"I'm glad I left when I did. It looks as though the Christmas events are bringing more people into Sapphire Bay."

"They are. Quite a few newspapers have run stories about what we're doing. Emma even gave an interview to a TV reporter yesterday."

Ben opened the tailgate of his truck. "The fundraising committee must be happy."

"They are. Thanks for bringing the tree into town."

"You're welcome. I can't supply the trees the fundraising committee want, but I'm hoping this one will brighten someone's day."

John grabbed one side of the tree as Ben pulled it out of the truck. "I'm sure it will. Can you do me a favor?"

"Sure."

"Next time you see Kylie, talk to her."

"It won't do any—" Ben followed John's gaze. Coming out of The Welcome Center was the woman he'd been dodging for the last week.

John cleared his throat. "Just so you know, I didn't plan this. Kylie called an emergency meeting."

"Can pastors tell white lies?"

"Only if they're very careful."

Ben ignored John's smile. His gaze traveled back to Kylie, absorbing everything about her in one earth-shattering sweep. She was, without a doubt, the most attractive woman he'd ever met.

She was also obsessed with everything Christmassy. Today, the fabric of her red knee-length dress had pictures of candy canes all over it. Her blond hair, normally caught in a ponytail, fell around her shoulders in soft, silky waves.

His eyes narrowed. She'd even dyed two wide strands of her hair, green. All she needed was pointy ears and she could have been one of Santa's elves.

She stopped in the middle of the sidewalk and frowned. It didn't look as though she wanted to see him, either. For someone who loved Christmas, it must be daunting to realize there was one person who didn't share her enthusiasm.

"Hi, Ben. I didn't expect to see you here." Kylie's gaze shifted to the tree. "Did you change your mind about supplying the Christmas trees for the party?"

He shook his head. The hopeful note in her voice made him feel bad. He knew how much the trees meant to her, but there had to be other decorations she could use. "This one is for The Welcome Center's living room."

She sighed. "It will look beautiful."

Ben gripped the string he'd wrapped around the branches. "I'm sorry I can't supply the trees."

Kylie walked toward him, the skirt of her dress swishing around her legs. "You've never told me why you can't donate them."

And he didn't want to. Admitting his business was going through a difficult time was like telling his family and friends they were right. Everyone had expected his business to fail, but he was still here. Just.

John adjusted his hands on the tree. "I need to leave for another meeting soon. Would you mind if we took this inside?"

"I'll help." Kylie stood beside the tree, her hands gripping the string that held everything tight.

Ben glanced at John, hoping he'd intervene and tell Kylie they could manage without her.

"That would be great," John said. "If you carry the top, we'll hold the sides."

Ben studied the innocent expression on John's face. If you didn't know him very well, you'd think he was being friendly. But John had an ulterior motive, and that motive involved Ben talking to Kylie.

With no excuse left, Ben repositioned his hands. When everyone was ready, they carefully carried the tree inside.

John nudged open the door to the living room. "We thought we'd put the tree between the piano and the sleigh."

Ben looked around the room. Someone had moved the sofas and chairs, creating a large open space in front of the glossy black piano.

His eyes widened when he saw the ornate wooden sleigh. With its high back, curved sides, and plush velvet seat, it was the perfect size for most of the children who stayed at the center.

He smiled when Mr. Whiskers, The Welcome Center's resident gray-haired cat, peeked his head out from under one of the runners. The children weren't the only ones who were enjoying the new piece of furniture.

John moved toward a bright red Christmas tree stand. "Mabel made sure everything was ready. She even mixed some of Kylie's special powder in the container beside the piano."

Ben frowned at the old juice bottle sitting on the floor.

"It's not illegal," Kylie muttered.

She was scowling so hard Ben almost smiled. "I didn't think it would be."

"It's the same powder I use to keep my flowers fresh. I thought it might stop the tree from drying out too quickly."

Ben lowered the trunk of the tree into the container. "If it drops too many needles, I'll bring the center another one."

When the tree was secure, Kylie stepped back and lifted her gaze to the ceiling. "It's the perfect height for this room."

"Let's see what it looks like out of its wrapping." He pulled out a knife and quickly cut through the string. As the branches fell into place, he walked around the ten-foot tree, making a few adjustments as he went. Thankfully, none of the branches were damaged on the journey here.

"Oh, my," Mabel said from the living room entrance. "That's one of the prettiest trees I've ever seen." As well as co-owning the town's general store, Mabel Terry spent many hours volunteering at The Welcome Center.

Ben's eyes widened. A red tinsel wreath sat on top of her hair and gold bells dangled from her ears. "You can thank the previous owners of the Christmas tree farm for that," he said. "It was planted more than fourteen years ago."

"Well, it sure is a beauty." Mabel picked up a remote control and pointed it toward the far wall. "We need some music. It will make it feel more like Christmas if we play some carols."

Stuffing the string into his pocket, Ben prepared to leave. After living with profound hearing loss in one ear, he knew when he was better off at home. The background noise would confuse his brain and make it impossible to hear what everyone said.

Kylie turned away and opened a box of decorations.

When she looked over her shoulder at him, he frowned. She was waiting for something, but he had no idea what it was.

"Kylie asked if you're selling many Christmas trees at the moment," John said.

Heat scorched his face. He should be used to missing parts of conversations. But he wasn't, not by a long shot. He hated not being able to hear what everyone said. Hated feeling as though he was damaged. That he was different.

He glanced at Kylie, hoping she didn't realize he was partially deaf. "It's too early for most people to buy a Christmas tree. Sales don't usually pick up until the end of November."

"I must order one for us," Mabel said with a smile. "Allan loves the smell of a real Christmas tree."

Ben picked up his gloves and looked over Mabel's shoulder. At least six children were walking into the room. "I'd better leave you to decorate the tree."

John beckoned the children forward. "This will bring a lot of joy to our guests. Thank you."

The children's eyes were wide with excitement.

"That's okay. With all the events happening around town, it would have been a shame not to make the center a little more festive." His gaze connected with Kylie's. She might think he was the Grinch, but he wanted everyone at the center to enjoy Christmas. "Good luck with the events you're organizing."

"Thanks. Would you mind if I walked back to your truck with you?"

That was the last thing he wanted. "I don't—"

John cleared his throat.

"Fine," he muttered. "But I have a lot of work to do."

Kylie took a piece of tinsel out of the box of decorations. "It will only take a few minutes."

And before he knew what she was doing, Kylie twisted the tinsel into a necklace and lifted it over his head. "Merry Christmas, Ben."

KYLIE KNEW Ben didn't want to talk to her, but she needed his trees more than ever. Without them, the old steamboat museum would look bare and uninviting—the last thing their guests would expect at a Christmas party.

She glanced at him. He hadn't said much since they'd left the living room. "How did you learn to grow Christmas trees?"

He opened the front doors and followed her into the parking lot. "When I was a teenager, I worked on a Christmas tree farm. The rest I've learned from the previous owners."

"You must be proud of what you've achieved."

Ben shrugged and she sighed. Most of the time, when she tried talking to him, he either changed the subject or didn't seem to hear her. He was one of the most frustrating people she knew, but that didn't mean she was giving up.

"We have to find another venue for the Christmas party."

His footsteps slowed. "Why aren't you having it at the community center?"

"One of the water pipes burst. It will take a few weeks to fix everything."

"Where will you go?"

"John suggested the old steamboat museum. It has the space we need and it's close to town."

"It's also full of half-finished tiny homes and all the tools and building materials the construction crews need."

"We don't have a lot of choice. Everything else is booked."

"There must be somewhere."

"Not that I've found." Kylie looked across the parking lot. The first stage of the tiny home village was well underway. Ten houses sat tall and proud on the large lot, each of them built by volunteers.

On the hardest days, when juggling her business and volunteering at The Welcome Center was too much, she thought of the people waiting for a house. The tiny home village was their last chance to feel a sense of belonging, of being part of a community that cared about them. And for some people, it was the first time they'd had anywhere to call home.

Ben pulled up the zipper on his jacket. "The steamboat museum is huge. How are you going to decorate it?"

"We'll have to rely on other organizations to help us. Emma is talking to the local business association tonight and Mabel will approach some of her suppliers. Hopefully, we can borrow or buy enough decorations to make the museum look less like a spaceship."

Ben grunted.

Did he just smile?

"You'll need a cherry picker to reach the high ceilings."

She'd need more than that to help fill the enormous space. "I spoke to Willow after my meeting with the fundraising committee. A friend of hers designs the lighting for her concerts. She thinks we can use some kind of laser system to create a holiday feel without spending thousands of dollars on decorations."

"So you don't need the Christmas trees?"

"We do. The trees will give a real Christmas feel to the party, especially if we don't have a lot of other decorations." Kylie bit her bottom lip. She was so excited when her friends had asked her to organize the Christmas fundraising party. She'd walked through the community center, imagined a winter wonderland, and begged and borrowed what she could to make the dream a reality.

But most of that was gone.

She took a deep breath. "I know you said you can't donate the trees. Would you change your mind if I helped recover the cost of them?"

"Each tree sells for seventy-five dollars. Multiply that by twenty and you have a whole lot of money I can't find anywhere else."

Kylie looked into his serious brown eyes. "I looked at your website. It needs a little work."

Ben frowned. "I'm not a web designer."

"You don't need to be," she said quickly. The last thing she wanted to do was offend him, but this was important. "I can't pay for the trees, but I can do something even better."

Kylie crossed her fingers, hoping Ben could see the benefit in what she was about to say. "I talked to my friend, Emma. She can update your website using mine as a template. All we need to do is take different photos and replace the text."

"That won't pay for the trees."

"No, but it will make it easier for customers to place online orders for your trees. I had some other ideas, too. What about selling a range of Christmas products? You could have wreaths, garlands, table centerpieces, and lots of other Christmas accessories for your customers to buy."

Ben's frown turned into a scowl. "I don't know how to make any of those things and I can't afford to buy them. And even if I could, I don't have the staff to organize everything."

She held onto Ben's arm. "I know it could work. No one else in Sapphire Bay sells Christmas trees, let alone locally made decorations. With all the visitors arriving for our events, it's the perfect opportunity to capture another market."

Ben's gaze focused on her fingers clutching his jacket.

Kylie dropped her hand. "Sorry. I get carried away where Christmas is concerned."

"I hadn't noticed."

A sinking feeling hit her chest. She'd said too much, tried too hard to make Ben see other ways he could earn money. "I need to get back to work. Thanks for listening to me." She had been so sure he would jump at the chance to have a new website and sell decorations, but she was wrong. Imagining the Christmas party without twenty glittering trees was difficult, but what choice did she have?

With a heavy heart, she opened the door to her truck. If she were lucky, Mabel might know someone who could—

"Do you know how to make wreaths and garlands?"

Kylie turned around. Ben was standing where she'd left him, scowling so hard that the end of the world could have been coming. "I do."

"Could you bring some samples out to the farm?"

Her mouth dropped open. "Okay."

"Call me first. If I'm working outside, I won't hear you arrive."

And before she said anything, Ben turned around and walked across the parking lot.

"Thank you!" she yelled.

He kept his head bowed, acting for all the world as if he hadn't heard her.

Kylie sighed. At least he was open to selling different products to make up for the cost of the trees.

And maybe, if she tried really hard to forget all the other times she'd talked to him, he wasn't so bad after all.

CHAPTER 2

*K*ylie held up a wreath decorated with silver ribbons and red berries. "What do you think?"

Bailey tilted her head to the side. "It's wonderful. If this doesn't encourage Ben to open a Christmas shop, I don't know what will."

For the last two hours, while Kylie put together samples to take to Ben, Emma and Bailey had been making decorations for the Christmas party. Even though Ben might provide the trees, they couldn't take his help for granted. With the party only three weeks away, they needed to work on the assumption that no one would help them decorate the museum.

Emma checked her watch. "I can only stay for another half hour. Jack is looking after the twins, but he needs to make some phone calls before nine o'clock."

Bailey placed a glittering table centerpiece on the counter. "It must be interesting living with a fiancé who looks for missing people."

"Some cases are heartbreaking. But, if I had to find anyone again, he would be the first person I'd call."

"That's because you love him," Kylie said with a smile.

"That's true, but he's also good at what he does. Do you want me to decorate the garland?"

Before her friends arrived, Kylie had made a three-foot garland from cedar and juniper branches. Glittery ribbons and small pine cones, twisted together with wire, were sitting in a box, waiting to be added.

"That would be great. If you need more decorations, there's some in the container beside the sink."

Emma slid off the stool. "I need to take some photos first. If you show Ben what his website could look like, it might change his mind about donating the trees." With her cell phone focused on the wreath Kylie had made, Emma snapped a series of pictures. "That should be enough. I'll do the same with the garland when it's finished."

"I don't know what I'd do without you both," Kylie said. "I didn't think Ben would be interested in my ideas for increasing his income."

Bailey picked up a metal frame. "It's not everyday someone comes to you with ways you can make more money."

Emma took a photo of Bailey's decorations. "Who works on the farm with him?"

Kylie had wondered the same thing until she'd spoken to Mabel. "Ben works on his own." Although, how he managed it, Kylie didn't know. The sign at the front of his property said he managed more than thirty acres of trees. Doing that on your own must be daunting, especially in the middle of winter.

Emma picked up a coil of fine wire. "Jack met Ben a couple of weeks ago. He said he used to be a builder. He worked in Los Angeles before coming here."

"I wonder why he bought a Christmas tree farm?" Bailey asked.

17

Kylie didn't know, but it wasn't because he liked Christmas. "Does anyone know if he has a problem with his hearing?"

Bailey shook her head. "I've only seen Ben in town a few times. We've never spoken to each other. What about you, Emma?"

"I haven't seen him very often, either. Why do you think he has a problem?"

"When we were in The Welcome Center, I asked him a question when he couldn't see my face. He had no idea what I'd said."

"The center can be noisy," Emma said. "Maybe he just didn't hear you."

"Apart from some Christmas music, the living room was quiet."

Bailey placed another bundle of foliage on the wreath she was creating. "He could have selective hearing. Mom keeps telling Dad he needs a hearing test, but he says he zones out when she talks."

Emma laughed. "I bet your mom had a few words to say about that."

"You've got no idea." Bailey glanced at the clock on the wall. "Sometimes Mom's reaction is more Italian than American. That was *definitely* one of those times. Didn't you say you wanted to leave by eight-thirty, Emma?"

Emma looked at her watch. "Oops. Thanks for the reminder. I wish I could stay longer."

Kylie took the clippers out of her friend's hand. "I appreciate everything you've done. I know how busy you are."

"How busy we all are." Emma hugged Kylie tight. "I'll work on a draft website for Ben tonight. When I've finished, I'll send you the link."

"Thanks. I'll let you know what he says."

Emma wrapped her arms around Bailey. "At least we can

say we've tried. If Ben can't supply the Christmas trees, we'll keep looking for another solution."

"He'll want to help after he sees the Christmas decorations," Bailey said. "Especially if the church has people who could make them."

That was what Kylie was hoping, too. But stranger things had happened, especially where their Christmas events were concerned.

THE FOLLOWING MORNING, Ben walked into The Welcome Center. Each month, a group of people got together who were dealing with PTSD. The only reason he was here was because John had sent him three texts, reminding him about the meeting.

As far as he was concerned, he'd dealt with the physical and emotional side of being beaten to a pulp. The doctors had told him he was lucky to be alive—if you could call a brain injury and permanent deafness in one ear being lucky.

After five years, he had come to the conclusion that his life was as good as it would get. He couldn't see the point of talking about the nightmares that filled his dreams or the bone-aching tiredness that sometimes overwhelmed him.

John walked toward him. "Glad you could make it."

Ben grunted. "You sent me enough reminders. Just so you know, I won't be at the next meeting. I can't afford to take any more time away from the farm."

"In that case, we're fortunate you're here today." John sent him a searching look. "You're tired. Is everything all right?"

He waved away John's concern. "I'm fine. It's busy on the farm, that's all." It wasn't all, not by a long shot, but his friend didn't need to know that.

John sighed. "Everyone's in the small meeting room. I just

need to get something from my office before I meet you there."

Ben's nose twitched as he walked across the foyer. The church's catering class always provided great food for their meetings. Whatever they'd cooked today smelled delicious.

He opened the door and glanced at the wooden sleigh sitting under the window. John must have wanted to add some Christmas cheer to their meeting.

Straight ahead of him, Gabe, Levi, and Zac were talking to each other as they sampled the food. James and Wyatt were deep in conversation with Georgia and, following Ben into the room, was Steven Butler, their newest member.

Steven stood on Ben's right-hand side. "I thought the food at the last meeting was for a special occasion."

"It's like this each month. Did you find someone to look after your daughter?"

"I didn't need to. She's back at school."

Like many people who moved to Sapphire Bay, Steven had been in the military. After serving two tours of duty in Afghanistan, he'd received an honorable discharge and found his way to the small Montana town. With no family or friends to support him, this group was as important to him as it was to everyone in the room.

"Have you started your new job?" Ben asked.

"This is my second week. The construction crews are completing the tiny homes almost as fast as we can plaster them."

Steven was working with a team of plasterers at the tiny home village. Because Christmas wasn't far away, Pastor John had moved the homes into the village as soon as they were weathertight. Not only did this free up space in the old steamboat museum for new construction, but it gave the plasterers, painters, and kitchen installers more space and time to finish the houses.

Ben pointed to the coffeepot. "Do you want a hot drink?"

"Sounds good."

While Ben poured two drinks, John walked into the room, holding a folder. Once everyone was seated, the reason for the paperwork became obvious.

"Before we catch up on what's been happening, I have a favor to ask. Over the past few months, the tiny home fundraising committee has spent a lot of hours organizing a series of Christmas events. At the same time, people are still sending us their Christmas wishes."

John opened the folder and handed each of them a copy of a spreadsheet.

Ben studied the first page. In between the stuffed toys, Lego sets, and new cell phones were wishes that wouldn't be so easy to answer. People were looking for jobs, money to pay hospital bills, and love.

John poured himself a cup of coffee. "The fundraising committee doesn't have a lot of time to make people's Christmas wishes come true. That's where we come in."

Georgia smiled. "You want us to play fairy godmother?"

"Fairy godmother on a shoestring budget," Levi said. "Some of these things are doable, but I wouldn't be much good at helping someone find happiness after their divorce. It took me nearly three years to realize Brooke was the woman for me."

"Could you help two teenagers with a building apprenticeship?" John handed Levi another folder. "Their resumés and letters of recommendation are in here. Each of them has completed the church's construction program. It would mean a great deal to them and their families."

"I'm sure it would, but it's October. As soon as it starts snowing, we won't be doing as much work." Levi frowned. "But we are starting the Montgomery project next month. If they're willing to work over Christmas, I could offer them apprenticeships."

"I'll arrange a meeting with Colby and Jess," John said, clearly relieved. "Once you talk to them, you'll see what great kids they are." He turned his attention to Ben.

This was one conversation John wouldn't win. "I read the spreadsheet. No one wants to work on a Christmas tree farm."

"If you're considering selling other Christmas products, I know four people who are looking for work. They would enjoy helping you."

"I'm not seeing Kylie until this afternoon," Ben told John. "I won't know until after our meeting whether her ideas will work."

"And if they're good ideas?"

Ben sighed. He really didn't want to work with anyone else, but John wasn't taking no for an answer. "Then maybe I could talk to you about employing some staff."

John handed him another sheet of paper.

His eyebrows rose when he looked at the photos printed on the page. A set of wooden Nutcracker soldiers, a miniature nativity scene, and intricately carved Christmas ornaments filled the sheet.

"I'm impressed. Are they locally made or imported?"

"They were carved by a seventeen-year-old boy who lives in Sapphire Bay." John nodded toward the wooden sleigh. "Nate made the sleigh for the center, too. His craftsmanship is better than anything I've ever seen."

Ben kept his gaze on John. "I'll keep him in mind if we talk about employing staff."

"Thank you."

By the time John gave each of them a list of the Christmas wishes they could help with, there wasn't a lot of time to talk about what was happening in their lives. For that, Ben was profoundly grateful. But for others, they needed the support and encouragement only this group could give them. For that reason, he stayed at the center long after he would have normally left.

As long as he didn't miss the meeting with Kylie, everything should be okay.

KYLIE PARKED her truck in front of Ben's home. The two-story wooden house sat at the end of a long driveway surrounded by pine and spruce trees. She'd only been here a couple of times. From what she'd seen, it was what her father would call a fixer-upper.

Before her last visit, she'd searched the Internet, trying to find information about growing Christmas trees. Unlike other forestry operations, Ben's trees needed lots of additional work, especially closer to Christmas.

It was no wonder his house needed a little work. He must work around the clock to make sure everything was ready for his busiest season.

Ben came out of the house just as she was opening the tailgate.

"You made good time."

"There wasn't a lot of traffic." Relax, she told herself, as he moved closer. Even if he didn't like the decorations, the new website Emma had created was incredible. "Could you give me a hand to bring these boxes inside?"

"Sure. We can take them into the living room. There's plenty of space in there."

After the last box was inside, she took a deep breath. If this didn't work, the old steamboat museum would look like a big empty cavern for the Christmas party.

Crossing her fingers, she hoped Ben could see the potential in the decorations she'd made. They would look amazing in a Christmas shop and even better in his customers' homes.

Cautiously, she sat on the sofa and opened her laptop. Before she showed Ben what was inside the boxes, she wanted him to see the website.

"Emma created a new website for you. It's still in draft format. If there's anything you want to change, she can easily do it."

Ben sat beside her, staring intently at the screen as she connected to the site. "She did all of this over the last few days?"

Kylie nodded. "Do you like it?"

"It's different."

"In a good way?"

"It's very...Christmassy."

Considering the whole point of the website was to advertise the Christmas tree farm and the shop, that had to be a good thing. Didn't it?

"We went with a red and gold theme. Emma couldn't find any branding for your business, so we created something that might work." Kylie pushed the laptop closer to Ben. The name of his business was The Christmas Tree Farm. Emma had played with different font styles and graphics. In the end, she'd settled on a logo that had a bright red background with gold swirls around the name of the farm. It looked like something Santa Claus would have used at the North Pole.

She pointed to the website. "Emma took photos of the decorations and ornaments we made. You might not want to sell all of them, but it gives you an idea of what everything could look like."

As he scrolled through the pages, Kylie watched for any change in Ben's expression. His only flicker of emotion was when he saw his own photo.

"We added an 'About the Farm' page so people can learn a

little more about you and the history of the farm. We'd need to add more text and photos." She pointed to a narrow box at the bottom of the page. "Emma also added a sign-up form so people can subscribe to your newsletter. Each month, you could send everyone information about what's happening on the farm."

"Does Blooming Lovely have a newsletter?"

Kylie nodded. "As soon as I launched my website, I created one. I only send out emails once a month or when there's something special happening."

"Like the Christmas fundraising events?"

"Exactly." While Ben studied the website, she opened the cardboard box closest to her. The sweet smell of pine helped to settle her nerves. The wreath she'd made was gorgeous. Sprigs of lavender decorated the deep green foliage, making its scent intoxicating—even to someone who was used to creating sweet-smelling bouquets.

Ben's hands stilled on the keyboard. "You made that?"

She held back a sigh. He was acting as though he was allergic to Christmas. "It's a wreath and, yes, I made it."

"How much does something like that cost?"

"Depending on the size and the decorations, between forty and sixty dollars. This one would sell for about fifty dollars. If you use foliage from the farm, the net profit on this item would be about twenty dollars."

After placing the wreath on the table, she opened another box. "These garlands look stunning over a mantelpiece or attached to the rail of a staircase."

Ben made room on another table. "How long does it take to make a garland?"

"It depends on the size. But for something this size, it could take an hour." Kylie pushed a small button. Solar powered fairy lights twinkled from between the branches. "Not everyone wants lights, but I think they look pretty. This garland would sell for about ninety-five dollars. The net profit, with lights, would be about twenty dollars."

"I wouldn't have to sell many decorations to make a reasonable amount of money."

"When you grow the basic materials, it makes each item less expensive to produce."

Ben peered inside another box. "I didn't see any photos of these ornaments."

"Emma didn't have time to take any." She waited until he was holding one of the decorations. The carving of the angel was exquisite. "A local teenager made everything in this box. His name is Nate."

Ben placed the angel on the table. "Is he the same teenager who made the sleigh in The Welcome Center?"

Kylie nodded. "He's really talented. If you're interested in his sculptures, you'll only be able to sell what he's already made. He doesn't have a lot of time to make anything at the moment."

"Because of school?"

"It's more complicated than that. A few months ago, his mom had an accident. Without her income, they don't have enough money to pay their rent and buy food. Nate has been working three part-time jobs to support them."

"And selling his sculptures through my store would give him more income."

"It would. His mom also makes beautiful quilts. If she made some with a Christmas theme, you could sell them in your store, too."

Ben picked up a carved set of wooden bells. "I can't afford to buy anything up front."

"You could sell on commission. That way, you won't pay for anything before it's sold."

"You've thought this through."

She placed her hands in her lap. "I had to. We really need the Christmas trees for our party."

He stared at the decorations for so long that Kylie thought he was going to say no. She only hoped somewhere, deep inside, he realized how important this was for everyone.

"If the website and the store help me sell more Christmas trees, I'll need more workers. But I can't afford to pay any wages until I sell the trees."

"Pastor John was happy to include your farm as one of the job placements on the church's youth employment program. If he gets approval from the county, they'll pay everyone's salary while they're working here."

"That sounds almost too good to be true."

"It's one of the benefits of living in a rural area. There's more help for companies wanting to employ local people."

Ben looked through the living room windows to the big red barn on the other side of the yard. "I'd need to use the barn for the Christmas shop. It's warm, but that's about it."

"It would be perfect." Kylie sat forward, excitement making her forget her promise to be cool, calm, and collected. She touched Ben's arm, smiling as her imagination created the most amazing Christmas shop ever. "The last time I saw your barn, it was gorgeous. All it needs is a good clean. We could push your machinery and tools to the back and build temporary walls and shelving. I don't think it would cost too much."

He looked at the wooden bells, the home-made decorations, and the laptop.

She knew that if he wanted to open a Christmas shop, he would have to be willing to take a risk—willing to work alongside other people to make a whole lot of Christmas wishes come true.

"What's the worst that could happen?" she asked softly.

Instead of answering, he placed the bells into their box and sighed. "Let's look at the barn. It will take a lot of work to change it into a Christmas shop."

"You'll do it?" she said excitedly.

"I'll think about it."

Kylie's smile dimmed, but she wouldn't let his caution dampen her enthusiasm. "If you decide to go ahead, you won't regret it. The whole town will be behind you."

She hoped her words reassured Ben, but she wasn't counting on it. Especially when there was so much at stake.

BEN OPENED the barn's heavy doors. The hinges creaked under the weight of half a ton of wood, strapped together with iron forged right here on the farm. "Be careful where you step. I was working in here this morning."

As Kylie followed him inside, she ran her hand along one of the doors. "How old is the barn?"

"Most of it was built in 1901. Sometime in the seventies, the previous owners added a tack room and two stalls."

Even though the late afternoon sun was pouring through the doors, he turned on the lights. Instantly, the shadows lurking at the edge of the building disappeared. The barn might have lost some of its magic, but it was better than Kylie tripping over something and hurting herself.

Lifting her chin, Kylie gazed at the thick rafters holding the barn steady. "How long do you think it took to build this part of the building?"

"Considering everything was milled by hand, it could have taken four, maybe five months to complete."

"It's incredible," she said softly.

Each time he stepped into the barn, Ben felt the same sense of wonder. He loved the way everything slotted together. Like an impressive jigsaw, each piece had its place, including the new tools he'd bought.

Kylie walked farther into the barn. She touched the rail on a stall and a leather saddle, cracked and worn with age.

He remembered the last time she was here. She'd stood just inside the doors, trying to convince him to part with twenty trees. He could have asked if she wanted to look around, but the barn was his sanctuary. He came here to unwind, to build furniture for his family and friends, and to pretend he was normal.

Creating a Christmas shop in here was a big deal. He would lose his privacy but, hopefully, sleep better knowing his mortgage would be paid.

Kylie stopped in front of his latest project. Under the fluorescent lights, her blond hair was a gleaming tumble of silk. When she flicked her hair to one side, her gentle smile took his breath away. Did she realize how beautiful she was?

"You're making a rocking horse?"

He returned one of his chisels to a shelf behind the workbench. "It's for my niece. She's four years old and crazy about horses."

Kylie didn't say anything. Instead, she leaned forward, her hair shielding her face from him.

He'd spent months looking for the perfect rocking horse design. In the end, friends in Seattle had sent him a template they'd used for their son. With its wide seat and a handrail to keep children safe, it was the perfect Christmas present for Lettie.

Kylie glanced at him.

He didn't understand why she was frowning. "What's wrong?"

"I asked if you were going to paint or stain the wood."

"Paint. Lettie likes anything that's pink, so I'm going with a pink body and white tail and ears."

"It sounds lovely." She looked more uncertain than ever. "Can I ask you a personal question?"

"Okay, but only one."

Kylie didn't smile at his half-baked attempt at being funny. Instead, she opened her mouth to say something, then stopped.

After a few seconds, she tried again. "Are. You. Deaf?"

Ben's heart sank. She'd spoken slowly, over-pronouncing each word—just like everyone else when they thought there was something wrong with his hearing.

"I'm completely deaf in my left ear. As long as I'm in front of a person or on their left-hand side, I can usually hear what they say."

Kylie took a moment to absorb what he'd said. "Do you lip read?"

"That's two personal questions."

"I'm sorry. I didn't mean to poke into your life."

"It's okay." Sometimes he could be a complete jerk. Anyone seeing the compassion on her face couldn't mistake it for anything other than genuine concern. "I only lip read when I'm in a crowded room or surrounded by lots of noise. Sometimes it works, other times I get it completely wrong."

"It must be frustrating."

Ben nodded. There weren't enough words to describe how bad it could be. "Tell me something. Why are you working so hard to raise money for the tiny home village?"

Kylie's gaze fell to the half-finished rocking horse. "Because it's important."

She paused, then looked straight at him. "When I was eight years old, my father left and never came back. Mom worked all day and night to put food on our table and pay our rent. It was hard. A lot of the people who will be living in the tiny home village have nothing. I know what poverty can do to a person's spirit, especially when you can't see your way out of it." She took a deep breath. "I want to make a difference. I want everyone who comes to Sapphire Bay to know we care about them, regardless of their situation."

"That's a big goal," he said softly.

"If everyone works together, we can make it happen."

Ben admired her pride and determination. From what he'd seen, he had no doubt she would do everything she'd set out to do. "You're a special person, Kylie Bryant."

"I'm no different from everyone else. Can I ask you another question?"

"Go ahead."

Instantly, her serious expression was replaced with excitement. "Can I climb into your hayloft?"

That surprised him. "Why?"

"I was born and raised in a city. Ever since I read *Little House on the Prairie*, I've wanted to sit in a hayloft. Besides, it would give me a good idea of the layout of the barn. We could work out where we'll place the Christmas shop."

Ben looked dubiously at the old ladder leaning against the loft. "I don't think the ladder's safe. We could measure the ground floor, then draw a plan from here."

"Have you been in the hayloft since you bought the property?"

"No."

Kylie sighed. "The view of your property must be amazing from up there. Aren't you even a little curious about what everything looks like?"

"No."

Her eyes narrowed. "Are you afraid of heights?"

First it was his hearing. Now she was digging a hot poker into his irrational fear of dropping like a lead weight from any height. "I prefer to keep my feet firmly on the ground."

"It's nothing to be ashamed of. Lots of people have an issue with heights."

"But not you."

Kylie looked wistfully at the loft. "Mom's nickname for me was spider. I used to climb everything. The higher I went, the happier I was."

"Did you ever get stuck or fall off?"

"A few times, but it didn't stop me from trying again."

He reached for the measuring tape. "Today, we'll use this. If I ever get around to replacing the ladder, you can climb into the loft."

Kylie smiled. "You've got a deal. You never know—by the time you replace the ladder, you might be ready to climb into the loft with me."

"I don't think so." Ben handed her a large notebook and pen. "I'll measure, you draw."

CHAPTER 3

*T*he next morning, Ben woke earlier than usual. He stood in front of the kitchen window with a hot cup of coffee in his hands.

One of the reasons he'd moved to Sapphire Bay was to get away from the chaos and noise of Los Angeles. But it had taken longer than he thought to get used to living in rural Montana. Sometimes, the silence that settled across the farm was like a heavy winter coat. It might keep out the cold, but it could also be suffocating.

After months of finding his way, he'd finally become used to the quiet, used to listening to his own thoughts instead of the noise from people around him.

But the silence came at a cost, especially when he couldn't sleep. There were no distractions, nothing to keep his mind from spinning in circles. Last night, he couldn't stop thinking about Kylie and Pastor John. Their knowledge of growing Christmas trees might be minimal, but he appreciated their skill at running profitable businesses.

Ben grimaced. John wouldn't like the church being

compared to a business. But without John's ability to balance the books, or his drive and determination, the church wouldn't be able to provide any programs. Relying on grants, sponsorship, and people's generosity to pay for their services was stressful and time-consuming and took more than good luck.

Then there was Blooming Lovely, Kylie's flower shop. As well as being a talented florist, Kylie knew a lot more than Ben about marketing and branding, and all the things he'd never considered before moving here.

But could he recreate her success? Maybe, but he couldn't do it on his own. If he wanted to sell a record number of trees this year, he'd need help, and lots of it.

He took another sip of coffee, his mind wandering back to a conversation with the farm's previous owners. They could have sold their property to a developer. The land was more valuable than the trees and, although it would have broken their hearts, they wanted a comfortable retirement.

To this day, he didn't know why they'd sold the farm to a man who knew next to nothing about growing trees. Maybe they sensed he would come to love the land as much as they did. Or maybe it was a way for their dreams to live far beyond their lifetime. Either way, Ben felt a deep sense of responsibility to the land and to the people who had come before him.

For someone who preferred to skip Christmas, it was ironic that the farm was the one thing he couldn't bear to lose. His counselor in Los Angeles would have pushed and prodded until Ben understood why he was so determined to make the Christmas tree farm a success. But for now, it was enough to know he wasn't giving up without a fight.

He checked the time. It was too early to call John or Kylie, but it wasn't too early to start work. The fundraising

Christmas party was only a few weeks away. If Kylie wanted twenty trees, he needed to prepare them now.

After rinsing his mug, he headed toward the mudroom. If Kylie's ideas about increasing his revenue didn't work, at least he could say he'd given it his best shot. It was better than lying awake each night, worrying about the farm.

KYLIE ADDED another lily to the arrangement she was making.

Today had been busier than usual. Between the online orders and the customers who came into Blooming Lovely, she hadn't stopped for a break.

The highlight of her day was seeing Megan and Brooke, two of her friends who owned the best candy and cake store in Sapphire Bay. They'd refilled the bags of fudge she sold in her flower shop and kept her up to date with what was happening in the town.

The bell over the front door jingled. Her hands stilled when she saw who was walking toward the front counter.

Ben's gaze drifted from one colorful bouquet to the next, absorbing everything inside her store like a connoisseur of fine wines.

She hadn't heard from him since their meeting yesterday. By four o'clock, she'd given up thinking he would call.

Kylie opened the workroom door and sent him a nervous smile. She didn't know what he was going to say, but she hoped it was good news. "Welcome to my flower shop."

Ben's surprised gaze dropped to her dress. With screen-printed images of Santa Claus across a black background, it was one of her favorites.

"How many Christmas dresses do you own?" he asked.

"I'm not sure, but I have quite a few. Do you like the fabric? I ordered it directly from the manufacturer."

"It's… colorful."

She wasn't sure whether he thought that was a good thing.

"I wanted to let you know I'm happy to provide the trees and mistletoe in return for some of your business advice. I think the Christmas shop is a good idea, too."

Relief surged through her. "That's awesome. Thank you so much. What made you change your mind?"

"It wasn't a hard decision. I need to earn more money. Otherwise, I won't own a Christmas tree farm next year."

She didn't realize his financial situation was so bad. "I'll do everything I can to help you. Wait here. I'll be back in a minute." Kylie rushed into the workroom and grabbed a folder off her desk. After she'd left Ben's house, she'd made a project plan incorporating everything they'd discussed. "I put this together last night."

Ben opened the folder.

"I was worried I'd overwhelmed you with my suggestions. So I reorganized what we talked about into a draft priority list. You can change it around if you like."

"Even your first bullet point is daunting."

Kylie moved closer and looked over the edge of the folder. After inspecting the barn, it was obvious why cleaning it could seem a little intimidating. "You don't have to do it on your own. There are lots of people at The Welcome Center who will help."

"I'm not sure that's a good idea. Some of the old machinery could be dangerous. I don't even know where we'd put it."

"All we need is enough space to create a Christmas shop. Besides, if your customers see the equipment, it will give them a more authentic shopping experience. Would you like a piece of caramel delight fudge? Brooke made it this afternoon."

"Are you bribing me again with food?"

Her eyes narrowed. Was he actually smiling?

Ben's eyes gleamed.

He was. The heat of a blush stole across her cheeks. "When I brought home-baking out to your farm, I wasn't trying to bribe you. I was being neighborly."

"I've lived there for two years. You could have been neighborly before you wanted the trees."

Kylie didn't know whether he was serious or joking. "If you'd given me the trees when I first asked, we wouldn't be having this conversation." She wiggled the bag of fudge under his nose. "Last chance."

He dipped his hand into the bag. "I'm only having this because I'm polite."

Kylie grinned. "Of course, you are. So, when do you want to clear out the barn?"

"Tomorrow is the earliest I can start. I'm seeing John about the youth employment program after I leave here."

"If John has extra people looking for work, tell him I could employ two part-time staff in my shop. I'll teach them how to make wreaths and garlands, and some other Christmas decorations. After the Christmas shop opens, they could work from there and serve the customers."

"Sounds good." Ben ran his finger down the list she'd given him. "After I've spoken to John, I'll ask Mabel about the other things we need."

"And I'll call my friend Natalie. She runs art workshops. There might be some students who want to sell their paintings through your shop."

"Are you sure you've got enough time?"

"I'll make the time. I appreciate you giving us the trees."

"You're welcome. I wanted to thank you, too."

Kylie frowned. "What for?"

"You didn't make a big deal out of my hearing issues."

Ben looked so vulnerable that she wanted to give him a hug. But that would only complicate everything.

So instead of wrapping him in her arms, she stuck her hands in her pockets. "That's okay. Apart from when people are standing on your left-hand side or you're in a crowded or noisy room, are there other times when you can't hear what's being said?"

"Not usually." He checked his watch. "If I don't leave now, I'll be late for my meeting with John. Let me know what Natalie says about her students' art."

"I will." She walked to the front door with Ben and watched him climb into his truck. It must be difficult living with a hearing loss. She wondered if he'd been born partially deaf or if it had only happened in the last few years. Either way, making new friends and adjusting to life in Montana must have been difficult. No wonder he kept to himself. It was probably easier than telling everyone he had trouble with his hearing.

With a heavy heart, Kylie turned back to her workroom. When she'd first met Ben, she was quick to judge him. But he wasn't the moody hermit she'd first imagined.

He was a man with a big heart who cared about his farm and the people of Sapphire Bay.

It was time for her to share a little kindness with him. And she knew exactly where she would start.

BEN KNOCKED on John's office door. "Are you ready for our meeting?"

John looked up from the papers he was reading and smiled. "You have perfect timing. We just received approval to include your business as one of our employment providers. The county has given us enough funding for five positions."

Ben's eyebrows rose. "That's incredible. I thought it would take weeks for them to make a decision."

"At this time of the year, there aren't a lot of job opportunities. They were grateful you wanted to employ our students."

"If it works out, I might be able to make some of the jobs permanent." He sat down and handed John a set of plans. "This is what I'd like to do in the barn. Do you know anyone who could help me create the partition walls and build some display units?"

John scanned the pages. "This looks fairly straightforward. Let me talk to the tutor who looks after our construction program. We should be able to provide the materials and labor at no cost."

Ben sat taller in his seat. Taking Kylie's advice was one thing, but relying on the church to pay for everything wouldn't happen. "I can pay for the job to be done."

"Leave it with me. When do you want to start?"

"The sooner the better. Kylie wants me to remind you that we'll need two part-time staff once the shop opens. Can we use some of the hours the county are financing to pay their wages?"

"If you're happy to have four full-time positions working on the farm, we could use the rest of the hours for Blooming Lovely and the Christmas shop."

"I would have been happy with one person helping me. Do I need to do anything before the students start?"

John picked up the papers he'd been reading. "I'll send you a list of the candidates. You can review their resumés and interview them. If you need any help, let me know. After that, I'll fill in the paperwork and then they can start. In the meantime, I'll see what we can do about helping you with the barn."

"Thanks." Ben rose from the chair.

"Before you go, I wanted to ask how you're feeling."

He slowly sat back down. "What do you mean?"

John frowned. "You still look exhausted. Have you had another meeting with the loan officer at the bank?"

"No." After their last meeting, Ben hoped he wouldn't see him again for a long time.

"What about Zac? You said you'd see him if you couldn't sleep."

Ben had nothing against doctors, especially Zac. By Sapphire Bay's standards, the clinic he'd set up was state-of-the-art. And compared to some doctors he'd visited, Zac knew better than most how PTSD could take over your life. But even after spending time with him and the other support group members, Ben had a hard time talking about his life.

When Ben didn't answer, John sighed. "I'll take that as a no."

"The nightmares are worse when I'm worried about something." He swallowed the knot of pride stuck in his throat. It wasn't easy admitting how tough things had become. "It's taking a lot longer than I thought to get the farm financially viable. Hopefully, with Kylie's ideas and your help, it will make everything a lot easier."

John looked even more concerned. "Apart from what we've discussed, is there anything else I can help you with?"

Ben shook his head. "Not at the moment. But I am thankful for everything you've done."

"I care about you. We all do. Will you talk to Zac if the PTSD symptoms get worse?"

Ben was going to say he didn't need Zac's help. But the

determined look in John's eyes told him he wouldn't get out of the office unless he agreed. "I'll see him if I need to."

When John raised his eyebrows, Ben smiled. "I promise. Besides, Kylie already thinks I'm grumpy. If I get any worse, she'll march me to Zac's clinic whether or not I want to go."

"She cares about people."

Ben didn't have to hear those words from John to know they were true. Through her work with the tiny home fundraising committee, Kylie was making a difference in many people's lives. Including his own. And as much as he hated to admit it, he was even getting used to her over-the-top love of all things Christmassy.

Maybe there was hope for him yet.

THE FOLLOWING SATURDAY, Kylie climbed out of her truck. She'd called Ben last night, hoping it was okay to bring a few friends to the farm to help clean the barn.

She just hoped his idea of 'a few friends' was the same as hers. Four pickup trucks and lots of eager helpers were driving onto the farm behind her and Bailey.

"I'm glad the snow stayed away," Bailey said as she zipped up her jacket. "It will make our jobs a lot easier."

"If we'd left it until next weekend, I don't think we would have been as lucky."

Bailey tilted her head to the side. "You look worried."

"I didn't tell Ben how many people were coming."

"He'll be fine. Once we get started, he won't realize how many of us are here."

Kylie hoped Bailey was right. Ben didn't like crowds but, in all fairness, twelve people could hardly be called a crowd—even by Montana standards.

"Talking about Ben," Bailey nodded toward the barn. "It looks as though he's already started."

The double-height doors leading into the barn were wide open. Old crates, boxes, and twisted metal had been placed in separate piles a few feet away.

Ben walked out of the barn. He stopped and stared at the number of trucks, then slowly focused on Kylie.

The closer she got to him, the more worried she became.

"This is a surprise."

Kylie cleared her throat. "Bailey, John, and Emma wanted to help. Mabel overheard our conversation and within a few minutes another five people said they'd come, too."

Before he could reply, Levi, William, and Steven, Ben's friends from the PTSD support group, joined them.

"Then we got involved," Steven said. "You should have told us you were opening a Christmas shop. We would have been here sooner."

"Where do you want us to start?" William asked.

Ben's gaze connected with Kylie's. Her heart pounded as a spark of awareness shot down her spine. Until a few weeks ago, she'd called him the Christmas Grinch. He never smiled, hardly spoke, and frowned each time he saw her.

Now look at him.

When Ben turned his attention to William, she breathed a sigh of relief. For some weird, totally irrational reason, she felt a connection with Ben that went far deeper than friendship.

After her last relationship ended in tears, she'd sworn she wouldn't fall for anyone she'd known for less than a year. But Ben was becoming an exception to her rule. And that worried her more than anything else that was happening in her life.

Bailey nudged her arm. "Are you okay?"

Kylie jumped. "I'm fine." She sent a reassuring smile to

her friend before focusing on what Ben was saying. Daydreaming wouldn't get the barn clean or keep her heart in one piece.

Ben's gaze captured hers. "A truck from the scrap metal yard will pick everything up this afternoon."

Levi pulled on his baseball cap. "Looks like we've got a lot of work ahead of us. Let's get started."

With a relieved sigh, Kylie looked away from Ben and followed Levi toward the barn.

"Not so fast, Tinker Bell."

The intensity in Ben's eyes made her mouth go dry. She looked down at her green trousers and bright red jacket and frowned. "I'm not Tinker Bell. I'm an elf."

Reaching forward, he gently tugged the bell on the end of her hat. "I found something you'll want to see."

Right at the moment, the only thing Kylie wanted to see was the inside of the barn. She looked across at her friends.

"They'll be okay for a few minutes. Come with me." Ben steered her toward his home. "The Christmas tree farm was in the same family for more than eighty years. The previous owners didn't do much in the way of advertising."

"I guess they didn't have to compete with artificial trees."

"Or small apartments." He pointed to a sign propped against the side of his home. "I don't know how old it is, but it's probably from the 1950s."

The round, tin sign was about three feet wide. Painted on the right-hand side was a cartoon-style Christmas tree, complete with multi-colored stars. On the left, two small children played in the snow. In faded green paint, the sign read, "Renwick's fresh cut trees. You choose 'em, we pick 'em."

Kyle moved closer. "I'm amazed it's in such good condition." She looked at Ben. "What will you do with it?"

"I thought I'd hang it in the Christmas shop. Do you think Emma could include a picture of it on my website?"

Kylie bent down and studied the sign. "That's a wonderful idea."

Ben's hand touched her shoulder. She looked into his confused face and sent him a quick smile. He hadn't heard her. "That's a wonderful idea," she repeated. "I'll take a photo and email it to her."

"I found some other things in the barn. If you're interested, I could show them to you later."

"I'd like that." Kylie took half a dozen photos and sent them to Emma. "If you find any old photos of the farm, let me know. We could add them to the website."

"If I don't find any, I'll ask the previous owners." Ben stuck his hands in his pockets. "Thanks for inviting everyone here. It's going to take longer than I thought to reorganize the barn."

"I was worried you'd think I was taking over."

Ben smiled. "I like assertive people. Even if they do wear elf hats and green trousers."

"I have other clothes, but they aren't as much fun." She twirled, showing off today's outfit. "I bought these clothes in a thrift store in Red Deer. Finding them was the highlight of my vacation."

Ben shook his head. "Apart from you, I don't know anyone who enjoys buying second-hand clothes on their vacation."

"You'd be surprised. It's like a treasure hunt, only the clothes don't cost a fortune." And for some people, she thought sadly, it was all they could afford.

Before she became too bogged down in her past, she looked at the barn. "We'd better get back. It looks as though Levi and John could do with a hand."

Ben followed the direction of her gaze. "They should have asked for help. That old plow weighs a ton."

Before Kylie knew what was happening, Ben sprinted across the yard. Grabbing one side of the plow, he helped pull it toward the large pile of twisted metal.

As Kylie joined her friends, she frowned. She knew how important this was to Ben. And regardless of what happened before and after the Christmas party, she would do whatever she could to help him.

CHAPTER 4

*B*en waved goodbye to his friends and the people he'd met from The Welcome Center. Over the last five hours, they'd pulled almost everything out of the barn. What wasn't thrown out or set aside to donate or sell, was rearranged. The space they'd created would give him plenty of room to build the partition walls and even more square footage for the Christmas shop.

Kylie walked out of the house with a picnic basket in her arms. Not only had she invited everyone to help them, she'd brought enough food to feed an army. "I've left everything we didn't eat in the refrigerator."

"You didn't have to go to so much bother, but thank you. I appreciate everything you're doing for me."

"You're the one who's donating twenty Christmas trees and lots of mistletoe for the party. Without them, it wouldn't be the same."

Her gentle smile made his heart beat fast. For the first time in a long while, he wasn't ready to say goodbye to someone. "Why don't I show you around the farm? We've still got another couple of hours before it gets dark."

"Are you sure it's not too much bother? You must have a lot of things you want to do."

Ben wasn't sure if she was being polite or didn't want to come with him. "There's nothing that can't wait until tomorrow. I could show you the trees I'm giving to the church."

Kylie bit her bottom lip. "I'd love to see them, but—"

"Great." Before she changed her mind, he took the basket out of her hands and pulled her toward the barn. "We'll take the four-wheeler. It will be faster."

This time, her eyes lit up. "Do you have an extra helmet?"

"You can use my sister's. There's a spare pair of gloves in the tack room that should fit, too."

By the time they were ready to leave, Kylie was even more excited. "I haven't been on a four-wheeler before. What do I need to do?"

"Just hold on tight and let me do the rest." As soon as they left the barn, Kylie's arms tightened around his waist. "Are you okay?" he yelled above the roar of the engine.

He felt her weight shift to his right-hand side. "It's fun!"

Ben smiled and surged forward, gathering enough speed to make it up the first rise.

As each row of trees gave way to the next, he breathed a sigh of relief. This was his happy place, the reason he'd moved away from everything he'd known.

After too many therapy sessions and countless hospital visits, he'd wanted to find somewhere he could be himself. Somewhere that could help him heal the scars that burned deep inside his soul.

When he saw this property, the tangle of trees, the rundown house and barn, he knew he'd found his new home.

Ben slowed down as they neared the trees he'd set aside for the church. Kylie's hands relaxed around his waist.

"The trees I'm donating are over there." He turned off the

ignition and pointed to the trees on their left. "What do you think?"

Kylie stepped off the bike. "They're perfect. Can I see them up close?"

"Of course, you can." With both of their helmets in his hands, he followed her across the firebreak. The only thing that worried him was the height of the trees. They were the perfect size for the average living room, but what they'd look like inside the old steamboat museum was anyone's guess.

Kylie ran her hand along the spiky branches. "What sort of trees are they?"

"Concolor Fir. I have Douglas Fir and Scotch Pine as well, but I thought these would be better for what you need."

"They're stunning. Once we've decorated them with fairy lights, they'll be even more incredible."

"What about the height?"

"They're going in a huge room, so the size of the trees won't matter." She leaned forward and inhaled their sweet scent. "They smell like Christmas."

"Or fir trees."

Kylie grinned. "Do you know what tree you're having in your house this Christmas?"

"I don't need one."

"Tell me you're joking."

Ben shook his head. "I'm surrounded by Christmas trees. By November, I'm working long hours on the farm. The last thing I want to do is bring one inside and decorate it." Or remember the night that changed his life forever.

"But it's Christmas. Do you put lights and tinsel around your house?"

When he shook his head a second time, Kylie groaned. "Really? Not even a sprig of mistletoe?"

"I'm not much of a Christmas person."

Kylie frowned. "What about when you were younger?"

"Mom and Dad filled the house with decorations. They still do. We made Christmas cookies and gave them to our friends and we always decorated the tree together."

"What happened?"

Ben looked away from her. At the best of times, it was hard talking about the assault. But, for some reason, today was even more difficult.

She touched his arm. "Are you all right?"

He pulled his gaze away from the trees and focused on Kylie. "Five years ago, I was working on a commercial construction site. We'd packed everything away for Christmas, but one of my crew left an expensive piece of equipment inside the building. When I went back to collect it, two men attacked me. They beat me so bad that I spent the next ten days in an induced coma, then another four months in the hospital, learning how to walk and talk again. The hearing in my left ear never returned."

The color in her cheeks disappeared. "I'm sorry that happened."

Ben scuffed the toe of his boot along the ground. "They were high on drugs. It wouldn't have mattered who they saw, they would have attacked them."

"Did they go to prison?"

He nodded. "They won't be out for a long time."

"And that's why you don't like Christmas? Because it brings back too many unhappy memories?"

Taking a deep breath, he nodded. "I can't remember what happened before or during the assault. My first memory was when I was lying on the floor, waiting for someone to find me. My eyes were almost swollen shut, but I could make out the shape of a Christmas decoration that had somehow fallen beside me. When I'm tired or stressed, I have nightmares about the decoration."

Kylie's eyes filled with tears. "Why did you buy the farm if Christmas is a difficult time for you?"

"It was my way of dealing with what happened. In some crazy way, doing something that makes other people happy gives me hope. It makes me feel that one day, I could have a normal, happy life, too." Ben looked across the farm, at the trees that had become his salvation. "Buying this property is the best thing I've ever done. I have fewer nightmares and I'm not as grumpy as I used to be."

Kylie sent him a wobbly smile. "You must have been *really* grumpy before you came here."

He gently wiped the tears off her face. "I'm a work in progress." A swell of emotion rushed through him. He wanted to kiss her, to be close to her in a way he never thought he'd feel again. But what if she didn't want to kiss him? What if—

Kylie's lips brushed his cheek. "If you need help with anything, let me know."

His heart pounded. Did she know what she was offering? How badly damaged he was?

"I mean it," she said sternly. "I'm only a phone call away."

Ben didn't know whether to be grateful or start running. Or hold her in his arms and never let go.

BAILEY TOOK the wrapper off her sandwich. "I still can't believe Ben agreed to open a Christmas shop. He must have been impressed with your ideas."

"He probably would have come to the same conclusion, I just nudged him along." Kylie added another rose to the bouquet she was making. Three days after cleaning out the barn, she was still unsure about what had happened between her and Ben.

"After you left the farm, Ben showed me the trees he's donating for the Christmas party."

"Will they look good?"

"They'll look fabulous. He has other trees that are huge. One of them would look amazing at the end of Main Street."

Bailey bit into her sandwich. "How much do they cost?"

"Six thousand dollars."

Her friend stopped chewing. "Each?"

Kylie nodded. "Two of the trees are already going to big corporations."

"The fundraising committee can't afford that much money."

"I know, but it's something to think about for next year. It would be amazing to hold the Christmas carol competition in front of one."

"Not if it snowed."

"That's true."

Bailey wiped her mouth with a napkin. "Did you take photos of the trees? They'd look great on Ben's website."

"Why didn't I think of that?"

"Maybe because you had other things on your mind? Ben hardly took his eyes off you all afternoon."

Kylie blushed at the teasing note in Bailey's voice. "He was watching everyone to make sure they didn't trip over anything."

"Of course, he was."

"Ben wasn't the only person who was being super careful."

Bailey smiled. "It's not a crime to like someone."

"It is if you promised yourself you wouldn't fall for someone you barely know."

"He isn't your last boyfriend."

"I know. It's just…"

Bailey's eyebrows rose.

Kylie sighed. "It's complicated."

"Most relationships are. From what I saw on Saturday, Ben seems like a nice guy."

"He is." Kylie glanced at Bailey, hoping her friend might help her understand how she was feeling. "Can I ask you a question?"

"Sure. I don't have to be back at the clinic for another half hour." She looked at Kylie and frowned. "What's wrong?"

"If I tell you something, can you keep it between the two of us?"

"Like a doctor/patient confidentiality clause?"

Kylie shook her head. With a degree in psychology, Bailey was probably the most qualified person in Sapphire Bay to talk to. "No. More like friend to friend. I'm worried about Ben."

"Why?"

"Five years ago, he was badly beaten. He still has nightmares about what happened. I want to help him, but I don't know how."

"Has he seen any therapists or psychologists?"

"I think so. He spent a long time in the hospital recovering from his injuries."

Bailey leaned her elbows on the table. "Let me ask you a question. Does he want your help?"

Kylie thought back over their conversation. "He didn't specifically ask for help, but he didn't tell me to mind my own business, either."

"How involved do you want to be in his life?"

Kylie put down the flower she was about to add to the bouquet. "What do you mean?"

"Each person who goes through a traumatic experience has different needs. Some people prefer to be wrapped in cotton wool until they're able to come to terms with what happened. Others want their friends to be their sounding board. In that case, it's important to take a step back and not get too emotionally involved. Sometimes, the best thing you can do is simply be there to support them."

"How do I figure out what Ben needs?"

"Ask him."

Kylie looked at the bouquet. She still wasn't sure if Ben would appreciate her help. He was strong and independent, and far too stubborn for his own good. "We talked about his hearing. He's completely deaf in his left ear."

"Did he become deaf because of the assault?"

Kylie nodded. "From what he said, he's lucky to be alive."

"It must have been a terrible time for him and his family."

"I imagine it was. If you were me, what would you do?"

Bailey sighed. "Do what you think is right, but promise me you'll speak to Ben first. And don't underestimate the value of a good friend. It can be the difference between being happy and feeling alone."

Kylie gave Bailey a quick hug. "Thank you. I appreciate your words of wisdom."

"They come from years of experience. I've seen too many relationships fall apart because one person thought they were doing what was best for everyone else." Bailey picked up her sandwich. "You should invite Ben into town for one of our Friday night get-togethers. It will be good getting to know him."

"That's a great idea. I don't know if he'll come, but it's worth a try." And as long as they didn't decorate anyone's Christmas tree, it would be even better.

FOR THE LAST HOUR, Ben had been reviewing the plans for the Christmas shop with Kylie. After pacing across every square inch of the barn and second-guessing each shelf and door option, they'd decided to focus on something else for a few minutes.

After they'd returned to his house for a cup of coffee, he'd shown Kylie the other things he'd found in the barn. But he had a feeling the last item would be the one she'd find the most interesting.

He handed her a framed picture of a pressed flower arrangement. "I found this behind an old dresser at the back of the barn."

Kylie's hand touched the glass, tracing the outline of the petals. "It's beautiful."

Ben watched in fascination as she studied each detail of the picture. "There's a date on the back."

Turning over the frame, Kylie read the hand-written numbers. "It's nearly one hundred years old. Do you know anything about it?"

"It probably belonged to the previous owner's mother or grandmother. Do you think the flowers were part of a wedding bouquet?"

"It's unlikely. Bouquets made around that time were huge. Brides loved using big flowers like calla lilies. The foliage often draped to the ground, and they added lots of decorative features like peacock feathers and ribbon. The baby roses and poppies are too small for one of those wedding bouquets."

With one last look at the flowers, Kylie handed the picture back to him. "This must have been special to the person who pressed them. Are you giving it back to the previous owners?"

"I've already called them. They don't want it."

Kylie's eyes widened. "That's like throwing away a family heirloom. I can't believe someone in their family doesn't want it."

"That's because you're a florist," Ben said with a smile.

"Would you like it for your flower shop?"

"I'd love it, but wouldn't you prefer to keep it here? It's an important piece of the farm's history. Especially since someone thought it was special enough to preserve."

Ben had found plenty of other things to remind him of the farm's colorful past. This one was meant for Kylie.

He left the picture on the kitchen table. "This is for you. I can enjoy it when I visit Blooming Lovely."

"On one of your infrequent trips into town?"

"I'll make more of an effort to come regularly." The grin on Kylie's face was almost his undoing. He enjoyed being with her, liked their easy banter and the teasing smiles she sent him. Sometimes, he worried that he liked it too much.

Kylie took a sip of coffee. "If you want a reason to drive into town, you could have dinner with Bailey, Emma and me on Friday. It's one of our regular get-togethers. Most of the time we order Thai takeout and watch a movie. It's nothing fancy, but it's fun."

He looked at the uncertainty in Kylie's eyes and felt himself drowning. He desperately wanted to say yes, but five years of insecurity and fear reared its ugly head. Apart from a massive mortgage and a brain injury that still affected him, he had nothing to offer her. No woman in their right mind would want a relationship with him, least of all Kylie.

When he didn't say anything, she frowned. "You don't have to come if you don't want to."

"Maybe another time," he murmured. "I've got a lot of work to do before the new apprentices arrive."

Kylie's cheeks turned red. "That's okay. I should have realized you'd be busy." She picked up her mug and pushed away from the table. "We've probably done all we can for now. If you have any ideas about what to do in the storage area, let me know. I'll see myself to my truck."

Ben grabbed the picture of the flowers. "Don't forget this."

Keeping her eyes on his hands, Kylie took the frame. "Thanks."

Without a backward glance, she placed her mug in the sink and left him standing in the kitchen, feeling like a complete idiot.

CHAPTER 5

$\mathcal{B}$y Friday night, Ben was still calling himself every fool under the sun. For the last two days he'd thought about calling Kylie, explaining why he'd panicked. But nothing he could have said would make a difference. She must think he was a lost cause, a loner who preferred his own company. But he wasn't, and he never would be.

He was grateful John was here to go through the list of people wanting to work on the farm. At least it was taking his mind off what Kylie was doing.

"This is the last resumé and cover letter," John said as he handed Ben a blue folder. "Marcus is originally from Polson, but moved here when he was eighteen."

Ben skimmed through Marcus' qualifications. His grades were average and apart from two part-time positions, he didn't have a lot of work experience.

John sat on the sofa. "He's a good kid and enjoys working outside. He's reliable and honest."

"Can he work as part of a team?"

"Absolutely. Marcus had a rough couple of years, but he wants to change. The youth employment program has given him a chance to make something of his life. He would be a good fit with the other young people you've selected."

Ben read Marcus' cover letter, recognizing something of himself in what he saw. When he was a teenager, he didn't know what he wanted to do with his life. His gran told him he could be whatever he wanted. All he had to do was make a plan and stick to it. But when he was eighteen, the only things Ben was interested in were girls and cars.

He should have listened to his gran.

John leaned forward. "You're scowling. The cover letter isn't that bad, so what's the matter?"

He placed the letter on the table. "Marcus reminds me of myself. When I was his age, I didn't know what I wanted to do."

"You ended up here, so you must have done something right."

"It was pure chance that I drove into Sapphire Bay."

John leaned back in his seat. "If there's one thing I've learned, it's that nothing happens by chance. We're all here for a reason. It just takes some of us a while to figure out what that reason is."

Five years after nearly dying, Ben was still trying to work that out. "I thought the farm was my chance to redeem myself, but I'm barely hanging on."

"No one said life was supposed to be easy."

"I get that, but why does it have to be so hard?"

John sighed. "Beats me. Before I joined the army, I thought I had my life sorted out. Then I saw what war does to the human spirit, and it almost broke me. I'd lived in a bubble for the first thirty-two years of my life. When it burst, I didn't know what to do."

"But you survived."

"We both did." John pointed to the folders. "Each of those kids has the weight of the world on their shoulders. They didn't ask for the things they have to deal with, but they keep going, keep trying to make a better life for themselves. If we can help them reach their full potential, then I'd say we're doing something right."

"Now I feel really old."

"Join the club. I thought I'd be married with at least four children by now. But look at me—forty-two years old and still single. If I ever meet a woman I can't live without, I won't know what to do with her."

"You and me both," Ben muttered.

A set of headlights shone across the living room.

Ben frowned.

"Maybe it's the woman you can't live without," John said half-jokingly.

"Wishful thinking." Thanks to his limited intelligence, Ben's woman was about twenty minutes away, eating Thai takeout with her friends. "I'll be back in a minute."

When he opened the front door, he stared at the truck parked in front of his house.

The woman he couldn't live without had just arrived.

BEN'S BREATH caught as Kylie stepped into the glow from the security lights. Tonight she was wearing a red tunic, black stockings, and a cute pair of ankle boots. If she hadn't been wearing an oversized green hat, she would have looked like anyone else.

But that wouldn't have been the Kylie who was getting under his skin and making him feel alive for the first time in years.

She held a brown paper bag toward him. "Hi. I was driving home from Bailey's and thought you might like some takeout. If you've already eaten, you could have it tomorrow."

"You didn't have to do that."

Color stained her cheeks. "I felt bad about leaving so suddenly on Wednesday night. I thought if you couldn't come to us, I'd come to you."

"Thanks." Whatever was in the bag smelled delicious. "Do you want to come inside for a cup of coffee? John's here, too."

She shook her head. "I don't want to interrupt what you're doing."

"It's okay. We've finished looking over the resumés."

"Of the people who might work on your farm?"

Ben nodded. "We've filled most of the positions."

"Was it difficult?"

"Not really. John had already gone through the list of applicants to see if they were a good fit. All I had to do was select the applicants I thought would work well together. Come inside. It's cold out here."

After a moment's hesitation, Kylie smiled. "Okay. But I won't stay for long."

As soon as she moved, the sound of bells filled the air.

Taking off her hat, she sent him a shy smile. "I visited the local elementary school today. We talked about the Christmas wish program."

"Why did you wear a hat with bells?"

"The children like hearing them."

As soon as they walked into the living room, John gave Kylie a hug. "My favorite Christmas elf has arrived. Thank you for what you did for Mabel."

Her eyes widened. "No one was supposed to know it was me."

John smiled. "You know what Mabel is like. She couldn't bear the thought of not knowing who had brought her daughters to Sapphire Bay."

Kylie turned to Ben. "Mabel's always showing me photos of her daughters, but they only see each other once or twice a year. We couldn't run the Christmas wish program without Mabel and Allan's help, so I paid for their daughters to fly home for a few days."

"For Mabel's birthday," John added. "It was a really kind thing to do."

"I was happy to do it. Ben said you've decided who will be working on the farm."

John nodded. "Now all we have to do is tell them."

"Before we talk about how that will happen, I'll get everyone a fresh cup of coffee," Ben said. "Do you want cream and sugar, Kylie?"

"Just cream, please. Can I help?"

"No—"

"That's a great idea," John said quickly. "I'll put the job applications away while you're in the kitchen."

Ben's eyes narrowed.

John handed Ben his empty mug. "I'll only have one sugar this time."

The innocent look on his face didn't fool Ben. John was up to no good and there wasn't a thing he could do about it.

Kylie looked in Ben's mug. "Would you like more coffee, too?"

He shook his head. "I'll switch to water. Otherwise, I won't sleep tonight."

She opened the kitchen door. "I hung the frame with the pressed flowers in my store. It's amazing how many people have stopped to admire it."

Ben checked the coffeepot. "I'm glad. It's better than it sitting in the barn."

"That's for sure. When I told my customers about your Christmas shop, they all wanted to come and see it."

"That's great, but we have to finish it first. It will take a few weeks to get everything organized."

"Just in time for the start of the Christmas tree season,"

Kylie said happily. "I think we should make some posters telling people about the store. A lot of the businesses in town would display them."

"I'll put it on my list of things to do." He poured Kylie's coffee and reached for the cream. "We could do the same for other businesses. Especially if they're selling different products from the Christmas shop."

Kylie waited beside the counter while he made John's coffee. "While we're talking about the Christmas shop, who did you choose to work there?"

"Because they'll be making the wreaths and garlands, *and* serving customers, John and I thought we'd talk to you and decide together. If you want, you could look through the short-listed candidates tonight."

"Are you interviewing them?"

Ben shook his head. "I trust John's instincts. I'm also employing them on a fixed-term contract. If it doesn't work out, I don't have to re-employ them."

"That sounds like a sensible thing…" Kylie turned toward the living room.

"Is something wrong?"

"I thought I heard someone knock on the front door."

He looked through the kitchen window and frowned. Another truck was parked beside Kylie's.

A few seconds later, John walked into the kitchen and handed him an envelope. "A UPS guy dropped this off for you."

"He's working late." Before Ben opened the envelope, he checked the return address. "It's from my lawyer in Los Angeles."

Kylie picked up her coffee. "Do you want us to leave while you read what's inside?"

"It won't be important." Using a pair of scissors, he cut open the flap. "The last time I saw Roger was two years ago. I don't know why he would contact me, unless..." He scanned the first page of the document, then re-read the first paragraph. "This can't be true."

John moved closer. "What is it?"

"My lawyer wants me to fly to Los Angeles to pick up my daughter." He looked at Kylie and John. "I don't have a daughter. I don't have any children."

"He must have sent the envelope to the wrong person," John said. "What else does it say?"

Ben turned to the next page and slowly read through the photocopies of the court documents and the birth certificate.

"This is crazy." His heart pounded and sweat trickled down his spine. He didn't know whether to be angry or upset but, either way, he was shocked.

He was a dad.

And, for the first time ever, he was lost for words.

KYLIE CARRIED a kitchen chair across to Ben. "Sit down. You look as though you're going to faint." His weight landed heavily against the wooden frame. "Is that better?"

Ben nodded. "Why didn't Heather tell me?"

John thrust a glass of water under Ben's nose. "I don't know but, from what you've said, your marriage wasn't easy on either of you. How old is your daughter?"

"Four-and-a-half." Ben handed her the documents.

She looked at the little girl's birth certificate. Her name was Charlotte Amber Thompson and she was born on November 20 at the Paradise Valley Hospital in San Diego. Although Ben wasn't listed as the father, Charlotte had his last name.

The rest of the words blurred as Kylie remembered reading her own birth certificate over and over again, trying to make sense of the chaos that had turned her world upside down. No one in Sapphire Bay knew she was conceived as the result of an affair. Her mom had sworn that her biological father meant nothing to her, but that hadn't changed the outcome. The man she'd called Dad for eight years had left and never returned.

Without his income, her mom had to work all hours of the day and night to pay their rent and put food on the table. If it weren't for their seventy-five-year-old neighbor, Kylie would have felt all alone in the world.

She left the papers on the table. "How long were you married?"

"Six years. Not long into our marriage, I realized Heather had a problem with alcohol. I tried to get her help, but she wouldn't listen to anyone."

The heartache on his face told Kylie just how hard it must have been.

Ben took a deep breath. "The day after I came out of my coma, Mom and Dad told me Heather had filed for a divorce."

Kylie was stunned. Even if their marriage was falling apart, most people would do anything to help their partner recover from their injuries.

As if reading her mind, John placed his hand on her shoulder. "Addictions change people. Heather may not have been able to process what was happening."

Ben frowned. "Even if she didn't want to tell me she was pregnant, her parents could have said something."

John picked up the papers. "According to this letter, your daughter has been living with her grandparents for most of her life. Did you know her grandfather died three months ago?"

"No. Robyn must be devastated." Ben walked across to his laptop and started typing. "I'll never know what happened unless I fly to Los Angeles. The next flight from Polson doesn't leave until Friday. I'll try Kalispell."

When he reached for his wallet, Kylie knew he'd found a seat. "When do you leave?"

"Tomorrow afternoon. I'll ask Roger to let Robyn know I'm coming."

Kylie was still confused about one thing. "If Heather's parents have been looking after your daughter, where's Heather?"

Ben's eyes filled with regret. "She died two years ago in a car accident."

CHAPTER 6

*S*pending Saturday morning searching for things a four-year-old might need was the last thing Ben thought he'd be doing. But here he was, walking the length of Main Street looking for bargains.

Last night he'd called his sister. Donna's daughter, Lettie, was about the same age as Charlotte. If anyone knew what he'd need to buy, Donna would. Without knowing what Charlotte already had, Donna had started with the basics.

She was as shocked as Ben when he told her he had a daughter. His sister wanted him to get a DNA test, but he was already one step ahead of her. After John and Kylie had left, he'd sent his lawyer an email. Not only had he asked for a comparison of his DNA against Charlotte's, he'd asked for Heather's mom's phone number.

What he didn't understand was why Robyn had told him about his daughter. The only reason he came up with was that the stress of losing her husband and looking after a young child was too much.

With a heavy heart, he crossed the road. If Charlotte was his daughter, he would do everything he could to give her a safe, loving, and stable home. If she wasn't, he didn't know what he would do.

As he walked into the general store, he maneuvered around sparkly Christmas trees, displays of local crafts, and colorful tinsel hanging from the shelves. Usually, when he was anywhere near Christmas decorations, his heart pounded and he had trouble breathing. But not today. Maybe some of Kylie's Christmas spirit was rubbing off on him. Or maybe he had too many things on his mind.

"It's lovely to see you, Ben," Mabel said from behind the front counter. "How can I help you?"

He pulled out his list. So far, he'd crossed off most things, but he still had a few things to find. "Hi, Mabel. I need to buy some toys for a four-year-old girl, but I don't know what she would like."

"Are they for your niece?"

Ben shook his head. "It's for a friend's daughter. I'm looking after her for a few days." Ben's cheeks burned. Who in their right mind would leave their four-year-old with him? He hated lying, but if he told Mabel he had a daughter, she wouldn't let him leave without telling her every detail. And before the sun went down, half of Sapphire Bay would know what was happening.

"How much money did you want to spend?"

"Not too much."

Mabel tapped her chin. "Let me see… Do the toys need to be new?"

Ben shook his head. "Secondhand is fine. As long as they're clean and safe."

"In that case," Mabel picked up the phone. "Let me call Allan. We have a container of old toys that used to belong to our girls. We've kept them for our grandchildren, but that hasn't happened yet. I'd be happy to lend them to you."

A weight lifted off his shoulders. He didn't have a lot of

extra money and he was thankful for any savings. "I'll take good care of them."

"I know you will." While Mabel called her husband, Ben crossed the store and studied the display of power tools. He wondered what Charlotte looked like. Was she a giggly little girl or did she take life more seriously?

He picked up an electric drill. Would she like spending time with him in the barn or would she get bored?

A light touch on his arm had him spinning around.

"Sorry," Kylie said, jumping clear of the drill. "I didn't mean to startle you."

"It's okay." He returned the drill to the display and glanced at Mabel. She was still talking to her husband. "I was thinking about Charlotte."

"It's a lot to take in. Is there anything I can do?"

"I think I've got everything I need. I didn't tell Mabel. She thinks a friend's daughter is staying with me."

Kylie leaned forward. "That's probably wise," she whispered. "But you might want to tell her at some point. She has a heart of gold and would understand what's happened."

"Before I tell anyone, I want to make sure Charlotte's..." He felt as though he was betraying his daughter by even thinking she might not be his biological child.

"It's okay. It's important to know the truth." Kylie looked at her watch. "Do you want to have an early lunch with me? There's plenty of extra food in my refrigerator."

Ben shook his head. "I'd like to, but I can't. After I take everything back to the farm, I'll have to leave straightaway for the airport."

"That's all right. How do you feel about meeting Charlotte?"

He sighed. "Scared. Worried. Guilty."

"Why guilty?"

"I let her down."

Kylie touched his arm. "You didn't know you had a daughter."

"It doesn't make me feel any better. I'm hoping Heather's mom will tell me why no one said anything."

Mabel came bustling toward them. "Allan is bringing the toys down now." Her smile widened for Kylie. "How's my favorite florist?"

"I'll be better once the fundraising Christmas party has finished."

"It will be over before you know it. Allan has pressed his favorite navy pinstriped suit and polished his shoes. It's going to be a lovely night to remember."

Kylie lifted the strap of her bag onto her shoulder. "I hope so." She turned to him and smiled. "I'd better get some lunch. Enjoy the rest of the day."

Ben nodded. He was grateful she hadn't mentioned anything about Los Angeles. "I'll call you on Sunday afternoon."

"Okay." With a final smile to Ben and Mabel, Kylie left the store.

At least his secret was safe for today. By next week, it could be a whole lot different.

As BEN WALKED out of the airport terminal in Los Angeles, the first thing he noticed was the smell. He'd forgotten how much the air irritated his throat and made his lungs burn. After two years of breathing the fresh mountain air of Sapphire Bay, he was glad he wasn't living here permanently.

"It won't take long to get to the parking lot." Roger led him toward a line of people waiting for a shuttle.

Either his lawyer was being optimistic or Ben had forgotten how quickly the ground transportation moved.

"Were you able to contact Charlotte's grandmother?" He was desperate for news about his daughter. On the four-hour flight, he'd worried about how Charlotte would react to being taken away from her grandma. It was a stressful situation for him, but for a four-year-old, it would be even worse.

Roger stood behind the last person waiting in line. "I called Robyn this morning." He looked at Ben. "When her husband died, it set off a chain of events that made it impossible for her to look after Charlotte."

"Why didn't she tell me about Charlotte when she was born?"

"You'll have to ask Robyn. She's meeting us in my office in an hour."

Ben's hand tightened on the handle of his suitcase. "Will Charlotte be there?"

Roger nodded. "You'll be able to take her back to the hotel with you."

"What if she doesn't want to leave her grandmother?"

Roger must have sensed Ben's rising panic. "She doesn't have a choice. Charlotte needs a home. Apart from going into foster care, you're her only option." He placed his hand on Ben's arm. "I know this is a lot to take in, but coming here was the right thing to do."

Ben took a deep breath. Knowing it was right didn't make it any easier—for him, Charlotte, or Robyn.

KYLIE WIPED her forehead with the back of her hand. For the last three hours, she'd been working in the barn on Ben's Christmas tree farm.

Last night, after Ben recovered from the initial shock of discovering he had a daughter, reality had set in. He was heading into the busiest time of the year. He had told her and

John that it was hard enough when he only had himself to organize. But with a four-year-old daughter living with him, he was worried it would be impossible to work the long hours the farm needed.

They'd told him it would be okay. The people he'd chosen to work on the farm would be his lifesaver. Without their help, he didn't stand a chance of harvesting enough trees to keep the business from foreclosure.

It didn't surprise Kylie when John called her at lunchtime. He'd spoken to Ben and organized a group of people to make a start on the Christmas shop. Knowing how much work they had to do, she thought it could only be a good thing. The sooner the shop was ready, the more income Ben could potentially make.

So here they were: John, Kylie, and ten of the church's construction students creating Sapphire Bay's first Christmas shop.

"Don't step backward," John warned as he leaned a sheet of drywall against the timber frame behind her.

She picked up the electric drill she'd been using. "I'll help you screw it into place."

"That would be great. Just give me a couple of minutes to stick the glue on the frame."

While John prepared the walls, Kylie's gaze traveled along the length of the barn. Pale gray drywall separated the new storage area from what would be the Christmas shop. It would be an amazing space. With all of Ben's equipment moved out of the way, there was so much more room than she'd imagined.

When John was finished, she screwed the drywall onto the frame. "I didn't think we would get so much done."

"All it takes is a little teamwork."

Kylie smiled. "And access to lots of builders."

John shrugged. "It's a great experience for the students."

It was so much more than that. John's heart was as big as his imagination. He connected people with unique opportunities that made a difference in the community. Even the most hardened souls gravitated toward the kindness that was in every cell of his body.

Take this morning, for instance. Without knowing anything about Ben, the construction crew in the old steamboat museum had built the frames that would separate the shop from the barn. Kylie knew for a fact that they were busy building the tiny homes, but that hadn't made a difference to their willingness to help. One word from John and they were happy to drop what they were doing for someone in need.

John picked up another drill and climbed a ladder. "I'll do the top screws and meet you in the middle."

"Okay." Kylie took more screws out of a container. Ben wouldn't arrive back at the farm until tomorrow afternoon. That gave them a few more hours to finish what they had started.

"Someone's looking after us," John said as he looked across the room.

Kylie glanced over her shoulder and smiled. Earlier in the day, she'd gone with John to let Nate know that Ben had chosen him to work on the Christmas tree farm. Shona, Nate's mom, was overwhelmed when Kylie asked her if she wanted to sell her quilts in the Christmas shop.

Now they were both here, emptying two picnic baskets of home baking onto a makeshift table.

Mabel followed them into the barn with even more food.

John grinned. "It looks as though no one will go hungry tonight."

Kylie looked at the people plastering the drywall, sweeping the floor, and assembling the secondhand shelves Mabel's husband had found. Everyone was here because they wanted to make a difference. And they would, not just to Ben, but to his daughter and the people he was employing.

She just hoped the fundraising Christmas party was as successful at bringing people together. With less than a week until the event, a lot of work still needed to be done.

CHAPTER 7

*B*en had never been this nervous. After he'd checked into his hotel, Roger had driven them to his office. Even though Charlotte and Robyn weren't supposed to be here for another ten minutes, Ben couldn't help rechecking his watch.

"If you keep pacing, you'll wear a hole in my floor." Roger handed him a cup of coffee. "Come and have a seat. I'll give you the name and address of the DNA clinic you'll be visiting tomorrow. Robyn will have her DNA tested at the same time."

"Why?"

"To make sure there's a maternal link to her granddaughter."

Ben took a moment to think through what Roger was saying. "You think Heather might not be Charlotte's mother?"

"At this stage, I'm not assuming anything."

Ben stared through the window. Under California law, he was presumed to be Charlotte's father because he was married to Heather when Charlotte was conceived. But if

Heather wasn't Charlotte's mother, where did that leave Charlotte?

He took a deep breath. "Do you send many people to have their DNA tested?"

"More than you might think." Roger pushed a folder across his desk. "Everything you'll need at the clinic is in here. I've included a copy of Charlotte's birth certificate, her hospital records, your marriage certificate to Heather, and other documentation that verifies, to the best of our knowledge, both your and Robyn's relationship to Charlotte."

A knock on the office door brought Ben to his feet. Unless his lawyer was expecting another client at seven o'clock at night, Robyn and Charlotte had arrived.

"Are you ready to meet your daughter?"

Ben wiped his hands on his jeans and nodded. He wasn't the type of person who prayed, but tonight was completely different. He desperately wanted to make sure Charlotte was okay; that what had happened between him and his wife hadn't destroyed a little girl's life.

Before Roger opened the door, he glanced at Ben. "It will be all right."

It was all very well for his lawyer to be so optimistic, but Ben was terrified.

"Hi, Robyn and Charlotte. Ben is waiting in my office." Roger held open the door.

A little girl stepped into the room. Dressed in a bright red coat, she looked at Ben with eyes that were so like his mom's his breath caught. Pale gold hair, the same shade as Heather's, fell to her shoulders, bouncing against her coat as she looked up at her grandma, then back at him.

Ben lifted his gaze to Robyn. When he'd booked his ticket for Los Angeles, he knew this moment wouldn't be easy for him or his ex-mother-in-law. They'd always had a good relationship. It wasn't until after his divorce that everything fell apart.

He held out his hand. Regardless of what had happened or how they felt about each other, he wanted this meeting to go as smoothly as possible. "It's good to see you again, Robyn. Roger told me Garry died a few months ago. I'm sorry. He was a good man."

"Thank you."

At least she shook his hand. It was a better start than it could have been. He had a lot of questions for her but, right now, they could wait. Giving his full attention to Charlotte was his main priority.

He knelt on the floor, hoping she didn't feel as overwhelmed as he did. "Hi. My name is Ben."

Instead of saying anything, Charlotte clutched her grandma's hand.

Ben's sister had warned him she may not want to talk to him. She was four years old, and he was a total stranger. So he pulled out Plan B. Hopefully, the small, gift-wrapped toy would help Charlotte feel more comfortable.

"This is for you."

Her blue eyes lifted to her grandmother's.

"It's okay," Robyn murmured. "This is the man I was telling you about."

"My daddy?"

Ben's heart slammed against his ribs. It was the first time anyone had called him daddy. Suddenly, everything that had happened over the last two days came crashing down around him.

Yesterday, Charlotte was a name on a birth certificate. Today, she was a living, breathing, human being who couldn't be anyone but his daughter.

Wiping his eyes, he held the gift closer to Charlotte. "Do you like purple dinosaurs?"

The wariness in her eyes was replaced with excitement. "I saw a dinosaur at the zoo."

"That must have been amazing."

Charlotte's short, sharp nod made him smile. "It had a long neck, like this." She stretched her neck high, straining every muscle in her little body.

He assumed Charlotte was talking about a giraffe. If he was four-and-a-half years old, he would get them mixed up, too. "You have a cousin named Lettie. She loves purple dinosaurs and thought you'd like one, too." He handed her the gift, hoping she would take it.

"Thank you." Charlotte sat on the floor and tore off the wrapping paper.

Her grin broke Ben's heart. He thought of all the birthdays, the Christmases, and the special events he hadn't spent with his daughter. All because Heather and her parents didn't want him to know about her.

Roger's secretary came into the room. She smiled at Charlotte and admired her gift. "Would you like to draw a picture of your dinosaur? I've got a box of color pencils in my desk."

Charlotte glanced at Robyn.

Her grandmother's nod was all the encouragement she needed. Jumping to her feet, she happily followed Roger's secretary into the other room.

Regardless of what happened next, Ben wouldn't miss another day of his daughter's life. She deserved the best of who he was and he would make sure she got it.

As soon as the door closed, Roger motioned to the seats in front of his desk. "Let's sit down and discuss where we go to from here."

Ben took the seat closest to the window. At least, that way, Robyn would be on his right-hand side. This conversation was too important to risk missing anything that was said.

"Perhaps if I start?" Robyn's words weren't so much a question, as a command. When Ben had known her, she was the manager at a large recruitment agency, and it showed.

"You probably think the worst of me, Ben. But no words can ever express how sorry I am for not telling you about Charlotte. Heather didn't want you to know. She was terrified you'd take her baby away."

"Because she was an alcoholic?"

Robyn lifted her chin. "Before she died, Heather had changed. She was sober and doing really well."

"When did you find out she was pregnant?"

"We didn't. The first we heard about Charlotte was after she was born. She was two months old when we saw her for the first time."

Ben rubbed his hand across his tired eyes. "What happened to Heather after she left Los Angeles?"

"She moved to San Diego. We thought she wanted to make a fresh start. She told us she wasn't drinking." Robyn glanced at Roger. "We were shocked when she introduced us to Charlotte."

Ben didn't know if he believed her.

"I know it sounds far-fetched, but Heather didn't want us to visit her."

"Even if that were true, it doesn't explain why you didn't tell me about Charlotte after Heather died." Suddenly, everything clicked into place. Ben felt sick to his stomach when he realized what Robyn and her husband had done. "Is that why you didn't tell me that Heather had died until after you held a funeral for her? Because you didn't want me to take Charlotte away?"

Robyn bowed her head. When she looked at him, there was a lifetime of regret in her gaze. "Heather came to live with us when Charlotte was a baby. Our daughter was a mess but, once she was living with us, she really tried to stop drinking. In between rehab and attending AA meetings, she was turning her life around. And then the accident..."

In a cruel twist of fate, a drunk driver had hit Heather's car head-on. She'd died two days later in the hospital.

Ben swallowed his bitterness. Even though his marriage hadn't been easy, he'd loved Heather. He would have given anything for a chance to say goodbye.

"You didn't answer my question," he repeated. "Why did you leave it so long to tell me Heather had died?"

Robyn's bottom lip quivered. "We couldn't tell you. You would have come to her funeral and someone would have told you about Charlotte."

"And when I visited Heather's grave? Where was Charlotte then?"

"We asked a friend to look after her. We thought we were doing what was best for our granddaughter. She was happy with us."

Ben ignored the pleading appeal in Robyn's voice. For four-and-a-half years, she'd kept Charlotte's existence a secret from him. He didn't know if he could ever forgive her.

"And now?" he asked.

"Three years ago, I was diagnosed with breast cancer. After my treatment, I went into remission. But the cancer has come back, only this time it's more aggressive. My oncologist said I have less than a year to live." Robyn took a deep breath. "If Garry was still alive, he would look after Charlotte. I know there will come a time when I can't look after my granddaughter. She needs to be with family, to be loved like every little girl deserves. You're her last hope."

Although they hadn't always agreed with each other, Ben

had always admired Robyn's strength. He could see how difficult it was for her to tell him she was dying, how hard it was to ask for help.

His anger was replaced with something he couldn't describe. He was devastated by Robyn's news, horrified by her actions. It was heartbreaking to know that the only reason she'd told him about Charlotte was because she was dying.

Roger cleared his throat. "Robyn has a couple of requests she'd like to make."

Robyn's chin lifted. "I couldn't bear to lose contact with my granddaughter. I'd like to bring Charlotte back to California in a couple of months to spend a week with me. If we could also talk on the phone and via the Internet, I'd appreciate it."

Tears rolled down her cheeks. "Regardless of what you think of me, I love Charlotte. I want to be part of her life for as long as I can."

Roger handed Robyn a box of tissues, then focused on Ben. "You don't have to decide what you want to do today." When Ben didn't reply, he continued. "There are a few more things we need to talk about. If you want to add your name to Charlotte's birth certificate, we need to complete several forms. Although you're presumed to be Charlotte's father, a judge will decide if your name can be added to Charlotte's birth certificate. The easiest way to prove your relationship is to do a DNA test."

"What if I'm not her biological father?"

Robyn's head shot up. "Heather wouldn't have lied about something so important."

"Ben's not suggesting she did," Roger said sympathetically. "Even if the DNA results tell us that Ben isn't related to Charlotte, he is still considered to be her presumptive parent because he was married to Heather when Charlotte was conceived."

Ben took a deep breath. Robyn was so upset she was trembling. He knew how close she'd been to Heather and how difficult it was to understand her daughter's addiction to alcohol. Regardless of how hurt he was, Ben couldn't keep Charlotte away from her grandmother—not after everything they'd been through.

"I want my name on Charlotte's birth certificate. And if you draw up some kind of visitation agreement, Roger, I'll sign it."

Robyn burst into tears. "Thank you."

Ben could only nod and hope that everything worked out for the best. Because right now, he didn't know what would happen.

If Ben thought yesterday was hard, today was worse. After they'd finished talking to Roger, they decided it would be better for Charlotte to go home with her grandmother.

By eleven o'clock the next morning, they'd completed the DNA test and Robyn, Charlotte, and Ben were waiting at the airport for the flight to Kalispell.

"I packed lots of snacks for Charlotte," Robyn said as she handed him a medium-sized backpack. "Before she goes to bed, she likes to listen to a story. Dinosaur books and fairy tales are her favorite, but keep an eye on the time. You'll be awake all night if she thinks you're happy to keep reading."

"I'll remember."

"And her favorite food is mac and cheese. If she has a temperature or feels unwell, it's one of the few things she'll eat."

"I know how to make mac and cheese."

Charlotte smiled at him. She knew she was going to live with Ben, but he didn't think she realized that meant leaving Grandma behind.

Robyn looked nervously around the departure area. "You've got my phone number. If you could call me when you arrive home, it would put my mind at ease."

Ben nodded. He wanted to reassure Robyn, to tell her everything would be all right, but he was just as nervous as she was. "I'll also send you plenty of photos and Charlotte can talk to you each night. If I have any questions about her, I'll call you right away."

A man's voice filled the concourse. Passengers on Ben's flight were being asked to make their way to their boarding gate.

Robyn's panicked gaze shot to his. "I'm not ready to say goodbye."

"We're only four hours away." Ben was the last person who wanted to come between Robyn and her granddaughter. When he'd calmed down, he realized they both only wanted the best for Charlotte.

Tears filled Robyn's eyes as she knelt in front of her granddaughter. "Grandma is going home now. Have a wonderful time with Daddy."

Charlotte's small hands touched Robyn's face. "Why you crying, Grandma?"

"Because I'll miss you. I love you very much." Pulling Charlotte into her arms, Robyn hugged her close. "I'll talk to you on the phone when you arrive at Daddy's house."

"Pinky promise?" Charlotte said with a wobbly smile.

Robyn wiped her eyes and held out her little finger. "Pinky promise."

Ben checked his watch. "We should go. I'm not sure how long it will take us to walk to the gate."

Robyn took a deep breath, hugged Charlotte once more,

then pulled herself to her feet. "Take good care of my grand-daughter, Ben."

"I will." For the first time in two years, he hugged Robyn. "It will be okay."

"I hope so," she said sadly.

Before more tears fell, Ben held Charlotte's hand and led her toward their gate.

One day, he would look back and see that this was a huge turning point in his life—the beginning of something wonderful. But right now, he felt as though he were treading water and trying not to drown.

KYLIE CAREFULLY CLEANED the last of the paint out of her brush. For the last five hours she, and most of the people who had been here yesterday, had been working in Ben's Christmas shop, painting the walls.

She couldn't believe the difference a few partition walls and two coats of paint could make. Instead of the big, cavernous space that had greeted them on Saturday, the barn finally looked like a Christmas shop.

They'd painted the new wall behind the front counter a bright, cheerful shade of red. The other temporary walls were a deep forest green. They were a perfect backdrop to the dark brown wooden shelving and the colorful Christmas decorations and ornaments that would fill the shop.

She hoped Ben liked what they had done. Pastor John had told him they would be making a start on the Christmas shop, but not how much they hoped to achieve.

John placed two empty buckets beside the water faucet. "The last truck just left. Mabel and Emma said they'd see you at nine o'clock tomorrow. They've cleared their schedules to give you a hand with the party."

"That's great. Did Levi make the last set of shelves before he left?"

John nodded. "He did and they look fantastic. We did good this weekend."

"I hope it's enough to help Ben."

"I don't think he'll have a problem selling any of the decorations. Besides, the farm already has a great reputation for producing beautiful Christmas trees. The shop will only encourage more people to come here." John tilted his head to the side. "Are you sure you aren't worried about something else?"

Kylie slowly dried the brush on an old rag. "Raising a four-year-old on the farm will be difficult. Where will she go when he needs to work?"

"Knowing Ben, he will already have a plan in place. It won't be easy, but he knew that before he left for Los Angeles."

"What if Charlotte isn't his daughter?" As soon as the words were out of her mouth, Kylie regretted them. Just because her biological father hadn't wanted anything to do with her, it didn't mean Ben would be the same.

John sighed. "I hope for everyone's sake she is. But, at the end of the day, she's a little girl who needs a home."

Kylie's eyes filled with tears. "You're a good man."

"So are a lot of people." John studied her face. "It's not like you to be so emotional. Not that you aren't emotional, but—"

"Don't worry. I know what you mean." She took a deep breath, fighting back another wave of tears. "I guess I'm a little tired. It's good that the Christmas shop is ready. Now I can concentrate on making sure the old steamboat museum is ready for next weekend's party."

"I'll be there on Wednesday but, if you need more help, let me know. I can postpone most of my appointments."

Kylie placed her brush in a bucket John had brought with

him. "Thanks, but at this stage, we're okay. As long as Willow's lighting team arrives on Thursday, we'll be fine."

She checked her watch. "Ben's flight arrived in Kalispell two hours ago. He shouldn't be too far away."

"I've been thinking the same thing for the last half hour," John said with a smile. "It wasn't easy making sure everyone left before he arrives home."

"You did well. Mabel and her husband would still be here if you hadn't asked them to order more fairy lights."

John laughed. "I've learned a thing or two about diversionary tactics since I've been living here. And talking about the fairy lights, I'd better turn on the ones we hung today."

While John rushed into the Christmas shop, Kylie carried the buckets to her truck. Everyone had worked so hard to make this dream a reality, now all they had to do was fill the barn with the magic of Christmas.

CHAPTER 8

*B*en stopped his truck in his driveway. Swinging from above the gate was a brand new, bright red sign. In large gold letters, it welcomed visitors to The Christmas Tree Farm. It was exactly the same shape and design as the logo Emma had created for his website.

He smiled as he remembered the conversation he'd had with Kylie and Emma about creating a brand for his company. They'd given him a crash course in marketing, covering things he'd never considered before now.

If he wasn't careful, they would make him wear one of the T-shirts they'd created for the Christmas shop staff. As much as he was getting used to Kylie's colorful wardrobe, it didn't mean he wanted to wear a black T-shirt covered in screen-printed candy canes.

He glanced over his shoulder at Charlotte. Unlike him, she would look adorable in the T-shirts.

During the flight to Kalispell, she'd told him about her favorite things, drawn lots of pictures, and listened to some stories he'd read. When she was tired, she'd sucked her two middle fingers and cuddled her toy bear.

It wasn't until they were in the truck that she fell into a deep sleep. He didn't know what she would think of the Christmas shop or the farm, but he hoped that one day she would be as proud of it as he was.

With one last look at the sign, he drove along the gravel driveway. John and Kylie were supposed to be the only people here. Just to be sure, he'd texted John before he left the airport.

When he saw the two trucks parked outside the barn, he breathed a sigh of relief.

Admitting that he'd missed Kylie was as foreign to him as running a Christmas shop, but that's what had happened. Somewhere between her quirky dresses and big blue eyes, he'd developed feelings for her that went far deeper than friendship.

He was more nervous about introducing her to Charlotte than he'd been when he'd met his daughter. What if Kylie didn't like children? What if she didn't want to spend as much time with him now that he had a four-year-old to look after?

But the worst and most devastating question in his mind had nothing to do with Kylie. What if Charlotte wasn't his daughter? What if everything Robyn and her husband had been told was a lie?

The results from the DNA test wouldn't be available for at least six weeks. A lot could happen in that time, including falling in love with a little girl who had the biggest smile and longest lashes he'd ever seen.

Ben's heart pounded as Kylie and John walked toward him. Kylie was wearing jeans. Plain blue jeans with a deep gray sweater. Mrs. Claus was nowhere in sight, but Kylie's smile was.

Relieved beyond belief, he parked his truck and quietly opened the door. He didn't want Charlotte to be startled when she woke. It was bad enough that she was in a different town, but not having her grandma to cuddle if she became upset would be worse.

John held out his hand. "Welcome home. How was your flight?"

"Quick, thank goodness. Charlotte was awake the whole time but, as soon as we drove out of the airport, she fell asleep."

Kylie looked at the truck. "I think she might be awake."

Ben turned around. Charlotte was rubbing her eyes and yawning. He opened the door and smiled at his daughter. "You had a good sleep."

Charlotte frowned, then glanced at Kylie and John. "Where's grandma?"

"She's at her house. This is where I live."

"I want to see grandma."

"We'll talk to her on the phone soon." Ben undid the car seat harness and lifted his daughter into his arms. "Would you like to meet my friends?"

Charlotte nodded. When she saw Kylie and John, her arms tightened around his neck.

Kylie smiled. "Hi, Charlotte. I'm Kylie."

"You have pretty hair."

Kylie's smile widened. "So do you. It's lovely to meet you."

Ben nodded to John. "And this is my friend, Pastor John."

"It's nice to meet you, Charlotte. Do you want to see what we've been doing in the barn?"

Charlotte's nod was more cautious than excited.

John grinned. "Did your dad tell you we're making a Christmas shop on his farm?"

"Like Santa's workshop?" Her eyes met Ben's. There was no doubting the excitement in her face now.

"Almost like Santa's workshop," Ben said as he followed John.

Kylie pointed to the sign above the doors. "What do you think?"

It was a replica of the one on the front gate. "The signs are amazing. I don't know how I'll ever repay you."

"You don't need to," Kylie said quickly. "Everyone pitched in to help. It's what we do."

Ben was incredibly grateful, but he didn't deserve everyone's thoughtfulness. For weeks, he'd told Kylie he couldn't give her the trees for the Christmas party. He felt worse than a fraud. "The trees and mistletoe I'm donating aren't enough…" As he stepped into the barn, a low whistle escaped his lips. "This is incredible."

John smiled. "I'm glad you like it. Everyone has worked long hours to get the barn to this stage."

Ben lowered Charlotte to the floor and held her hand. They'd painted the wall in front of him bright red. Fairy lights hung from the rafters, draped down the walls, and twinkled from the wreaths above the wooden shelves.

He walked across to an ornate, gilt-framed mirror. It must have been six-foot wide and nearly as tall. "Where did you find this?"

John smiled. "It was in Mabel and Allan's attic. They're lending it to you until you find something else you want to place on the wall."

It would be hard to find anything that looked as good. The mirror reflected the light coming through the barn doors. Combined with the soft glow from the fairy lights and the old-fashioned pendant lights, it gave the shop a magical quality that fluorescent lights would never achieve.

Even though most of the shelves were empty, Ben could imagine what the shop would look like in the next few weeks. "How did you get everything done so quickly?"

Kylie refolded a quilt. "We had a lot of help. After tomorrow, everyone will be busy making Christmas decorations and ornaments you can sell. By the end of the week, you won't recognize the barn."

Charlotte tugged Ben's hand. "Where are the toys?"

"They won't arrive for a few days, but I've got some other toys for you."

"Are they from Santa's workshop?"

Ben shook his head. "They're from somewhere even more special. Do you want to see them?"

Charlotte's head nodded furiously. "Yes, please."

Kylie smiled. "I'd better go home but, before I do, there's something else we want to show you."

John lifted a circular piece of metal off a shelf. "Natalie restored the original Christmas farm sign for you."

Ben couldn't believe how good it looked. Instead of repainting everything, she'd only fixed the worst areas. Despite the cracks and faded paint, the sign kept its classic, vintage appeal.

He couldn't have been happier. "It would look amazing on one of the green walls."

"We thought the same thing." John climbed a stepladder and placed the sign over a heavy-duty picture hook. "What do you think?"

"It's perfect. Everything you've done is better than I imagined." Ben looked around the barn. "It's incredible."

Kylie knelt in front of Charlotte. "We'd better go so that you can play with your toys. It was really nice meeting you."

Charlotte reached out and touched Kylie's hair. "Will you come back?"

"I'd like that very much, but it won't be for a few days. I've got a Christmas party to organize."

"Can I come?"

"You'll have to ask your dad," Kylie whispered.

Charlotte's big blue eyes lifted to Ben's. "Can we go to the party?"

Between John and Kylie's amused expressions and Charlotte's excitement, Ben didn't stand a chance. "Yes, we can go to the party. But sometimes it's hard for me to hear what people are saying."

Charlotte frowned. "It's okay, Daddy. I'll look after you."

And just like that, Ben fell in love with his daughter.

❄

KYLIE LIFTED another bag of pine tree branches onto the workbench. "This should be enough for the next hour. Does anyone need more holly or lavender?"

Emma shook her head. "Not me. But I'll need another red bow soon."

Kylie took a bag of bows off a shelf and left a handful in front of Emma. "How about you, Bailey?"

"I'm okay at the moment. Does anyone want a cup of coffee?"

"I'll get it," Kylie said quickly. "I need to spray more pine cones with gold paint, anyway."

"I can get the coffee." Bailey stood and stretched her arms above her head. "You've been running around after us for the last hour. Why don't you sit down and have a break?"

"There's too much to do." Monday was always busy, but today had been frantic. In between showing her new part-time staff how to create Christmas wreaths and garlands, she'd helped customers and made a lot of bouquets. After everyone had gone home, Emma and Bailey arrived to make decorations for the Christmas party on Saturday night.

Bailey pulled out a chair. "Sit down and leave the coffee to me. Have you had anything for dinner?"

"I'll grab something later."

Bailey stuck her hands on her hips. "You have to look

after yourself. After we've finished, I'll help you cook something for dinner."

"Are you always this bossy?" Kylie asked.

"Only when you aren't listening to me."

Emma laughed. "You know you won't win, so give in gracefully."

Giving in gracefully wasn't something Kylie was used to. For more years than she wanted to remember, her destiny had been in her hands. If she didn't put in the hard work, nothing got done. But now that the trainees were working in Blooming Lovely, she had to trust that everyone would do a good job.

Bailey stopped in front of the small kitchen in the workroom. "What do you want me to do with the lavender that's sitting in the sink?"

"If you can work around it, leave it there," Kylie said as she added more branches to Bailey's wreath.

"Okay."

With five days left until Sapphire Bay's biggest Christmas party, everyone was working super hard to get everything finished. Today, Pastor John's construction trainees were clearing out the old steamboat museum. It was such a big job that no one expected it to be finished until Wednesday morning. By Thursday they needed all the decorations in place so that the lighting team could set up their equipment. Friday was sound check day and completing anything that hadn't been done during the week. It was enough to make Kylie's head spin.

"You look as though you're a million miles away," Emma said as she placed another finished wreath on a shelf.

"I'm just thinking about everything that needs to happen before Saturday. It will be a busy time."

"Just think about the tiny home we'll be able to build from the money we raise."

Sometimes, it was the only thing that kept Kylie going. "The construction team moved another house into the village today."

"Pastor John must be really pleased."

"Especially with winter not far away. That's one less family that will be homeless." Kylie held two bows against the wreath she was finishing. "Gold or red?"

Emma looked at the wreath. "Gold. It looks better with the pine cones. We didn't get a chance to see Ben after he arrived home. What did he think of the barn?"

"He was impressed. I don't think he realized how much we could do in two days."

"Neither did I. I can't believe we haven't had a Christmas shop in Sapphire Bay before now. Especially with The Christmas Tree Farm being so popular."

"I guess it's the same as most towns. You get used to what's there. It isn't until you need to find other ways to make money that you realize how much potential you have."

"And Ben's Christmas tree farm has loads of potential," Bailey said as she placed hot cups of coffee in front of Emma and Kylie.

"What about Ben?" Emma asked. "Does he have potential, too?"

Kylie felt her cheeks burn. "Maybe."

Emma grinned. "From what I've seen, you and Ben are more than a maybe. The man adores you."

"No, he doesn't. We're friends, that's all." Kylie threaded a piece of thin wire through a gold bow and hoped her friends started talking about something else.

"Friends with potential," Bailey said wistfully. "I don't think I'll ever find someone like that."

Emma gave Bailey a hug. "It will happen when you least expect it. Jack and I are a good example of that. He lived in New York City and I was here, but we still found each other."

Bailey grinned. "And look at you now—planning a wedding and raising two beautiful children. It's no wonder you're glowing."

Emma lifted her hands to her cheeks. "It's all the talk about love and potential. Imagine if we could sprinkle a little love onto each flower Kylie sells. People would order bouquets for everyone they know."

"The extra money could build tiny home villages across America," Bailey added. "People wouldn't be homeless, children wouldn't go to school hungry, and there would be lots of wrap-around services to help people get back on their feet."

Kylie's eyes widened. "That's not such a crazy idea."

Emma frowned. "Building tiny home villages everywhere?"

"That, too. But I was meaning sprinkling a little love on the flowers I sell. We have a lot of people whose Christmas wishes won't come true because they're too expensive. What if we sold flowers for different wishes? People could choose which wish they want to support. In return, they receive a flower and know they've made a difference in someone's life."

"We could have three or four wishes happening at once," Emma said enthusiastically. "I could run the fundraising event through Blooming Lovely's website and change the flowers and wishes each week."

Bailey frowned. "What if you don't get enough donations in one week for a wish?"

"We could keep it going for longer." Kylie picked up a gold-painted pine cone. "I think it could work really well."

"I agree," Emma said. "What about you, Bailey? Do you think it would make a difference?"

"I think it would make a huge difference, but I wouldn't

start it until next year. We've still got a Christmas party, a carol competition, and a train trip to organize."

Kylie looked at the Christmas decorations stacked on the shelves. They were already working long hours to raise money for the tiny home village. The last thing they needed was another project. "You're right. Let's get the next two months out of the way before we begin something else."

And for Kylie, her 'something else' would have to include Ben.

ON TUESDAY AFTERNOON, Ben drove into Sapphire Bay, hoping The Welcome Center would be the answer to his prayers.

For the last two days, he'd been training the young people who had joined him on the farm. The first day was relatively easy. Charlotte had stood beside him as he'd run through the health and safety briefing. Then, as they'd toured the farm, she'd sat silently beside him as he'd explained what happened to the trees at each stage in their growth. From there it had gone downhill.

When they'd walked between the rows of trees, Charlotte was in her element. He'd spent a good ten minutes chasing her as she'd darted between the trunks. The trainees thought it was hilarious, but Ben was worried she'd get lost. From then on, her little hand never left his.

On Tuesday, he found a length of twine and made a harness for her. If his mom and dad saw him, they would be shocked, but he didn't know what else to do. It wasn't until Kylie told him about a child care service at The Welcome Center, that he saw a way he could still work on the farm.

With a weary sigh, he checked the rearview mirror. Charlotte still had her eyes closed, but he didn't expect that to last for long. In the last forty-eight hours, he'd learned that she had boundless energy and chatted nonstop about anything and everything around her. In a lot of ways, she reminded him of Heather. At other times, all it took was one look and she could have been his sister.

As soon as he stopped his truck in the parking lot, Charlotte's eyelids fluttered open.

"Is Grandma here?"

"Not today. We've come to see Pastor John. Do you remember him?"

Charlotte shook her head. "I want Grandma."

"I know you do. How about we call her after dinner? She enjoyed talking to you last night." He undid the car seat harness and lifted Charlotte into his arms. With her puffy jacket wrapped around her little body, she felt as light as a marshmallow.

"I want to see Grandma." Charlotte's eyes filled with tears.

"Grandma is at her house. We'll see her another day." Before she could ask what day, Ben pointed to the old gray cat that had wandered out of the center. "Look over there, Charlotte. That's Mr. Whiskers."

She squealed in delight, then wiggled like a fish on the end of a line.

Ben winced as he placed her on the ground. Being deaf in one ear had distinct advantages, especially around an excited four-year-old.

"Be careful. Mr. Whiskers is very old and has sore bones."

"Like Grandma?"

Ben held back a smile. Robyn wouldn't be impressed if she heard Charlotte comparing her to a cat. "Not quite. Mr. Whiskers is much older than Grandma."

Charlotte pulled him toward the doorway. "Does Mr. Whiskers live here?"

"He does. No one knows where he came from, but he's lived here for a long time."

Her steps slowed. "Can I pat him?"

"You can try. Mr. Whiskers will let you know if he doesn't want to be patted."

Charlotte studied the well-loved cat who was sitting beside the entrance to The Welcome Center, lazily scratching an itchy spot under his chin. "How will I know if he wants a pat? Cats can't talk. They meow. I don't know what meows mean."

"Mr. Whiskers has other ways of letting you know how he's feeling." Ben knelt on the wooden veranda. They were close enough to see what Mr. Whiskers was doing, but not close enough for Charlotte to leap on him.

Ben hoped Mr. Whiskers was in a good mood. "Do you see how his tail is curled around his body?"

Charlotte's solemn smile was endearing.

"That means he's happy. If his tail was standing straight up, he would be scared or angry."

"Is he happy because he wants me to pat him?"

"I think so." Ben stood and walked slowly toward Mr. Whiskers. Without so much as a blink, the fluffy gray cat stretched and moved toward them. When he rubbed his furry body against Charlotte's legs, she closed her eyes and a look of utter bliss filled her face.

Mabel opened the door and smiled. "It looks as though someone's found a new friend."

Ben held back a sigh. He was hoping Mabel wouldn't be volunteering today. "Charlotte and Mr. Whiskers are getting to know each other."

"I'd say they're doing a mighty fine job. If you rub between his ears," Mabel said softly, "Mr. Whiskers will be your friend forever."

Charlotte's blue eyes connected with Ben's. "Can we take him home, Daddy?"

Ben's heart sank.

"Charlotte is *your* daughter?" Mabel looked as though she was about to fall over in shock.

"We've just found each other. Charlotte, this is Mrs. Terry."

Charlotte smiled. "Hello. Is Mr. Whiskers your friend, too?"

"He's everyone's friend. He enjoys living at The Welcome Center because he gets lots of cuddles."

"I've never had a cat to cuddle," Charlotte said wistfully. She wiggled forward, wrapping her arms around Mr. Whiskers' large tummy.

Ben stayed beside her, just in case the old gray cat decided he didn't like a four-year-old wrapped around his body.

"I'm heading back to the general store," Mabel told them. "If you need more toys or anything else for your daughter, come and see me."

"That's kind of you, but we should be okay." If Ben went to the store, Mabel wouldn't let him leave until she knew everything about Charlotte. "Is John in his office?"

"He was there ten minutes ago. Is Charlotte staying with you for long?"

Ben ran his hand over Charlotte's hair. "She'll be here permanently."

Instead of looking surprised, Mabel beamed. "That's wonderful. I'll add your names to the list of people coming to the children's event in December." She checked her watch and sighed. "I'd love to chat for longer, but I need to help Allan in the store. It was lovely meeting you, Charlotte."

And before they could say goodbye, Mabel hurried across to the parking lot.

To say he was surprised was an understatement. Ben had

expected Mabel to ask a lot more questions. Although, knowing how her mind worked, it wouldn't be long until he saw her again.

KYLIE LOOKED AROUND BLOOMING LOVELY. With most of the flowers packed away for the night, it was just about time to close the shop. It had been another busy day. Between creating custom made bouquets, filling online orders, and the tourists exploring Sapphire Bay, business was booming.

It didn't seem that long ago that she was worried about starting a business in a small town. Even now, she doubted she would have been so successful in a big city. The overheads alone would have left her bankrupt within twelve months. But here, in her little store overlooking Flathead Lake, she could create beautiful flower arrangements for her customers at affordable prices. Even if her income stayed the same, she would have her mortgage paid off in three years. For someone who had come from so little, it was a huge achievement.

Kylie took a vase of roses into the workroom. Not all the flowers needed special care, but these did. Tomorrow afternoon, one of her regular customers was celebrating the birth of her son. The roses would be part of a large floral centerpiece and Kylie wanted them to look perfect.

The bell above the front door jingled. She checked the time, then moved into the store to greet her last customer of the day. She smiled when she saw Ben and Charlotte. "How are my two favorite people?"

"We saw a kitty cat," Charlotte said excitedly. "His name is Mr. Whiskers and he likes lots of cuddles."

Kylie smiled. "I've met Mr. Whiskers. Did he show you his favorite hiding place?"

Charlotte nodded. "Pastor John said he likes to hide in the…" She looked up at Ben.

"Sleigh," he whispered.

"… sleigh," Charlotte said confidently. "And he likes to play with mice, and eat cheese and Pastor John's chicken."

Kylie laughed. "He sounds like a very busy cat."

Ben unzipped Charlotte's jacket. "We looked at the Little Sprouts Daycare Center, too."

"What did you think?"

"Sheryll and Naomi are great people. The children seem happy and were busy doing things."

"I made a picture," Charlotte added. "But I couldn't bring my sparkly pine cone home 'cos it's for a party." She tugged on her dad's hand. "Can we show Kylie my picture?"

"Sure." He took a folded sheet of paper out of his pocket and gave it to Charlotte.

Kylie knelt beside Ben's daughter.

"That's Mr. Whiskers and that's the sun and the snow and the trees."

"That's a wonderful picture. Are you visiting Little Sprouts again?"

Charlotte nodded happily. "We're making cookies tomorrow."

Ben seemed relieved that Charlotte had enjoyed herself. "I'll take Charlotte there each morning and pick her up at three o'clock."

"Will that give you enough time on the farm?"

"There's never enough time, especially this close to Christmas. But with the extra people John helped to organize, we should be okay." Ben cleared his throat. "Charlotte and I thought we'd eat something in town before we drive home. Would you like to have dinner with us?"

Kylie bit her bottom lip. She had promised herself she wouldn't get involved in Ben's complicated life. But with

Charlotte's big blue eyes pleading with her, and Ben's hesitant smile making her heart pound, she couldn't say no. "I've got another idea. I made a big dish of lasagna last night. You could have dinner with me."

"I love lasagna," Charlotte said.

Ben's smile widened. "In that case, we'd like to accept your invitation. Where do you live?"

Kylie looked up at the ceiling. "About fifteen feet away."

"You live above your store?"

"It was one of the reasons I bought the building." She smiled and locked the front door. "And I have the most amazing view of the lake."

"Do you have a cat like Mr. Whiskers?" The hopeful note in Charlotte's voice made Kylie smile.

"No, but I have a cuddly teddy bear called Fred." And, for the first time in years, she had a feeling that Fred was about to make another little girl extremely happy.

CHAPTER 9

*A*fter they'd shared a delicious dinner, Ben went into the kitchen and poured himself and Kylie a cup of coffee. He couldn't remember the last time he had felt so relaxed, and he wasn't the only one.

Charlotte had chatted nonstop about the children she'd met at Little Sprouts. Fred, Kylie's well-loved teddy bear, hadn't left her side all night.

When he walked back into the living room, Kylie and Charlotte were sitting on the sofa, reading a children's book. Although, looking at the way Charlotte's eyes were slowly closing, he didn't think it would be long before she was asleep.

He placed a cup on the table beside Kylie. "Here you go," he said softly.

"Thanks. If you'd like something sweet to eat, there's fresh shortbread in the pantry."

"I'm okay." He sat on the sofa opposite Kylie and listened to the last few pages of the story. Her voice drifted across the words like a gentle ocean breeze. He didn't have to close his eyes to imagine the far away castle and the feisty princesses saving the kingdom.

Ben smiled when he thought of the fairytales he'd grown up with. Unlike those stories, this one had no white knights in shining armor, no damsels in distress, and no handsome princes. The princesses had their own adventures and brandished their swords with as much accuracy as any male.

If Charlotte grew up with the same confidence, the same sense of who she was and what she wanted out of life, he would be happy.

By the time Kylie said, 'the end', Charlotte was sound asleep.

He left his coffee on the table. "It looks as though it's time for us to leave."

"You're welcome to stay for longer. If you move Charlotte to the other end of the sofa, I'll find a blanket for her."

Carefully, he picked up his daughter and placed her against the cushions. She was so small, so dependent on the adults around her for love and support. He hadn't known her for long, but he loved her as if she had always been in his life.

A knot of sadness lodged in his throat. He was still devastated that Heather and her parents hadn't told him about her. But he couldn't wind back time and do things differently. He had to focus on the future, on providing a stable and loving home for his daughter.

Kylie came back into the room and draped a red blanket over Charlotte, tucking it around her like a soft cocoon.

She sat on the sofa and curled her legs under her. "Charlotte has beautiful hair. Did her mom have blond hair, too?"

Ben picked up his coffee and nodded. "Heather used to add silver streaks in the middle of winter to make her feel as though summer wasn't far away."

Kylie smiled. "That sounds more sensible than the red and green streaks I put in my hair."

He looked at her blond hair and frowned. "They aren't there anymore."

"I don't use permanent dye. The color comes out of a spray can and only lasts for a few washes. I found the most amazing wig to wear to the Christmas party on Saturday."

Ben groaned. "Is it shaped like a Christmas tree?"

Kylie laughed. "You'll have to wait and see."

"Do you want Charlotte and me to pick you up? We have to drive straight past your apartment to get to the party." He was disappointed when Kylie shook her head.

"Normally I would say yes. But I want to be there early to fix any last-minute emergencies."

"That's okay. If you change your mind, let me know. Do you still want me to deliver the Christmas trees and mistletoe on Thursday morning?"

"That would be fantastic. John and his team have nearly finished clearing out the building. By lunchtime tomorrow we'll be hanging all the other decorations."

Ben imagined that Kylie would be incredibly busy preparing for the Christmas party. "How are you keeping Blooming Lovely open and organizing everything for Saturday night?"

"The two part-time staff John sent me are wonderful. Jackie and Paris already have retail experience, so helping in my flower shop has been an easy transition. It just means I need to get out of bed a little earlier to make bouquets and do some on-the-job training. I'll miss them when they start working in the Christmas shop. How are your new recruits doing?"

Ben took a sip from his coffee. "Nate and Marcus are picking everything up a lot quicker than I thought they would. They're quick to ask questions when they don't understand something. Helena and Andrew are a lot quieter, but just as motivated to do a good job. They're good kids."

"How does it feel to have people helping you?"

"It's…different." Ben looked at Charlotte. The person he used to be was slowly disappearing. Would Kylie understand just how profound the changes were? "I didn't realize how much time I spent on my own until we started planning the Christmas shop. Most weeks, I was lucky if I saw two or three people. And that was only when I came into town to see John. I guess I'd become a bit of a hermit." He glanced at Kylie and smiled. "A grumpy hermit."

"At least you were consistent," Kylie answered with a cheeky grin.

"That's true." His hands tightened around his cup. "It feels good to be part of the community, to help the young people who are working with me."

"That's why I'm on the fundraising committee."

"Why did you move to Sapphire Bay? You could have helped people when you were living in San Francisco."

Kylie's smile disappeared. "I was engaged to someone I thought was incredible. We were planning our wedding and doing all the things most people do when they're in love. But my fiancé had second thoughts about getting married. Instead of telling me how he felt, he slept with someone we both knew." She took a deep breath. "Trust is a big thing for me. After my dad left, I constantly worried that mom would leave, too. When Matthew told me what he'd done, I freaked out. I needed to sort out what was going on inside my head, so I jumped in my truck and started driving. When I saw Flathead Lake, I felt as though I could breathe again. I rented a cottage beside the lake and decided to live here for a few months."

"Is that when you saw the store that would become Blooming Lovely?"

Kylie's shoulders relaxed and her smile returned. "I used to visit Brooke's candy shop at least once a week. She knew I was a florist, so when the owners of this building said they were moving, she called me. Within two weeks I was the proud owner of an old pet store and an apartment that needed a serious makeover."

Ben looked around the living room. With its white-painted walls, polished wooden floors, and colorful art, it was a bright, happy interior that suited Kylie's personality. "Whatever you did, it looks great."

"Thanks. The previous owners didn't live above the store, so it was a mess. The first thing I did was get rid of the rats' nests. Then I knocked down a wall, replaced all the wiring, and installed a new kitchen. I was living in a construction site for a few months, but it was worth it."

"And in between the remodeling, you opened Blooming Lovely?"

Kylie nodded. "Everyone in the community has been really supportive. I can't imagine living anywhere else."

"You work hard."

"So do you." Kylie leaned her head against the back of the sofa. "Is Charlotte enjoying living with you?"

"I think so. She loves talking to her grandma and helping on the farm. She keeps asking Robyn when she's coming to see her."

"What does Robyn say?"

"That she has to work, but she'll see Charlotte before Christmas."

"How do you feel about that?"

Ben sighed. "Before I left Los Angeles, we agreed on set times when Robyn would visit Charlotte. I want my daughter to have a good relationship with her grandma. But, at the moment, it's hard on both of them. Robyn isn't due to see Charlotte until the second week in December."

"If they're missing each other, can you bring the date forward?"

"If Robyn is happy to fly to Montana, I could. But I'm worried that once Charlotte sees her, she'll want to go back to Los Angeles."

"I hate to tell you this, but that will probably happen, anyway."

Ben knew Kylie was right, but that didn't make him feel any easier about Robyn coming to Sapphire Bay. "What if Robyn doesn't agree with putting Charlotte into day care?"

"It sounds as though Charlotte had a great time today. If she's happy, I can't see why her grandma would want to change that. Besides, Charlotte will start kindergarten soon."

All the stress, the frustration, and the emotion of the last few days hit Ben like a ten-ton weight. "I want what's best for Charlotte, but I don't know what I'm doing."

Kylie changed seats and sat beside him. "From what my friends have said, most first-time parents feel exactly the same. You don't have to be perfect. All Charlotte wants is your love."

"What if it isn't enough?"

She held his hand. "It's always enough. You're a good man. Charlotte's lucky to have a dad like you."

His heart pounded as he stared into Kylie's serious blue eyes. He hoped like crazy she was right because, right now, he didn't know where this journey into fatherhood would take him.

BAILEY PICKED up a box of decorations and carried them across to Kylie. "Where would you like these wreaths?"

"In the foyer." Kylie picked up some drawings she'd made of the old steamboat museum. With so many people helping to decorate the building, she'd made things easier by drawing a plan of where everything was supposed to go.

She handed Bailey the foyer design. "While you're there, could you stick this on the wall? It tells everyone where the decorations need to go. All the fastenings are in the green box beside the main doors."

Bailey saluted her before walking across the room.

As soon as she left, Kylie took a deep breath. So far, everything was going according to plan. But plans, she knew, could go astray at any moment. All it took was a damaged water pipe and the entire event could be in jeopardy.

"Cheer up. It can't be that bad." John was wearing his favorite, bright yellow hard hat. "But if it is, you've got twenty people who can put their collective brains together and come up with a solution."

"I was thinking about the community center. Imagine if the water pipe had burst a few days before the party. It would have been a disaster."

"As long as nothing happens in here, we'll be all right. The first banner is going up. Come and have a look."

Kylie picked up her clipboard and followed John. They were doing something different to decorate the main hall. She only hoped it looked as good as they'd imagined.

As well as being a wonderful singer, her friend Willow was a talented photographer. Last winter, she'd taken a series of photographs of Flathead Lake. To help create a feeling of grandeur and opulence, Willow had paid for one panoramic photo to be printed as a series of enormous banners that were twenty-five feet high.

A team of people had traveled from Polson to hang the black and white images on the wall.

Once the panels were in place, another team would hang sheer drapes about a foot in front of the picture. After the lighting crew worked their magic, and the Christmas trees were in place, Kylie was hoping it would make everyone feel as though they were dancing in the middle of a snow-covered wonderland.

Two cherry pickers sat side-by-side, slowly lifting the first panel into place. Kylie held her breath. If this panel wasn't perfectly square, the whole design would look wrong.

"Breathe," John told her. "These guys know what they're doing."

"I hope so." Someone appeared beside Kylie. Someone who smelled as amazing as the winter scene she was trying to re-create.

"It looks as though I've arrived at the right time."

Kylie smiled. Ben didn't like heights, so he wasn't talking about standing in one of the cherry pickers. "If you're looking for a job, there are plenty of ways you can help."

Ben shook his head. "I'm busy today, but tomorrow I'm all yours."

She shouldn't have blushed, but she did. And the worse thing was that John saw her face flaming brighter than a red-hot chili.

John smiled at Kylie. "Ben has spent too much time on his own. It's just as well you're reintroducing him to the world."

"He's not too bad once you get to know him."

Ben sighed. "I'm delivering the Christmas trees and mistletoe tomorrow. I'm here to make sure I know exactly where everything's going."

"Oh. That's okay, then." Kylie fanned her face with the clipboard. "Haven't you forgotten someone?"

"Charlotte's still at Little Sprouts. I'm picking her up after I've finished here."

John's cell phone rang. "While you're sorting out the Christmas trees, I'll answer this call."

While John moved away from the noisy room, Ben wandered closer to the wall.

"Did you see the email I sent you? The one with the picture of where the trees need to go?"

Ben didn't hear her. Kylie caught up with him and repeated what she'd said.

"Did you have to ask me that twice?"

She nodded. "It doesn't matter. Between the machinery and everything that's happening in here, there's a lot of background noise."

"I'm sorry."

"Don't worry about it." But no matter how hard he tried to hide his disappointment, she could tell he was upset. Before Kylie could reassure him it really didn't matter, he pulled a piece of paper out of his pocket.

"I've got the drawing you sent me. Come and show me where you want the first tree." With the picture in his hand, he continued walking across the room.

Kylie followed him and touched his arm. "Why are you upset that I had to repeat myself?"

Ben frowned. "I'm not upset with you. It's just..."—he looked down at the piece of paper—"The downside of having people around me is that there are more times when I can't hear what's being said. I'm worried a trainee will hurt themselves, or Charlotte will wander off and I won't know she's gone."

"Is there a hearing aid or something else that could help?"

"I saw my specialist last week. He's looking at different options."

"That's good."

"I hope so."

Kylie studied Ben's face. Either he wasn't telling her the whole story or he was worried. Regardless of what he was thinking, he looked as though he needed some moral support. "If you need to see your specialist again, I could go to the appointment with you."

Ben gently kissed her cheek. "I'll be okay, but thank you."

Kylie looked into his eyes. "I haven't done anything."

"Just being able to talk to you is important." He looked up as a loud beep erupted from one of the cherry pickers. "You'd better tell me where you want the trees. Otherwise, we might leave them where you don't want them."

She smiled at Ben before looking at the drawing. Hopefully, once he found something to help with his hearing, his life would be less stressful. But for now, they both had lots of things to do, and not much time to finish them.

BEN DIDN'T SEE Kylie again until Friday afternoon. The last couple of days had been crazy. Between delivering the Christmas trees and making sure everyone knew what they were doing on the farm, he hadn't had a lot of spare time.

"Can I give Kylie her picture when I see her?" Charlotte asked.

Ben checked the rearview mirror and turned into the parking lot. "She'll like that. If she's not here, we'll visit Kylie in her flower shop."

"Okay." Charlotte's smile was as carefree as a spring breeze.

He was surprised at how well everything had gone this week. Robyn's nightly phone calls and positive encouragement had helped Charlotte overcome some of her anxiety. The Little Sprouts Daycare Center had given Charlotte something to focus on. She'd made friends, spent a lot of time drawing, and enjoyed all the other activities the center offered.

It was almost as if Charlotte had always lived here.

He looked around the parking lot and saw Kylie's truck. "It looks as though Kylie is here," he said to Charlotte.

"Yeah!"

His daughter wasn't the only person who was happy. It had only been two days since he'd last seen Kylie, but he missed her. "Don't take off your seatbelt until the truck has stopped," he warned Charlotte.

"But I can't reach my picture."

"It will be all right where it is." Charlotte had a habit of jumping one step ahead of where she needed to be. Yesterday, when they'd parked in front of the general store, she was almost out of the truck before he opened the driver's door. For the first time ever, he was grateful the back doors had child locks.

"Do you think Kylie is wearing one of her pretty dresses?" Charlotte asked.

"Probably." Ben parked the car and turned off the ignition. "Would you like to wear a special Christmas dress to the party tomorrow?"

Charlotte nodded. Even though she was only four-and-a-half years old, she loved dressing in bright, colorful clothes. And she knew exactly what she wanted to wear each morning.

He smiled as he opened the passenger door. "Good girl for staying in your car seat."

"Grandma told me I had to be careful." She unbuckled the restraints and wiggled to the edge of the seat. With the drawing clutched in her hand, she said, "I'm ready to get out now."

Charlotte wrapped her arms around Ben's neck. Carefully, he lifted her out of the truck and locked the doors. The parking lot was full of trucks, cars, and vans. John had told him they were fixing some last-minute lighting issues, but he didn't expect this many people to be here.

"Hold on tight, Charlotte. I'll carry you across to the main doors."

"Okay, Daddy."

Hearing her say the word 'daddy' still made Ben feel emotional. After Heather left, he never thought he would be a father, let alone live in the middle of rural Montana. But here he was, checking on the trees he had delivered yesterday and hoping the woman he was falling in love with was inside the building.

As he walked into the large foyer, he took a moment to admire the decorations. A wide red carpet ran the length of the room and a row of glittering Christmas trees lined each side. It was a walkway worthy of any grand palace or a fairy-tale castle.

Charlotte sighed. "It's so pretty."

"It is," Ben murmured. And it would be even more spectacular tomorrow night when everyone arrived. His friend, Levi, walked out of the main hall. "Hi. I didn't expect to see you here."

Levi smiled. "Neither did Kylie, but the lighting crew needed some last-minute adjustments to the scaffolding. I don't believe I've met this beautiful little girl."

Instead of being overcome with shyness, Ben's daughter grinned. "I'm Charlotte."

Levi held out his hand. "It's nice to meet you, Charlotte. I'm Levi. I hope you enjoy living in Sapphire Bay. Are you coming to the party tomorrow night?"

Charlotte nodded. "We're going to dance with Kylie and I'm wearing a pretty dress."

"That sounds exciting. I'll make sure I come and say hello." Before he left, Levi studied Ben's face. "You look tired. How is the Christmas shop coming along?"

"All I'm waiting for are some products we'll be selling."

"If you need another pair of hands, call me. Have you seen the main hall since you dropped off the trees?"

Ben shook his head.

"You're in for a surprise, then. See you tomorrow."

Ben lowered Charlotte to the floor and they walked toward the double doors. By the time he'd left yesterday, two of the black and white panels were on the wall, the scaffolding for the lighting was almost finished, and the temporary stage was ready for Willow's band.

Even then, the room had looked impressive.

Kylie stepped into the foyer, talking on her cell phone. When she saw Ben and Charlotte, she smiled. "Okay, Mom. Yes, I'll make sure I send you some photos. Love you, too." When she'd finished the call, she walked up to Charlotte and gave her a hug. "How's my fairy princess doing?"

"I got a wiggly tooth."

"Really? Can I see?"

Charlotte poked her finger in her mouth and wiggled one of her front teeth. "Daddy said the tooth fairy will come and see me."

"I bet you're looking forward to that. Did you come to see the Christmas trees?"

"And the lights," Charlotte whispered. "'cos they're my favorite."

"Well, you've come at the right time. We've just turned them on to make sure they work."

Charlotte's eyes widened.

Ben laughed. "Okay. We'll go inside."

Kylie rushed ahead of them. "Before you go any farther, close your eyes."

"Like a surprise?" Charlotte asked.

"That's right," Kylie said with a smile. "Come on, Ben. You can hold my arm so you don't trip on anything."

He looked at his daughter. She already had her eyes tightly closed. "It looks as though I've been outnumbered."

Kylie held her elbow toward him. "I won't lead you astray."

He grinned into her gleaming blue eyes. "That's not much fun."

"You haven't seen anything yet. Prepare to be amazed."

Ben sighed. With one hand holding Charlotte close and the other wrapped around Kylie's elbow, he walked into the main hall.

Even with his eyes closed, he was already amazed. Not because of the decorations. Because of Kylie.

WHEN BEN STEPPED through the double doors, the first thing he heard was the sound of a guitar. Someone on his right-hand side was strumming a tune that was vaguely familiar.

"Just a little farther," Kylie said beside him. A couple of steps later, she stopped. "You can open your eyes now."

Ben blinked as his eyes adjusted to the dim light.

Charlotte started clapping. "It's so pretty."

He stared at the room in amazement. The trees he'd delivered yesterday were covered in twinkling fairy lights. A blanket of rocks and pine needles covered the floor, setting the scene for the enormous photograph behind the trees.

"What do you think?" Kylie asked.

"It's extraordinary." Soft, sheer fabric fell from above the enormous black and white panels. Willow's photograph was stunning. At the bottom of the image, the swirling waters of Flathead Lake gently lapped against the shore. In the background, a towering mountain range ran from one side of the room to the other, adding height and grandeur to an image that was already breathtaking.

And the lighting brought the room to life. Spotlights shone from behind the trees, illuminating the panels and making the fabric transform into a fine mist. Suspended from the ceiling, other lights shone on the tables, on the dance floor, and against the other walls.

Ben moved closer to Charlotte. She was sitting under a tree, holding a pine cone in her small hands.

When she looked up, the light from hundreds of twinkling fairy lights shone against her face. In that moment, he could have sworn he was looking at a younger version of Heather.

"Can we stay here forever?" she asked.

Kneeling beside his daughter, he pushed a stray lock of hair off her face. "We can stay for as long as Kylie needs us, then we have to go home. But we'll be back tomorrow night for the Christmas party."

She hugged the pine cone close to her chest. "Is Santa Claus coming?"

Ben smiled. He didn't know about Santa, but a lot of other people would be here. "He's busy getting everything ready for Christmas. I don't know if he's coming to the party, but lots of other wonderful people will be here."

"Like us."

He held out his hand. "Exactly."

Charlotte placed the pine cone on the ground and clambered to her feet.

When her hand slipped into his, Ben smiled. "Do you want to have a look at the rest of the room?"

With a happy nod, Charlotte tightened her hold and waited beside him.

"Look at the stage," Kylie said to Charlotte. "The lights are amazing."

Ben turned around. Sitting in the center of the stage was a lone guitarist, quietly playing a song as a rainbow of lights swirled around him.

"We're testing the lighting sequence Willow uses when

she's performing. This stage is smaller, so the lighting team is making some adjustments."

Finally, Ben recognized the music. "Is that one of Willow's songs?"

Kylie nodded. "The band will play the instrumental version of 'Smoky Mountain River' after we've announced the recipients of another four Christmas wishes."

"You've been busy."

"I didn't do anything this time. Santa's Secret Helpers have been working overtime to make people's wishes come true." Kylie nodded toward the stage. "Watch what happens next."

When the music ended, a drummer and someone on an electric keyboard joined the guitarist. As the first notes of a different song filled the room, a single beam of light cut through the air, exploding into a giant firework on the back wall. As the music gained momentum, more colorful bursts of light filled the room.

Charlotte jumped up and down, pointing to each star as it flared into life.

Just when Ben thought it couldn't get any better, the song ended and Willow walked onto the stage. Even though she rarely performed in public, her presence was electrifying.

The first words of the song drifted across the room, bringing everyone around them to a standstill. Willow's voice was amazing and no one, including Ben, was immune to the sweet country ballad.

Charlotte tugged on his hand. "Dance, Daddy."

"Now?"

She swung his hand in hers and nodded. "Just like Grandma does."

Ben had no idea how Robyn danced, but he was willing to try. He picked up his daughter and held her close.

Charlotte wiggled her fingers toward Kylie. "Kylie, too."

"I'll watch," she said quickly. "Your daddy will enjoy dancing with you."

Ben wasn't letting her get away that easily. With his free hand, he reached for her fingers and pulled her close. "It won't be for long. Willow must be halfway through her song by now."

Kylie sighed. "I don't dance."

He wrapped his arm around her waist. "I promise not to step on your toes." He could have sworn she muttered something under her breath. "It's probably a good thing I didn't hear that. Let's dance."

Kylie linked one arm around Charlotte's waist and the other around Ben.

It had to be the most unusual dance ever, but he wasn't complaining. As they slowly swayed to the music, he thought he was the luckiest man alive. Even if it was only for a few minutes.

CHAPTER 10

"*Y*ou look amazing." Kylie handed Bailey a red velvet cape that she was borrowing for the night. "I can't believe you had such a beautiful dress hanging in your closet."

"My sister invited me to her accounting firm's Christmas dinner last year. I thought it was only the staff who were going, but they invited all their major clients. You know what Shelley's like. Nothing in my closet passed her inspection, so we went shopping."

"Well, I'm impressed with what you found. How is Shelley? Is she still thinking about living in Sapphire Bay?"

Bailey sighed. "I don't know. Two weeks ago, she was ready to pack her bags and move here. The next day, she accepted a fixed-term contract in Boston. I don't know what she wants to do."

"It's a big decision, especially when you're used to earning lots of money. But one of the good things about living here is that it's not expensive."

"Shelley's an accountant. Her life revolves around

investing the thousands of dollars she makes each week. I don't think she could cope with a limited income."

"You might be surprised. I didn't know what I was going to do after I left San Francisco, but look at me now."

Bailey smiled. "I am looking and you're gorgeous. You definitely didn't buy your gown in Sapphire Bay, either."

Kylie ran her hands over the skirt of her pale gray floor-length dress. With its fitted bodice, sparkly straps, and satin skirt, it was the prettiest piece of clothing she'd ever bought. "A friend got married last year and I was one of her brides-maids. It doesn't look too wedding-ish, does it?"

"It's perfect. Especially with your wig. You look like an ice princess."

Kylie had told Ben he would be surprised when he saw her, and she wasn't joking. Instead of wearing a Christmas-themed dress, she'd wanted to find a snowflake costume. But everything she saw would be too hard to move around in. With the Christmas party getting closer, she'd decided to wear the bridesmaid's dress with a sparkly snowflake sitting on the top of a large silver wig.

Her biggest worry was that her wig would fall off and hurt someone. "If you see the snowflake tilting at an odd angle, let me know."

Bailey picked up a pile of green and gold envelopes sitting on the kitchen counter. "You've got a deal. Are you ready to leave?"

Kylie walked into the living room and looked around her apartment. She'd already packed her truck with a box of emergency supplies. If she'd forgotten anything, it would be too late to do anything about it.

With her keys in her hand, she took a deep breath. "Let's go."

"It's going to be a fantastic night," Bailey assured her. "Just remember to enjoy yourself. There are enough volunteers in the room to fix anything that goes wrong."

Kylie hoped so. It had taken a monumental effort to get this far and she wanted everything to be perfect.

BEN RAN his fingers around the edge of his collar. He hadn't worn a tie in so long that it felt like a noose around his neck.

"Oh, my. Don't you look handsome." Mabel smiled at him from below a headpiece that could only be described as a Christmas wreath on steroids. Her eyes lifted to a pine cone that was drooping over her forehead at an alarming angle. Lifting her hand, she straightened the rogue decoration. "That's better. Where's your beautiful daughter?"

Charlotte peeked around Ben's legs. "Here I am."

"You're not Charlotte," Mabel said in mock confusion. "You're a Christmas angel."

"No, I'm not." Charlotte giggled. "My name is Charlotte Amber Thompson and I live with my daddy."

"Are you sure?"

Charlotte nodded and looked up at Ben.

He placed his hand on her shoulder and smiled. "Do you want to show Mrs. Terry your dress?"

Charlotte gripped the leg of his trousers as she showed Mabel what she was wearing.

"It's very pretty," Mabel said with a smile. "I like your wings."

Charlotte's grandmother had mailed them the costume after she'd heard about the party. With a full tulle skirt and a white, fluffy jacket, Charlotte could have easily been a number of things. But the glittering red and green angel wings screamed Christmas. As soon as Charlotte saw the costume, she'd loved it.

"The wings go up and down," she told Mabel. "See." With a tug of the cord at her waist, Charlotte fluttered the glittery wings.

"That's amazing. After dinner, I'll bring Mr. Terry across to your table so you can show him your wings."

Charlotte nodded, then stared at Mabel's head. "I like your hat."

"Well, thank you. I'm thrilled with how it turned out." She looked at Ben. "Have you found where you're sitting?"

He shook his head. "We only arrived a few minutes ago. Have you seen Kylie?"

Mabel's smile softened. "She was in the kitchen when I last saw her. You'll want to keep her close. She's stunning. Every single man in the room will want to dance with her."

Ben looked across the room at the kitchen door. Most of the people in that area were talking and laughing with friends. The waiting staff were handing out glasses of wine and the finger food the catering company had provided.

He couldn't see Kylie.

Mabel rested her hand on his arm. "I asked if you knew about the seating plan."

Ben apologized. "Sorry, Mabel. I didn't hear you. And yes, I do know there's a seating plan. Kylie told me about it yesterday, but I don't know where it is."

"It's on your left-hand side, beside the first Christmas tree." She looked across the room at a handkerchief waving in the air. "That's my friend, Doris. She's come all the way from Bozeman to spend the weekend with me. I'll see you both later. And remember...watch out for the mistletoe!" With a little wave, Mabel disappeared into the crowd.

He smiled at Charlotte. "Let's find our table."

"Can we sit beside Kylie?"

"We'll see." He hoped whoever had organized the tables

had seated them together. With everything that was happening tonight, it might be the only time he saw—

"You made it."

He turned and his eyes widened. "Kylie?" He couldn't believe this was the same woman who wore candy cane dresses and elf hats.

She smiled and spun in a slow circle. "What do you think?"

"You're beautiful." No wonder Mabel told him to stay close. Kylie's silver wig, shaped like a beehive, made her eyes look as blue as a summer sky. Her dress hugged her upper body, then fell to the ground in a soft cloud of shimmery fabric.

Charlotte touched Kylie's hand. "You look pretty."

"Thank you. I love your dress, too." Kylie knelt on the ground. "Are your wings real?"

"I can't fly," Charlotte said sadly. "But I can do this." And with one tug, the sparkly wings started flapping.

"That's amazing. You look like a beautiful butterfly."

Charlotte grinned. "I'm a Christmas butterfly."

"Well, Miss Butterfly, how do you feel about finding our table?"

"We're sitting with you?"

Kylie nodded. "I didn't want to sit beside anyone else."

Charlotte smiled. When she looked up at Ben, the happiness shining from her face made his heart melt. "We're all sitting together."

He breathed a sigh of relief. "That's great." He helped Kylie to her feet, smiling as her other hand reached for her wig. "Don't worry. It hasn't moved."

"Thank goodness for that. The snowflake is a lot heavier than I thought. If I tilt my head too far in one direction, it starts to slip."

Ben wrapped one hand around Charlotte's fingers and

held his other arm toward Kylie. "You could always take it off."

"I'll try to keep it on until after dinner. Are you ready to sit at our table? We're on the right-hand side of the stage."

Ben looked across the crowded room. With so many people around them, he was already having problems hearing what was being said. When he looked down at Kylie, she smiled.

"Don't worry," she said. "I'll look after you."

And for the first time since he'd arrived with Charlotte, he relaxed.

AFTER DINNER, Kylie looked at the Christmas party schedule, then checked her watch. So far, everything was on time. Bailey was working with the catering staff, and Pastor John was keeping the speeches and entertainment on track.

Bailey tapped her on the shoulder and handed her a cup of coffee. "Santa Claus has just arrived," she whispered.

Kylie's eyes widened. "He was supposed to be here half an hour ago."

"His truck wouldn't start. He's getting dressed and should be ready in ten minutes."

With a relieved sigh, Kylie sat back in her seat. "Does he need us to help with anything?"

"It's all under control. Just sit here and enjoy yourself."

Kylie wished it were that simple. Throughout the main course she had compared notes with John, making sure he was comfortable with what was happening over the next part of the evening. She'd also checked that all their special guests were here to receive their surprise Christmas wishes. And in-between all of that, she'd enjoyed Charlotte and Ben's company.

"How are you feeling?" Ben asked.

"A little nervous." She bit her bottom lip. "Don't be surprised if John asks you to come onto the stage."

Ben frowned. "To thank me for donating the Christmas trees?"

"Something like that," she murmured.

Gently, Ben placed his finger on her chin and lifted it toward him. "I didn't hear you."

Kylie looked into his eyes. Ben had told her it was difficult to hear people talk in a noisy room, but until tonight she hadn't realized just how hard it was. "John will be thanking you, but it's for something else, too."

His eyebrows arched. "Should I be worried?"

Butterflies danced inside her tummy. "I hope not." She was used to seeing Ben wearing jeans and a sweatshirt. The jet-black suit and crisp white shirt he'd worn tonight had left her speechless. Instead of being able to relax around him, she felt on edge, as if she were about to leap into something she couldn't get away from. "When John gives you an envelope, all you have to do is say thank you."

Fortunately, John chose that moment to walk onto the stage. "I'd like to begin the next part of the evening by thanking everyone for being here. With your support, the tiny home village is becoming one of the most talked about community projects in Montana. By December, we're hoping to have fourteen tiny homes rented to families in desperate need of accommodation."

Everyone in the room clapped and cheered.

John picked up the envelopes that had been sitting in Kylie's kitchen. "As well as raising money for the tiny home village, the church has another project we're working on. Most of you know that two months ago, the Christmas events fundraising committee posted a message on Facebook. Within hours, hundreds of people had replied to the post, telling us about their Christmas wishes. Over the last few weeks, Santa's Secret Helpers have been working hard to make a lot of dreams come true. Before I announce the next Christmas wish recipients, I'd like to ask Ben Thompson to come onto the stage. Ben donated all the trees and mistletoe you see here tonight."

"Come with me," Ben whispered to Kylie.

She shook her head.

"I thought you were going to look after me?"

"I am. Just smile and accept the envelope." Kylie's heart pounded. Ben was the most attractive man she'd ever met and it was getting in the way of her common sense. She shouldn't have agreed to John's meddling. But it would make such a difference in Ben's life that she didn't have the heart to stop him.

"Can I come, too?" Charlotte asked.

Ben's gaze dropped to his daughter. "Okay."

Charlotte wiggled out of her chair and held her dad's hand.

With a final look at Kylie, Ben guided Charlotte onto the stage.

John smiled at his unexpected guest. "You look lovely, Charlotte. Would you like to say hello to everybody?"

Charlotte shook her head and hid behind Ben's legs.

Kylie smiled. It was hard for most people to stand in front of two hundred people, but it was even more intimidating when you were four-and-a-half years old.

Ben placed a reassuring hand on his daughter's shoulder.

John turned to the audience. "As well as providing some of the wonderful decorations for tonight's event, Ben has also made six Christmas wishes come true. He recently employed four full-time and two part-time employees on his Christmas tree farm."

The audience burst into applause.

A dull red blush skimmed along Ben's cheeks.

Kylie knew he didn't enjoy being the center of attention, but there was no way around it tonight. John wanted to thank him publicly for what he had done and nothing, barring a burst water pipe, would stop him.

John cleared his throat. "As you know, Ben, Santa's Secret Helpers are working incredibly hard to make people's dreams come true. The other day, a Christmas wish was made on your behalf."

Ben's shoulders stiffened.

Her fingers gripped the edge of the chair. He must be wondering what's going on.

John sent him a reassuring smile. "On behalf of Santa's Secret Helpers, I would like to present you with this Christmas gift. You don't have to open the envelope now. But when you do, I want you to know how much we appreciate everything you've done for tonight and for the young people you've taken under your wing."

Ben took the envelope and shook John's hand. After a quick wave to the applauding audience, he made his way back to the table with Charlotte beside him.

After they were seated, Kylie touched the sleeve of his jacket. "Are you all right?"

He held the envelope in his hands and nodded. "Do you know what it is?"

She studied Ben's face. "I do, but I only found out about it this afternoon."

He turned over the envelope and frowned.

More applause erupted as John asked three other people to come onto the stage.

"Leave it until later. I can explain—" Kylie's cell phone vibrated. She read the text message and sighed.

"Bad news?"

"Santa can't find his hat. I need to go." She glanced at the envelope, then lifted her gaze to Ben's. "Don't worry. It's good news."

Ben's frown turned into a scowl. It didn't look as though he believed her.

BETWEEN THE MAIN course and dessert, Santa Claus made an unexpected visit to Sapphire Bay. Ben didn't know how Pastor John had done it, but every child at the party was being given a small gift. By the time Charlotte reached the front of the line, she was hopping on the spot with excitement.

Ben was thankful Santa was sitting in a smaller room away from the main hall. Without the noise from the music and people talking, he could enjoy seeing Charlotte interact with the other children.

He was so proud of his daughter. She hadn't pushed or shoved her way to the front of the line. When one of the other little children started crying, she was the first person to ask if she was okay. No matter what he thought of Heather or her mom, they had done a great job of raising her.

With his cell phone focused on his daughter, he took a photo of her face as she grinned at Santa Claus. After a few whispered words, Santa handed her a small red box. Ben captured the moment when Charlotte's excitement turned to wonder. He didn't know what had been said but, whatever it was, his daughter was holding the box as if it contained the most precious gift in the world.

She looked at the people around her, searching for Ben. He waved and started moving toward her. "That's a pretty box," he said as they sat on a sofa. The red wrapping paper sparkled under the fluorescent lights.

Charlotte ran her fingers over the big gold bow sitting on

top of the gift. "I told Santa I miss Grandma. He said this present would make me feel better."

Ben glanced at Santa and hoped he was right.

"Can I open my present now?"

He placed his hand around Charlotte's shoulders and kissed her forehead. "You can open it whenever you like."

"Will you help me?"

"Sure. Where do you want to start?"

"Here." Charlotte plucked the gold bow off the top of the box. With a happy grin, she stuck it on Ben's jacket. "You look pretty."

"I thought I looked good before you added the bow," he joked.

"Now you look better."

Ben smiled. He would wear a lot more than a gold bow if it made his daughter happy.

Charlotte only took a few seconds to rip the wrapping paper off the present. After she lifted the flap on the box, she glanced at Ben. "It's a picture." Her little fingers grasped the edge of the frame and turned it over. "Grandma." Tears filled her eyes as she hugged the photo close to her chest.

Ben tightened his hold around her shoulders and gave her a hug. How on earth had Santa found a photo of Robyn? And how did he even know Charlotte was missing her Grandma?

He took a closer look at Santa. With all the white hair, it was difficult to see who was under the costume. But when Santa winked at him, Ben sighed. It was Zac. Not only was he the only doctor in Sapphire Bay, he was also one of Ben's friends.

A grin appeared from behind the fluffy, white beard. "Ho, ho, ho."

Last week, Ben had visited Zac to see if he'd received any information from his specialist. They'd talked about a lot of things, including Charlotte and Ben's ex-wife and her family.

"I thought you'd still be here," Kylie said, sitting down beside them. "Did you enjoy seeing Santa?"

Charlotte held up the photo frame. "Look what Santa gave me. It's a picture of Grandma and me."

Kylie admired the photo. "You both look so happy."

"We were at the park. I wish Grandma was here."

Kylie's eyes lifted to Ben's.

He knew exactly what she was thinking. "You'll see Grandma soon. In the meantime, you could put the photo beside your bed."

Charlotte looked disappointed. "Okay."

Kylie glanced across the room. "Bailey is making jelly and ice cream for everyone. Would you like some?"

"Yes, please."

"What about your dad? Do you think he'd like some?"

Charlotte smiled at Kylie. "Daddy loves ice cream."

Ben laughed. "I do, especially if it's vanilla."

"Well, in that case, you'd better follow me." Charlotte held Kylie's hand as they walked toward Bailey.

Ben slowly followed them. Having to fit into an adult world was hard when you were a child. It didn't matter why Robyn wasn't here. Charlotte missed her and nothing would change that.

Bailey was standing behind a table, scooping ice cream into empty bowls. She grimaced when she saw them. "I've got five minutes until Santa invites everyone for dessert and I'm only halfway through."

"We're here to help," Kylie assured her. "Charlotte and I could spoon the jelly onto the plates."

Ben didn't think that was a good idea, but Charlotte was ready to go.

"She'll be okay," Kylie said when she saw his expression. "If you'd like to help, you could open the packet of paper napkins and leave them on the table beside Bailey."

Ben was glad to have something to do. With all the noise in the main hall, it was a relief to be in a quieter area.

When Kylie and Charlotte came back from washing their hands, he placed the last packet of napkins on the table. "I'll help with the jelly, too."

Kylie handed him a spoon and a bowl of green jelly. "That would be great."

When Bailey took Charlotte to the kitchen to find more dessert spoons, Ben moved closer to Kylie. "Can I ask you a question?"

"Sure."

"How did the photo of Robyn become Charlotte's present?"

"When we were planning Santa's visit, we wanted the children to have gifts that were special. John and I saw Charlotte's birth certificate. Thankfully, your ex-wife's maiden name was on the piece of paper. From there it was a matter of finding Robyn and asking if she could send a photo to us. I think she would have come here in person if we'd asked."

"Is that a gentle hint?"

"Maybe."

He looked over Kylie's shoulder at Charlotte. She was climbing onto a chair beside Bailey, getting ready for the first group of children to collect their dessert. He didn't know how Robyn was coping without her granddaughter. Even though Charlotte hadn't been living with him for long, he would miss her like crazy if she ever left.

Kylie added more jelly to the bowls. "You look worried. Did you think Charlotte wouldn't enjoy herself?"

Ben sighed. "I worry about everything. I keep thinking that one day I'll wake up and discover I did the wrong thing when I brought Charlotte here."

"Why would you think that?"

"She loves Robyn."

"She loves you, too."

Ben's heart clenched tight. "She's four-and-a-half years old. She doesn't know how she feels."

"I wouldn't be too sure about that. Charlotte is happy. That's all most people want."

He filled the last bowl with jelly. "Are you happy?"

Kylie paused before she answered. "Yes. Especially while we're in this room."

"Why?"

"Because we're away from the music. While I'm here, no one can ask me to dance."

Ben tapped the end of her nose. "That's a challenge I can't refuse. I'll be back soon."

He rushed across to Bailey and asked if she could look after Charlotte. When that was organized, he returned to Kylie. "Would you dance with me?"

"I can't dance."

Ben spun her in a circle. "We managed okay yesterday."

"That's because we weren't really dancing."

Ben held out his arm. "We'll make it up as we go along. Shall we?"

"I hope you're wearing steel-capped boots."

"It won't be as bad as that."

Kylie sighed. "I hope not."

Before she changed her mind, Ben gathered her close and led her onto the dance floor. They might not be Ginger Rogers and Fred Astaire, but he didn't care. As long as Kylie was beside him, he would be the happiest man in the room.

And if they danced under a sprig of mistletoe, he'd be even happier.

CHAPTER 11

$\mathcal{B}$y nine o'clock, most of the families with young children had gone home.

Ben smiled as Willow's voice filled the old steamboat museum with an old rock 'n' roll classic. All the people he'd spoken to had enjoyed themselves. It was a night everyone would remember, not only for the music and entertainment, but for what they'd achieved.

"Penny for your thoughts," Kylie said as she sat beside him.

"I was just thinking about the tiny homes. Twelve months ago, the village was only a dream." Charlotte stirred in his arms but quickly fell back into a deep sleep. "It just goes to show what good planning and a lot of perseverance can do. Are you happy with how everything went tonight?"

"It was better than I thought. When the community center flooded, I thought we would have to cancel the Christmas party. But this is so much better. Thank you for giving us the trees and mistletoe."

Ben shrugged. "I felt like a fraud when I was accepting

everyone's thanks. If it wasn't for you thinking about the Christmas shop, I might not have agreed."

"If I'd known how much the trees cost, I wouldn't have asked. Have you opened your envelope?"

"I'll leave it until I get home."

Kylie nodded and pushed a lock of hair away from Charlotte's face. "She's like a porcelain doll."

Ben studied his daughter's face. "She's been through a lot in her short life. I thought about what you said. About Robyn. I think you're right."

"You're going to ask her to visit Sapphire Bay sooner than December?"

"She might not be able to come, but it's worth a try. It might help Charlotte and Robyn feel happier if they can spend some time together."

"That's a wonderful thing to do."

"I hope so." Ben was worried it could backfire, that Robyn would have an issue with something he was doing. But what choice did he have? He wanted Charlotte to spend as much time as possible with her grandma. If Robyn's cancer was as aggressive as she thought, they wouldn't have a lot of time together.

Kylie leaned back in her chair. "Have you heard anything about the DNA test results?"

"Not yet. My lawyer doesn't think they'll be available until mid-December at the earliest." He looked down at Charlotte and sighed. "I'll go home soon and put this little munchkin to bed. Do you want to come back to my house for coffee?"

When Kylie's eyebrows rose, he shook his head. "I didn't mean…" Ben cleared his throat. He would die a happy man if she wanted more from him than friendship. But his life was getting complicated. Asking anyone to start a long-term relationship with a man who was half-deaf and had a four-year-old daughter to look after was a challenge. Especially when his Christmas tree farm was barely making enough money to pay the mortgage.

Taking a deep breath, he tried again. "Coming home for a cup of coffee wasn't a secret code for anything else. Unless you want something to happen, but I don't expect anything and even—"

"It's okay," Kylie assured him. "I'd like to have a cup of coffee with you, but I still have a few things I need to do here."

"Are you cleaning everything up tonight?"

Kylie shook her head. "That's one of the benefits of having the event in this building. John is bringing a group from the church here tomorrow. They'll take down the decorations while the lighting team removes the scaffolding. On Monday morning, the construction crew will bring the half-finished tiny homes back into the building. From then on, it's business as usual."

"You could drive out to the farm once you've finished. I'll be awake for a few more hours."

"That sounds like a great idea. I shouldn't be too long."

Ben gathered Charlotte close to his chest. "I'll put the coffeepot on. If something changes and you can't come, just call me."

"I will." Kylie hesitated before leaning toward him. "Thank you for coming tonight."

When she kissed his cheek, Ben smiled. "I hope your intentions are honorable. A man could read a whole lot of somethings into that kiss."

Kylie laughed. "That's why I kissed your cheek."

"To limit my somethings?"

She nodded and grabbed the snowflake off her head as it slipped sideways. "If I'd kissed your lips, you might have enjoyed it too much."

"Would that be a bad thing?"

A blush skimmed along Kylie's cheeks. "No, but it—" She pulled her cell phone out of her pocket and read the screen. "I need to go. The dishwasher has stopped working. I'll see you soon."

And before he could offer to help, Kylie rushed across the room.

Ben sighed. He didn't know where their relationship was heading, but maybe it didn't matter. As long as Kylie wanted to spend time with him and Charlotte, they could figure out the rest as they went along.

KYLIE STOPPED her truck outside Ben's home. It hadn't taken long to fix the dishwasher and do a few other last-minute jobs before she left the party. She was looking forward to spending some quiet time with Ben. They had been so busy this week, she'd hardly seen him.

Reaching across the cab, she picked up a box. A lot of the people who'd come to the Christmas party had brought food for The Welcome Center. What couldn't be distributed the next day was being wrapped and frozen. But before Kylie left the party, John had given her four muffins to take to Ben's house.

"That didn't take you long," Ben said as he stepped off the front porch.

"Everyone pitched in to help." Kylie closed the truck door and smiled. Ben was wearing his jeans and a thick, red, padded jacket. He looked handsome, carefree, and more relaxed than he had all night. "Did Charlotte go to bed okay?"

He took the box out of her hands. "She woke up for a few minutes, then went back to sleep. What did you bring with you?"

"Chocolate chip muffins. John thought we would enjoy them with our coffee."

As they walked toward his house, she smiled at the fairy lights surrounding the veranda. "The lights are beautiful, but I thought you didn't like Christmas decorations."

"After Charlotte saw the lights inside the old steamboat museum, she wanted me to buy some for our house. She's helping me choose a Christmas tree next weekend."

"Will you be okay decorating it?"

Ben held open the front door. "We're making our own decorations, so I should be fine. You're welcome to join us."

"Can I let you know later in the week? The next fundraising event we're organizing is a Christmas carol competition. Bailey has done most of the work, but she's had a few last-minute cancelations and needs some help."

"That's fine. If you can come, we'll be decorating the tree on Sunday afternoon."

"I'll try my hardest to be here." While Ben hung up their jackets, Kylie looked around his living room. "You've moved the furniture."

"I made a castle with the sofas and chairs and a few sheets from the linen closet. When we'd finished, Charlotte wanted to put the sofa opposite the fireplace. She enjoys looking at the flames while I'm reading stories to her." He moved some books onto a table. "Have a seat while I make the coffee."

Kylie wasn't ready to sit still just yet. "I'll come with you. If I get too comfortable, I might fall asleep."

Ben's smile made her toes curl. "That wouldn't be a problem."

Kylie kissed him lightly on the lips. "You might regret those words, especially when I start snoring."

"As long as you're on my left-hand side, I won't hear you." His answering kiss wasn't as light or as playful as hers. But it was really, really, good.

Kylie sighed when Ben led her into the kitchen.

"Coffee first. You're cold."

Kylie rubbed the goosebumps on her arms. "I only took a light jacket to the Christmas party. The storm that everyone has been predicting mustn't be too far away."

Ben turned on the coffeepot. "Hopefully, it stays away for a few more days. I'll get one of my sweaters for you."

"You don't need to—"

"Yes, I do. I'll be back soon."

While Ben was gone, she found a plate for the muffins, then looked around the kitchen. With its floor-to-ceiling windows, white sparkling counter, and colorful art on the walls, she could have stayed here forever.

Ben returned with a sweater in his hands.

"Is that what I think it is?"

He held it against his chest. In the center of the bright red, hand-knitted sweater was a large snowman. It was the last thing she'd expect Ben to wear.

"Mom made it for my first Christmas in Sapphire Bay." He unclipped the silver snowflake in Kylie's hair and pulled the sweater over her head.

The soft wool felt wonderful against her skin. "Have you ever worn it?"

Ben grinned. "For about five minutes when Mom first gave it to me." He kissed the end of her cold nose. "It looks good on you."

"Thanks, but if this is your way of finding a new home for your sweater, you're out of luck. Your mom knitted it for you. Besides,"—Kylie flapped her arms inside the long sleeves—"it's too big for me."

Ben rolled up the cuffs. "There's always a way around a problem."

At his mention of a problem, Kylie's thoughts turned to the Christmas events they were organizing. By working together, they were finding creative solutions to homelessness, social isolation, and poverty.

Ben frowned. "That was a deep sigh."

"I was thinking about how generous everyone has been. Take Willow, for instance. She gave up a successful music career to become a photographer, but she didn't hesitate to help us. How amazing is that?"

"It is special." Ben took two mugs out of a cupboard and poured their coffee. "It must have been a big decision to leave Nashville."

"I guess we all make choices that might not make sense to other people."

"Like moving to Sapphire Bay after living in a big city all your life."

"Or buying a Christmas tree farm when you know almost nothing about growing trees."

Ben's smile made her stomach do cartwheels. "We're more alike than we think."

"Is that a good thing?"

"It could be."

Ben studied her expression. "How do you feel about children?"

His question surprised Kylie. "I think they're great. Why?"

"I've always wanted a large family. I know we're friends and that's great, it really is. But if we were ever going to be... you know...more than friends, I thought it would be good to see where we stand."

"On children?"

"On lots of things."

"Oh. Okay." Carefully, she took the mug he handed to her. "Well, I don't mind having a large family, but time isn't on my side. Not that I'm ancient, but it takes a while to find..." It was her turn to feel flustered. Finding someone who could be the father of her children wasn't hard. She could imagine

Ben running around with their children, reading them stories, and cuddling them after they'd skinned their knees or fallen off their bicycles. But having a vivid imagination could get her into trouble. Especially at ten o'clock at night when she was sipping coffee with a man who left her tongue-tied.

She tightened her grip on her mug. "What else were you wondering about?"

Ben looked even more uncertain than he had a few minutes ago. "I love what I'm doing. I work hard, but I don't make a lot of money. Is having lots of money important to you?"

"How long have you been thinking about these questions?"

Ben's eyes clouded over with something close to regret. "A while. You said trust is important to you. These questions are important to me."

"Because of Heather?"

"No. Because of Charlotte. I want to give her a stable home. If that's only with me, then that's all right. But if you and I were to become more than friends, I need to know that we value the same things, that we aren't going to tear each other apart."

A warmth spread through Kylie. It was as if a bright beam of sunlight had hit her heart and was lighting all the dark places she'd locked away. Ben Thompson, the man she'd originally thought was cold and uncaring, was more human than anyone she'd ever met. He wanted to protect his daughter, protect himself and, quite possibly, protect her.

She walked toward him and took the coffee mug out of his hands. "I used to think that if I worked hard and saved lots of money, I'd be happier than I'd ever been. And for a while, I was. But I lost sight of who I was and why I was working so hard." She held his calloused hands in hers. "My relationship with my family and friends suffered and my fiancé left me. I didn't know who I was anymore. Then I came to Sapphire Bay and everything made sense. I realized I get more joy out of helping people than having a large bank balance. So, to answer your question, having lots of money isn't important to me. As long as I can pay my bills and put something away for a rainy day, I'm happy."

Ben's hands tightened on hers. "That's a good answer."

Kylie smiled. "It was a good question."

His gaze never left hers. "Can I ask you something else?"

"Okay."

"Would you be my girlfriend?"

Kylie's heart pounded. "Are you sure?"

With a slow nod, Ben wrapped his arms around her. "I'm more certain of what's happening between us than anything else. But if we take this first step, I don't want it to be our last. I'm falling in love with you, Kylie Bryant."

Her eyes filled with tears. "I'm falling in love with you, too." And before she lost her courage, she kissed Ben until she couldn't think straight. Until the last thing she ever wanted to do was leave his arms.

LATER THAT NIGHT, Ben held Kylie in his arms as they watch the flames dance inside the fireplace. Everything about tonight felt so right. Being close to Kylie and knowing they both wanted a future together made him feel like the luckiest man alive.

Kylie rubbed her cheek on the front of his shirt. "I can see why Charlotte likes sitting here. It's so peaceful."

He kissed the top of her head before reaching for his jacket. "It's even better with you here." He fumbled inside one pocket before searching another.

Kylie levered herself away from him. "What are you looking for?"

His fingers found the envelope John had given him. "I should have opened this before you came. Do you know who made a Christmas wish for me?"

"No. John wouldn't tell me."

Ben frowned as he took a piece of paper out of the envelope. There was nothing he needed, apart from lots of sales from his trees and the products in The Christmas Shop.

His eyes widened as he read what the wish involved. "A trust in Chicago wants to give me a cochlear implant. Zac must have spoken to them."

"How do you know it was Zac?"

"I've talked to him about my hearing. He sent my specialist the results from some tests I had in Polson." Ben rubbed his hand across his eyes, still not believing what was in his hands. "Why would someone pay for a cochlear implant for me?"

"Did Zac think it would improve your hearing?"

Ben nodded. "So did the specialist I saw after I was attacked."

Kylie seemed confused. "If it would help your hearing, why didn't you get one?"

"The doctors I spoke to said an implant would cost about thirty thousand dollars. I didn't have that kind of money and my insurance wouldn't cover it."

"Did you try other hearing aids?"

Ben left the envelope on the table. "I used a CROS hearing aid for three months. It's where you have two devices; one on your bad ear that picks up sound, and a receiver on the other ear that helps transfer the sound. But it was worse than being deaf. All I heard was a high-pitched beeping when someone talked to me." Instead of being excited, he felt sick to his stomach. "I can't accept the implant."

"Why not?"

"It's too expensive. There must be other people who need the surgery more than I do."

Kylie frowned. "This could change your life."

"It could change many people's lives, not only mine."

"What about Charlotte? She doesn't understand why you don't always hear what she says. What if she got into trouble or you stepped into the path of a truck because you couldn't hear anything? What would happen to Charlotte, then?"

Ben knew the risks of not accepting the generous offer, but he didn't take handouts. "I haven't had an accident in five years. I'm careful."

"You say that now, but all it takes is one distraction and you or Charlotte could be hurt."

"I'm not accepting it."

"Oh, for goodness' sakes," Kylie huffed. "You're too proud for your own good. This is a once-in-a-lifetime opportunity. Are you seriously going to turn it down because you don't want anyone to help you?"

"There are lots of people who are in a worse situation than me. At least I have partial hearing." Ben didn't know how he could make it any easier for Kylie to understand why he wouldn't accept the implant. Until now, he had managed just fine with limited hearing.

Kylie touched his arm. "I understand why you won't accept it, but can't you see what a difference it would make?"

"It would make a huge difference. But my specialist might have other devices we could try." He slid the piece of paper into the envelope. "I'll call my specialist on Monday."

"And that's it? You're not going ahead with the implant?"

"The trust probably has a waiting list of people they can help."

Kylie sighed. "Just promise me you'll think about having the surgery."

Ben had already made up his mind, but Kylie wasn't ready to accept his decision. "I'll think about it, but don't get your hopes up."

"Thank you." She gave him a quick hug. "I need to go home. I promised Bailey we'd meet at her house in the morning to do some work on the Christmas carol competition."

When Ben started to lift himself out of the sofa, Kylie shook her head.

"Stay here where it's warm. I can see myself out."

He ignored what she'd said. "Call me when you arrive home. I'd like to know you got there safely." Ben took her jacket out of the hall closet and wrapped it around her shoulders. "And be careful on the road. There's black ice everywhere."

The troubled look on Kylie's face softened. "I'll be extra careful."

Ben opened the front door and walked with her toward her truck.

The still night air was so calm and peaceful. Kylie wanted to hold on to the serenity and never let it go. "Thank you for a wonderful evening."

Ben's eyebrows rose when Kylie unlocked the truck. "We don't have much crime in the middle of nowhere."

Kylie smiled. "Old habits are hard to break. Thank you for a wonderful evening."

"I enjoyed myself as much as you did."

Kylie pulled on her seatbelt. "I'll call you tomorrow."

He stuck his hands in his pockets and nodded.

"Say hi to Charlotte from me." And after a quick wave, Kylie drove away.

Ben returned to the house. He knew why Kylie wanted

him to accept the gift, but it was too expensive. If he could have afforded the surgery five years ago, he would have had it. But even then, thirty thousand dollars was a lot of money. So instead of dwelling on what could have been, he'd learned to live with his deafness.

Before he went upstairs to check on Charlotte, he looked around the kitchen. Sitting on the table was the snowflake Kylie had worn on her head.

He picked it up and held it in his hands. Kylie looked at life through rose-tinted spectacles. She thought everything could be fixed with a kind word or a thoughtful gesture. But real life—the hard, gritty, messy side of life—couldn't be fixed with band-aids or money.

His hearing loss was a constant reminder of everything that had happened since he was attacked. And nothing, including a thirty-thousand-dollar implant, would make him forget how far he had come. Or how far he still had to go.

CHAPTER 12

ylie took two daisies off the workbench in Blooming Lovely. "I can't believe he's being so stubborn. Who in their right mind would give up the chance of fixing their hearing?" She shoved one of the daisies into the floral arrangement she was making. "It was a Christmas gift, not charity."

Bailey watched her from across the workbench. "Perhaps to Ben, there isn't much difference."

"That doesn't mean he can't accept help when it's offered. I looked on the charitable trust's website last night. They donate lots of medical equipment to people across America."

"He might change his mind." Bailey twisted a piece of wire around some pine branches and added them to a wreath.

Kylie sighed. The chance of that happening was about as likely as the moon turning red. "I doubt it. Ben thinks he's indestructible, but his superpowers only go so far."

"Superpowers?"

She ignored Bailey's amused smile. Convincing Ben that he needed to accept the cochlear implant was important. The trust had given him six months to have the operation. After that, they would donate the implant to someone else.

"Ben thinks he can conquer any obstacle in his way. I don't know how he's going to fix his hearing without an implant." She picked up a rose and took a deep breath. If she kept jamming the flowers into the bouquet, it would look like something you'd see at the Mad Hatter's Tea Party.

"What if he doesn't want to fix his hearing?"

Kylie's hand froze. "No one would willingly stay deaf if there was a way they could regain their hearing."

Bailey shrugged. "Ben might not see his hearing loss in the same way you do. It could be his badge of honor."

"From when he was attacked?" Kylie couldn't imagine anyone wanting a constant reminder of such a horrific crime.

"No. To what happened afterward. Ben's wife left him, he learned how to walk and talk again, and he reinvented himself in a small Montana town. People don't go through all of that without some kind of psychological damage. But he survived and, from what you've said, he's proud of what he's achieved."

"And you think an implant will make what he's done seem less important?"

"It could. Or it might take away the one thing that sets him apart from everyone else."

Even though Bailey had worked with a lot of trauma victims, Kylie found it difficult to believe that anyone would want to hold on to something that caused them so much pain.

"Do you think there's anything I can say or do to change his mind?"

Bailey reached for a silver bow. "If I knew the answer to that question, I'd be a rich woman. All you can do is listen to what he's saying and support him."

"And if I don't?"

"Then he might not spend time with you. Is that what you want?"

Kylie shook her head.

"In that case, listen and learn." Bailey stood back and peered at the wreath. "When I've finished, do you want me to make another wreath or a garland?"

With a worried scowl, Kylie looked at the Christmas decorations sitting on a shelf. "A wreath would be great. If someone offered you a free cochlear implant, would you take it?"

"I'm not Ben," Bailey said softly. "Everyone does things for different reasons. Just because you don't agree with him doesn't make his reasons any less valid."

Kylie bit her bottom lip. "I want him to be happy."

"I know you do."

With a heartfelt sigh, Kylie added another rose to the bouquet. Perhaps Bailey was right. It was Ben's decision to make, not hers. Regardless of what she thought, she didn't have to live with a hearing loss or the memory of what had happened.

She just hoped Ben decided to have the operation.

BEN GLANCED at Charlotte in the rearview mirror. So far, on their ride into Sapphire Bay, she'd chatted about last night's party, about the spiders she'd found in the garden, and the Christmas trees surrounding their home. He had a suspicion she thought Santa Claus lived on the farm, especially with the Christmas shop filling up with gifts.

From the moment Charlotte jumped out of bed, she'd been a ray of sunshine. Ben knew she missed her grandma, but she didn't let that stop her from exploring the world around her or finding joy in the smallest things. Without a doubt, she was the most incredible little girl he'd ever met.

He turned into the old steamboat museum's parking lot. He'd told Kylie he would talk to John on Monday about the cochlear implant. But after tossing and turning all night, he'd called him this morning. Sunday was the busiest day of the week for John, but he'd still found time to get together.

The old steamboat museum was bustling with activity. Not only were trucks arriving with the half-finished tiny houses, but lots of smaller trucks were parked on the grassy bank surrounding the building.

It wasn't until Ben and Charlotte stepped inside the museum that he saw why the parking lot was so full. The volunteers who worked on the tiny homes were carrying tools and building materials back into the main hall. The massive panels Willow had donated were still on the wall, but the fabric, fairy lights, and trees were all gone.

John was standing on a ladder, removing Christmas decorations from a wall.

"Do you need any help?" Ben asked.

John looked over his shoulder and smiled. "I should be okay." With a final yank, he pulled the last of the tinsel off the red brick. "You've timed our meeting perfectly. Levi and his team are about to bring in the tiny homes we're still building. Hi, Charlotte."

Her small hand tightened around Ben's fingers. "Hello."

John climbed down the ladder and shook Ben's hand. "Mabel's here. She's happy to look after Charlotte while we talk."

Ben looked at his daughter. "Do you want to show Mrs. Terry your drawings of Mr. Whiskers?"

Charlotte's face broke into a dimpled grin. "Yes, please. She loves Mr. Whiskers 'cos she says he reminds her of Mr. Terry."

John laughed. "Because he's cute and cuddly?"

Charlotte shook her head. "No. It's because his whiskers are prickly."

Ben glanced at the grin on John's face. "Let's find Mrs. Terry before Pastor John says something he's not supposed to."

"Who me?"

For someone who'd spent half his life looking after people who were traumatized, John still had a good sense of humor. "Where did you say Mabel had gone?"

"She's checking the Christmas wreaths we took off the walls. One of our church groups is giving them to families to decorate their homes."

"Just like Kylie," Charlotte said excitedly. "She gives people flowers sprinkled with fairy dust to make them feel special."

"Does it work?" John asked.

Charlotte nodded solemnly. "And sometimes the fairy dust makes magic happen."

"We could all do with a little magic in our lives. I'll have to ask Kylie to make a special flower for me."

"You could have a pink one. They're my favorites."

John smiled. "That sounds good to me. Let's find Mrs. Terry. You can tell her about the fairy dust."

When John opened the door to a large room, Charlotte gave an excited squeal. "It's just like Kylie's flower shop."

Ben had to admit that the room did look and smell a lot like Blooming Lovely. The wreaths that had been taken off the walls were stacked on one side of the room. Mabel and three other women were busy working around some large wooden tables, repairing damaged branches and bows.

Charlotte tugged on Ben's arm. "I can see Mrs. Terry."

Mabel waved at Ben. "Charlotte will be okay. Just find me after you've finished talking to John."

He knelt on the floor beside Charlotte. "Be good for Mrs. Terry."

"I will." Charlotte's pack bounced against her back as she ran across the room.

"We can talk in the kitchen. I'll make the coffee." John held open another door. "If you'd like something to eat, help yourself. Mabel and her friends made lunch for everyone. There are more leftovers in the refrigerator."

Someone had stacked sealed containers of food on the counter. At least a dozen of them.

John noticed his surprised reaction. "They brought far too much food. I'll take whatever's not eaten to The Welcome Center." He handed Ben a mug of hot coffee. "You said you wanted to talk about the cochlear implant."

"I can't accept it."

"Why?"

"There are a lot of people worse off than I am. It doesn't seem right."

John opened a container of cookies and handed it to Ben. "There will always be someone who's worse off than you. It was a gift."

"I didn't ask for it. Zac shouldn't have said anything."

"He didn't. Months ago, you told me about not being able to afford a cochlear implant. I spoke to a friend who works with the trust and they agreed to fund what you need."

"But I can't pay it back."

John bit into a cookie. "You don't need to. Paying it forward is more important, and you're doing that by helping the young people who are working on the farm." He stopped munching and studied Ben's face. "You're serious about turning it down?"

"Kylie thinks I'm crazy, but I've never taken a handout in my life. Besides, there could be something else that will give me a similar result."

"What's the likelihood of that?"

Ben didn't know and, after the last attempt to help his hearing, he wouldn't guess. "I'm waiting to see what options my specialist recommends."

"And if a cochlear implant gives you the best solution?"

If that happened, Ben still wouldn't feel comfortable accepting the trust's help. "I'll have to think about what I'll do next."

John picked up his coffee. "Did I ever tell you about a woman who had her leg blown off by a landmine?"

The coffee in Ben's mouth turned to acid. "Not that I remember."

"She was twenty-eight years old and working for the UN in Afghanistan. After half a dozen surgeries and a prosthetic leg, she was struggling to find some kind of normal. She'd seen too many people lose limbs because of landmines and felt guilty about all the help she was receiving. She was a lot like you."

"What happened to her?"

"She thought she was coping but, when her husband left her, everything fell apart. The only thing that meant anything to her were the children she'd met in Afghanistan. So, instead of unpacking the emotional and physical trauma of what she'd been through, she threw herself into raising money for other amputees. When she traveled back to Afghanistan to set up a prosthetic clinic, she was humbled by the gifts she received. No one had any money. The war had destroyed everything they owned. But the children and adults came to see her, even though they didn't know if she could help them. She gave them hope, even when war was still raging around them."

Ben held his coffee mug in both hands. He hadn't been in a war, hadn't seen the carnage and bloodshed that changed so many lives. But he knew what it felt like to hit rock bottom, to be scared to close your eyes at night, and to be terrified of the same thing happening again.

"Is she okay now?"

Slowly, John nodded. "She's able to talk about how she feels and, most of the time, she's happy. She still goes to counseling to help with the PTSD. Being with other people who have gone through similar things keeps her focused on living her life to the fullest."

"Is she a friend of yours?"

"She's my sister." John lifted his troubled eyes to Ben. "No one else in our support group is deaf, but we all carry the weight of something we're dealing with. If you could help one of our friends overcome some of what they're going through, even though there are probably hundreds of people worse off, would you?"

Ben ran his hand around his neck. "Of course, I would."

"So would I. And that's where the gift of the cochlear implant has come from. No one expects anything in return except to know it's made a difference."

"What if it doesn't?"

"Then at least you tried."

KYLIE SPENT most of Monday thinking about Ben. She knew how proud he was but, regardless of what Bailey had said, not accepting the cochlear implant was plain crazy.

She glanced at her watch and looked around the store. With only three days until Ben's Christmas shop opened, the two part-time staff were working hard to provide as many decorations as they could. But that wasn't the only event Kylie was organizing. Willow and Zac were getting married on Saturday. Hopefully, the flowers she'd ordered would arrive on Wednesday morning. That would give her three full days to concentrate on the bouquets, reception flowers, and headpieces Willow had ordered.

The front door flew open and Brooke rushed inside. "You forgot to collect your caramel fudge." She handed Kylie the gift-wrapped box of deliciousness. "I can't stay long, but did you have a good day?"

"It was quieter than usual, but I'm not complaining. This week is going to be busy."

Brooke's eyes crinkled at the corners. "We finished wrapping Willow's table favors today. It's going to be such an awesome wedding. Have you asked Ben to come with you?"

"I'm not sure he'll be able to. Willow hasn't said anything about children coming."

"Give her or Zac a call. I don't think she'd mind." Brooke checked the time. "I've got to go. Levi's making dinner."

Kylie smiled. "Has he set off the smoke alarms, yet?" Last week the fire department had raced to Brooke and Levi's apartment above Sweet Treats. It was a false alarm, if you didn't count overheating a pan of oil and creating a cloud of smoke in the kitchen.

"Not yet, but I'm not taking any chances. Can you still meet for coffee tomorrow?"

"I'm looking forward to it. Enjoy your dinner."

The front door opened again, and Ben and Charlotte walked into Blooming Lovely.

Ben smiled at Brooke. "It's good to see you again."

"You too. Are you enjoying living in Sapphire Bay, Charlotte?"

Charlotte nodded. "We made a chocolate cake at Little Sprouts today. It was really yummy."

"You should ask your daddy if you can visit us at Sweet Treats. Megan could show you the cakes she makes. We might even have a little cake you could try."

"Can we, Daddy?" Charlotte pleaded.

Ben stroked her hair. "Okay, but not today. Brooke's store is already closed."

"You could come another day after Little Sprouts. I'll show you how we make fudge, too." Brooke smiled at the excited look on Charlotte's face. "It's time for me to go home. I'll see you all later."

Kylie followed her friend to the front door. "Say hi to Levi from me."

"I will." When she was standing on the sidewalk, Brooke nodded toward Ben and whispered, "Ask him about the wedding."

Kylie frowned. She wouldn't ask him if he could go until she found out if Charlotte could come. "I'll do it later. Now go home before Levi sets off the smoke alarms."

Brooke gave her a hug. "Tell Ben I'll drop off the bags of Christmas fudge for his shop tomorrow."

"I will." Kylie smiled as Brooke waved and disappeared into her candy store. Taking a deep breath, she returned to Blooming Lovely. Hopefully, Ben had spoken to John and Zac and felt more comfortable accepting the cochlear implant.

"Is it okay to visit you?" Ben asked.

"I was hoping you would come and see me. I'll just close the shop and then we can go upstairs. Have you had dinner?"

"Not yet, but don't worry. Charlotte and I can grab something when we get home."

Kylie flicked the deadbolt across the door and turned the sign to Closed. "I'm happy to make you something. If you like mac 'n' cheese I can easily bake enough for the three of us."

Charlotte grinned. "That's my most favorite dinner ever."

"That settles it," Kylie said with a smile. "It's mac 'n' cheese night."

"Yeah!" Charlotte jumped up and down like a Jack-in-the-box.

Ben's eyes lit with laughter. "You've made a friend for life. If you like, we could go to the general store after dinner and buy something for dessert."

"Ice cream?" Charlotte asked excitedly.

"I think that could be arranged." He looked at Kylie, then at the flowers sitting in vases. "Is there anything I can do to help you close the store?"

She shook her head. "Everything is already done. Those flowers will be all right until tomorrow." She held out her hand to Charlotte. "Did I tell you I bought more pink cushions the other day?"

"Like my ones?"

"They aren't as good as your cushions, but they're still amazing. Come and see." Kylie led them upstairs to her apartment. She had no idea what Ben would say about the implant, but he didn't seem too upset. If anything, he was more relaxed than she'd seen him in a long time. For now, she'd take that as a good sign.

AFTER DINNER, Ben helped Kylie with the dishes while Charlotte drew pictures at the kitchen table. Her feet swung above the floor as she sang along to the children's music they'd found online.

He opened the cutlery drawer and placed some forks in the tray. "I spoke to Robyn this afternoon."

Kylie turned toward him. "How is she?"

"She's missing Charlotte. I asked if she wants to visit Sapphire Bay this weekend." He didn't have to read Kylie's mind to see that she was surprised.

"I thought you wanted to wait a few more weeks before they saw each other again."

"I did, but John said something that made me realize that

the only person who still had to get used to Charlotte living here was me. I can't change what happened, but I can make Charlotte and Robyn happier."

"Are you still worried that Charlotte will want to go home with her grandma?"

Ben looked at Charlotte. "A little, but I'm hoping it will work out for the best."

Kylie handed him a plate. "For what it's worth, I think you've done the right thing."

"So do I." He dried the plate and left it with the other clean dishes. "I thought about the cochlear implant, too. I'll call my specialist tomorrow and ask him if it's still the best option. If it is, I'll talk to the trust and let them know I want to go ahead with the operation."

Instead of looking happy with his decision, Kylie frowned. "What made you change your mind?"

"You. Having a cochlear implant won't change who I am. If anything, it will make working on the farm easier, especially with more staff. And Charlotte deserves a dad who can hear what she says."

"I'm sure it will all work out."

"It's better than doing nothing." Ben leaned against the cupboards. "While I was at the old steamboat museum, I saw Zac. He reminded me I still haven't replied to his wedding invitation."

"I didn't realize you had one."

Ben smiled. "He gave it to me last month. Would you like to go to the wedding with me?"

Kylie bit her bottom lip. "I was going to ask you the same thing. But what about Robyn? Isn't she arriving on Saturday?"

"Her flight gets into Kalispell airport at four o'clock on Friday afternoon. She's happy to babysit Charlotte while we're at the wedding."

"That was nice of her."

Ben leaned forward and kissed Kylie. "That's because she's a nice person."

Kylie grinned. "In that case, I'd love to go to the wedding with you."

His heart pounded as he looked into her eyes. "Thank you for making me rethink the cochlear implant."

"I didn't want you to regret turning it down."

"I know. I just needed someone to remind me about what's important. And you're important to me. I can't imagine my life without you."

A soft sigh escaped Kylie's lips. "I feel the same way."

He wrapped a strand of Kylie's hair over her ear. "Does it worry you that I have a daughter?"

"Charlotte is one reason I love you so much. A lot of people wouldn't have welcomed her into their home. But you did. That makes you an extra special dad and Charlotte a very lucky girl."

He breathed a sigh of relief. "That's good, because I'd like to—"

"Daddy! Come quick. There's a spider and he's ginormous."

Kylie shuddered. "She likes spiders?"

Ben smiled. "It's in our genes. I loved any creepy crawly I could find when I was younger. Come and admire Mr. Spider with me."

"Do I have to?"

He smiled at Kylie's worried frown. "No, but you'll miss out on witnessing first-hand the Thompson fascination for eight-legged creatures."

When Kylie still didn't move, he laughed. "You can stand behind me with your eyes closed if that helps."

"That sounds perfect," Kylie said with gratitude. "As long as he isn't a jumpy spider, I'll be okay."

Ben wasn't promising something he couldn't deliver. Especially when it involved a spider. When he saw what Charlotte was pointing at, he laughed. "You might want to take a look at this," he said to Kylie.

Cautiously, she stepped from behind him and stared at the table.

Filling an entire piece of paper, was a drawing of the happiest, hairy spider Ben had ever seen.

"It's a Christmas spider," Charlotte said proudly. "And he's wearing a pair of wings, just like Grandma sent me."

Kylie breathed a sigh of relief. "He's beautiful."

Charlotte handed her the sheet of paper. "I made him for you."

"Thank you. I'll put the picture on the front of my refrigerator. That way I'll see your spider whenever I'm in the kitchen."

Ben didn't know how long it would stay there, but Charlotte didn't seem to care. She was so proud of the picture that her smile would have lit half of Montana.

Ben held out his arms to his daughter. "How about we go to the general store to buy some ice cream?"

"Yeah!" Charlotte stood on the chair and jumped into his arms. "This is the best dinner ever."

He smiled at Kylie. "I think so, too."

CHAPTER 13

*B*y Thursday afternoon, Ben felt like he was swimming upstream in a tsunami. So far, the opening of The Christmas Shop was a huge success.

Earlier in the week, Emma had launched the website and used lots of social media sites to invite people to the opening. With only seven weeks until Christmas, everyone within a fifty-mile radius of Sapphire Bay had gone crazy. From nine o'clock this morning, the parking lot had been full of eager shoppers.

It was just as well the community had rallied behind him. Without their support, he wouldn't have had enough products to fill the store to overflowing. Looking at the shelves now, he was seriously worried about having anything left for the weekend.

Kylie walked into the barn carrying some blankets. "These just arrived from one of the local craft groups. They're hand-woven mohair blankets. Would you like me to put them on the shelves or take them into the storeroom?"

"We'd better leave them in the back. Hopefully, there are still enough products to keep everyone happy."

Kylie nodded toward Emma. She was busy placing signs on the shelves that were empty. "We're letting people know they can order more items online."

"Will we have enough stock to supply their orders?"

"Jackie created a spreadsheet of all the products we had in The Christmas Shop and in the storeroom. She also added a column for products that are being made. As long as you don't have the same number of people arriving tomorrow, you should be fine."

When someone asked Kylie a question, Ben looked around the barn. There were still a lot of people buying gifts for themselves and their family and friends. Never in a million years did he think The Christmas Shop would be so popular.

He didn't know what he would have done without the young people he had employed. Take today, for instance. Instead of working on the farm, everyone had lent a hand to make sure their customers went home happy. Jackie and Paris were looking after the front counter. Nate, Marcus, and the other trainees were restocking shelves, selling Christmas trees, and taking orders for more.

After working on his own for so long, he was still getting used to having people around him. People who were happy to do what was necessary to make the farm a success.

Someone tapped him on the arm. Ben turned around and smiled at Nate's mom, Shona. Not only had she delivered more quilts this morning, but she'd stayed to direct people to the products they wanted to buy.

"I just wanted to say thank you. I'm overwhelmed by what people are saying about my quilts. Apart from the extra income, it's made me feel as if I'm a valuable part of the community again."

Ben was happy it had worked out so well for her. "We

couldn't have done this without you and Nate. You've been amazing."

"That's very kind, but all of this is because you wanted to make a difference. I need to go home but, if you want me to work in the shop again, just give me a call."

"I will. Thank you."

Shona zipped up her jacket. "If I don't see you tomorrow, I'll be back in a few weeks with more quilts."

After Shona left, Kylie sighed. "You're a big softy, Ben Thompson."

"I know what it's like to lose your self-confidence. Sometimes, all it takes is a kind word to change your life."

"Well, speaking on behalf of everyone who's been part of creating The Christmas Shop, you've changed a lot of people's lives." She looked at the blankets in her arms. "I'd better take these into the storeroom so we can sell them another day. Is there anything you need while I'm there?"

"I think we're all right. If I'm not here when you get back, I'll be at my house. I want to make sure Charlotte and Mabel are okay." Knowing that it would be a long, busy day, Ben had accepted Mabel's offer of looking after Charlotte. From what he'd seen, his daughter was having a great time. "I'll bring everyone back a cup of coffee. Would you like one?"

Kylie gave him a quick kiss. "That sounds divine. After I've dropped off the blankets, I'll be in the workroom making more wreaths."

"Thanks for giving me a hand this afternoon. I never thought we would be so busy. You and Emma have done an incredible job."

"We had a lot of help." She looked across the barn and pulled the blankets close to her chest. "Oops. Someone is making a beeline for me. I'll see you soon."

And before Ben could move, Kylie rushed toward the

back of the store, narrowly avoiding a determined-looking woman.

If the number of people coming here today was an indication of the shop's future success, he wouldn't have to worry about his mortgage payments. And, hopefully, the young people he'd employed would have a job that went far beyond the initial contract period.

LATE ON FRIDAY NIGHT, Kylie jumped when someone knocked on Blooming Lovely's back door. She glanced at her watch before rubbing her tired eyes. She didn't know who it could be. It was too late for any delivery trucks, and Ben and Charlotte were with Robyn on the farm.

She pulled open the door and frowned. "Bailey? What are you doing here?"

"I know I said I was going away for the weekend, but my sister is driving me insane."

Kylie smiled. "Which one?"

Bailey rolled her eyes. "It definitely isn't Sam. It's the other opinionated, controlling one who's nuts."

"What has Shelley done?"

"It's more like what she hasn't done. She was supposed to come home for Mom and Dad's wedding anniversary, but she said she's too busy. Who in their right mind would cancel their flights a week before a big family event?"

"Come through to the workroom. I'll make you a cup of coffee."

Bailey stomped into the building. "Shelley is being totally inconsiderate."

"Maybe she didn't have a choice?"

Bailey groaned. "That's what she told me, but everyone

has a choice. She doesn't have to stay in Sapphire Bay for the full week."

Kylie knew the wedding anniversary was a big deal. Bailey and her two sisters had been planning what would happen for months. It must be incredibly disappointing to know that her middle sister wouldn't be there. "How do your mom and dad feel about Shelley missing their anniversary?"

"That's the problem. They don't know."

"Oh."

"Exactly. And what makes me even more annoyed is that Shelley is too scared to tell them. She wants me to say something."

"That's a little—"

"Cowardly, spineless, uncaring."

Kylie's eyebrows rose. "That sort of covers it. Are you sure you aren't annoyed about something else, too?"

"It's nothing a magic wand and a stick of dynamite wouldn't help." Bailey sank onto a stool. "Have you ever tried to organize nineteen choirs?"

Sensing that Bailey was on the verge of hysteria, Kylie placed a hot cup of coffee in front of her. "I can't say I have."

"Well, let me tell you something. Everyone thinks they know what's best for the Christmas carol competition. No one is happy with the program. I've lost a special guest singer, and the brass band is refusing to learn six new songs."

Kylie looked closely at Bailey to make sure she wasn't joking. "I thought musicians enjoyed learning new songs."

Bailey threw her hands in the air. "That's what I thought, too, until I tried to introduce something different into the competition. Anyone would think I was asking them to change the day we celebrate Christmas."

"So, Shelley's a no-show for your parents' wedding anniversary is only half the problem?"

"A big half," Bailey said begrudgingly. "She's my sister. She should know better."

"Have you talked to Sam?"

"Not yet. She'll be even more upset than I am."

Kylie reached for a container she kept for emergencies. "It sounds to me as though we need all the help we can get. Cake?"

Bailey peered inside the container. "Is that what I think it is?"

"Yep. It's Megan's divine chocolate fantasy cake. I bought it yesterday."

"Because?"

Kylie only bought this cake when she was feeling stressed. And this week had been a doozy. "I've spent more time than I should have at Ben's Christmas shop. That made me run behind with Willow's flowers and a hundred-and-one other things I was supposed to do."

"Is that why half the cake is missing?"

"You're lucky the whole lot didn't disappear. Would you like a slice?"

Bailey jumped off the stool and took two plates out of a cupboard. "Yes, please. Can I have a piece with a caramel swirl on top?"

Kylie found a knife and cut off an enormous slice for Bailey.

"Oh, my goodness. I'll weigh an extra ten pounds if I eat all of that."

"I can cut it in half if it's too much?"

Bailey handed Kylie a plate. "It's too late. I'm already drooling." With a happy sigh, she bit into the cake. "This is so decadent. I should have ordered one of these cakes for Mom and Dad's party."

Kylie slid another piece of cake onto a plate for herself. "It wouldn't have lasted that long."

"You're right." Bailey sighed. "I would have eaten the whole thing myself. I'm sorry I didn't make it to the opening of Ben's Christmas shop. How did it go?"

"It was an enormous success. The online orders for trees and decorations are unbelievable, and lots of people were still visiting the shop today."

"That's great. You must be relieved."

Kylie was more than relieved. "It was a lot of work, but Ben now has another revenue stream apart from the Christmas trees. I don't think he'll ever be disappointed that he started the shop."

"I don't think he will, either. Do you still have a lot of work to do for Willow's wedding?"

"Not anymore. I just finished the bridal bouquet before you arrived."

"That's good." Bailey picked up her coffee cup. "Are you taking Ben to the wedding?"

Kylie frowned. "How did you know I was going to ask him?"

"I saw Brooke yesterday. Did he say yes?"

"In the end, he asked me. Charlotte's grandmother has come to Sapphire Bay for the weekend. She'll babysit Charlotte while we're at the wedding."

"That worked out well."

Kylie pushed away her half-eaten plate of cake. "I've fallen in love with him."

"Of course, you have."

"You said that as if it were a given it would happen."

"Maybe it was. When you first met Ben, you butted heads so often you were either going to murder each other or fall in love."

"What if I'd just walked away?"

"You needed twenty trees and lots of mistletoe. You

wouldn't have walked away." Bailey licked her fingers. "So, what are you doing about Ben?"

"There's nothing I can do except see what happens."

"Take my advice. That's a recipe for disaster."

Kylie frowned. "Why?"

"When was the last time Ben was in a relationship?"

"Five years ago, before his wife left him."

Bailey sighed. "That proves my point. You've both been single for so long that you've forgotten what it's like to be in a relationship. If you wait to see what happens, you'll still be waiting in twelve months' time."

"Is that a bad thing?"

"It depends on what you want out of your relationship."

"Is this where you suggest I make a list of everything I want, then talk to Ben to see if it matches his expectations?"

"Wow, you should be a family therapist," Bailey said with a grin. "When you see him next, take one of these cakes. It will help him overcome the shock of talking about his feelings."

"He's already told me how he feels. He loves me, too."

"That's wonderful. A lot of men don't like talking about the L word." With a satisfied sigh, Bailey ate a caramel swirl off the top of the cake. "Apart from falling in love, my nutty sister, and the mutiny of the choirs, there's another urgent matter we have to discuss."

"The Christmas wishes?"

Bailey shook her head. "No, but I had an update from Emma. A company in Red Deer is donating the uniforms for two of next year's Little League Baseball teams. Isn't that awesome?"

"It's wonderful. What else is on your mind?"

"Something incredibly important. Do you know what you're wearing to Willow and Zac's wedding?"

Kylie frowned. "I've been so busy that I haven't thought

about it." She waved her spoon over her half-eaten cake. "But at the rate I'm going, I won't fit anything in my closet."

"I'm glad you're not always super organized. If you want to borrow any of my clothes, let me know. I'll be home all morning."

"What would I do without you?"

Bailey nibbled on the last piece of her cake. "You would have eaten this entire container of deliciousness and felt incredibly sick."

"But what a way to go," Kylie said with a smile.

BEN MOVED his legs so another couple could take the seats beside him and Kylie. The Connect Church was the perfect venue for Zac and Willow's wedding. With its cathedral ceiling and large arched windows, it was a wonderful space to enjoy their friends' special day.

Watching people get married wasn't his favorite thing to do. Since his divorce, he'd avoided any invitations to weddings. But today was different. Zac was more than a good friend. Over the years, he'd been his doctor, his confidant, and his sounding board. And, right now, he looked as nervous as a man who was about to step off a one-hundred-foot cliff.

Every few minutes, Zac looked over his shoulder toward the back of the church.

It was just as well John was marrying Zac and Willow. Without his calming presence, Zac's stress levels would be through the roof.

Ben smiled as he remembered meeting Willow for the first time. She was a free spirit, an eternal optimist, and the most talented person he'd met. It was easy to see why Zac had fallen in love with her.

"You look as though you're a million miles away," Kylie said.

His smile widened. "I was thinking about the first time I met Willow. I'm glad she's marrying Zac. They'll have a wonderful life together."

"I saw Willow yesterday. She was a bundle of nerves, but excited to be getting married." Kylie looked at her watch and frowned.

"What's wrong?"

"She was supposed to be here ten minutes ago. I hope nothing's happened."

Ben tightened his grip on her hand. "I'm sure she's okay. Tell me about the flower arrangements in the church. They're lovely."

Kylie's face relaxed. "Willow didn't want anything too formal. She loves roses, baby carnations, tulips, and lots of color. We tried different combinations and came up with a theme she loved."

"I'm not much of a flower expert, but don't tulips bloom in spring?"

Kylie grinned. "Willow knows a lot of people. Those people knew other people who grow flowers. Finding exactly what she wanted was like a treasure hunt."

Ben studied the smile on Kylie's face. "You enjoyed every minute, didn't you?"

"It took a long time, but it was fun. Everyone was happy to help."

Kylie's flower arranging skills weren't limited to the vases overflowing with flowers. The rose and tulip covered arch at the front of the church was a work of art.

The same band members who performed at the Christmas party were seated on the right-hand side of the church. With the kind of skill that Ben could only dream about, they played country music ballads as everyone waited for the bride.

When John asked the wedding guests to stand, Ben looked down the aisle and smiled. Willow had arrived.

As the bride walked past them, Kylie sighed. "Oh, my goodness. Willow's beautiful."

Ben agreed, but it was the unconditional love shining from his friend's face that humbled him and made him think twice about his own life.

For a brief moment, before Zac's nerves returned, he looked as though his entire world began and ended with the woman walking toward him.

A heavy weight settled over Ben's heart. He'd never felt that kind of connection with his ex-wife. They were teenagers when they'd met, too young when they married. They'd thought they were indestructible, that loving someone was their right, and nothing could go wrong. They were wrong.

Kylie's hand tightened around Ben's.

He looked at her and frowned.

"I asked if you're okay."

Taking a deep breath, he pushed his unhappy memories aside. "I will be." The tenderness in Kylie's gaze brought tears to his eyes. She had become one of the most important people in his life. There was nothing he wouldn't do for her and no one he would rather be with.

Saying a silent vow, Ben promised to be as much of a rock to her as she was to him. He would stand tall and proud beside Kylie and never let her forget how important she was in his life. Because, regardless of what had happened with his ex-wife, he didn't want history repeating itself. His daughter and Kylie deserved the best of who he was, and he wouldn't let them down. Ever.

LATER THAT NIGHT, Kylie anxiously watched the people on the dance floor. "You're serious, aren't you?"

Ben grinned. "It's a waltz, not a walk down death row. It will be fun."

She'd pushed her comfort zone when she'd danced with Ben and Charlotte last week. Not that you could really call what they'd done, dancing. They'd moved to the music, spending more time laughing and talking than thinking about what they were doing. But this was different.

As Zac and Willow glided past them, Kylie's palms began to sweat. "Everyone knows how to dance."

Ben tightened his hold on her waist. "Not everyone. Most of the people are making it up as they go along."

"You're just saying that to make me feel better."

"It's true. I've watched three seasons of *Dancing with the Stars*. I know a waltz when I see it."

Kylie didn't know whether to laugh or cry. "Is that how you learned to dance?"

"You can thank my dad for that. He told me he swept Mom off her feet with a waltz. It's the only dance he ever taught me."

Kylie bit her bottom lip. "Did he think it might come in handy for you, too?"

"Maybe. Do you want to see if he's right?"

Kylie didn't care if he was right or wrong. Either way, she was terrified she'd spend most of the time untangling her feet from Ben's.

The band started to play another song. As soon as she heard the first few notes, she sighed. It was another waltz. "Okay, I'll dance with you. But don't do any fancy moves."

"I only know the basics," Ben whispered in her ear as he pulled her into his arms. "Don't worry. You're safe with me."

Taking a deep breath, Kylie relaxed her shoulders and stumbled through the first couple of steps. After a few minutes, the rhythm of the music and the movement of Ben's body made sense.

"You're doing great. Keep your hips pressed against mine. That way if I change direction, you'll change direction, too."

"Did you learn that from your dad or *Dancing with the Stars?*"

Ben turned her slightly to avoid colliding with another couple. "Dad. And it works."

Kylie was glad he thought so. It might stop them from bumping into anyone, but it wasn't helping her to stay focused. Ben's body was one hundred percent hard-packed muscle. Dancing hip-to-hip with him made her heart pound and her blood pressure soar.

Just when she thought the four minutes of torture was over, the band began another number. She dropped her head to Ben's shoulder. "I'm doomed."

Ben's laughter sent shock waves through her body. "Just relax and let me do all the work."

"That's easier said than done," she muttered.

"What a shame I couldn't hear you."

Kylie frowned. "It's just as well you're getting a cochlear implant, then."

"I could always change my mind."

She knew Ben was joking. He had been just as excited as she was after he'd spoken to someone from the trust. The operation would go ahead; all he had to do was make an appointment with his specialist.

Closing her eyes, Kylie let the music drift over her. She forgot about where their feet were going, didn't worry about stepping on Ben's toes, or banging into one of the other couples. She simply enjoyed the moment—and realized that dancing with Ben wasn't so bad after all.

"Don't go to sleep."

Ben's laughter vibrated through his chest. Kylie snuggled closer and sighed. "I'm imagining that I'm floating on a big, white fluffy cloud."

"Where are we going?"

"Somewhere warm and exotic. What about Bali or Thailand?"

"They'll definitely be warm. What about adding another destination? I've always wanted to go to Jamaica. We could walk along the beach and swim in the water with Charlotte."

Kylie snuggled closer. "I'm sure we could make it work."

Ben kissed the top of her head. "As long as we're together, we can make anything work."

If that wasn't enough to make Kylie fall in love with him all over again, she didn't know what would.

When the music ended, she reluctantly stepped out of Ben's arms. "You're a good dancer."

"Right back at you, ma'am."

Bailey grinned at them as she walked along the edge of the dance floor. "If you feel like something sweet to eat, the dessert buffet is ready."

"We'll follow you." Kylie looked up at Ben and smiled. "Unless you want to spend more time on the dance floor?"

"I heard a rumor that Megan and Brooke baked all the desserts, so I vote for following Bailey."

"What you heard is true. Brooke showed me the menu and you won't want to miss it."

Ben held out his arm. "In that case, would you do me the honor of accompanying me to the dessert table, my lady?"

Kylie held the edge of her dress and curtsied. "I would be honored, my lord. If you see the strawberry cheesecakes before I do, let me know. They're delicious."

With her arm linked in Ben's, they made their way across the room.

Kylie's eyes widened when she saw the tables filled with mouth-watering desserts. "This is amazing." The three flower arrangements she'd delivered this morning were each placed in the center of a table. Now she understood why Willow had wanted such bright, bold flowers in each vase.

The cakes, bars, cheesecakes, and towering stacks of profiteroles had been color-coordinated with the flowers. Kylie smiled when she saw the bright pink tulips she'd ordered from a supplier in Chicago. And beside the gorgeous flowers were plates of the small strawberry cheesecakes she'd tasted yesterday.

When they joined the line of wedding guests waiting for dessert, Kylie nudged Ben's arm. "The cheesecakes are on our right."

Ben looked over her shoulder and smiled. "They look delicious. If you like chocolate, you won't want to miss the table behind me."

Kylie turned around and stared at the chocolate Ferris wheel dripping with silky smooth chocolate. Bars of fudge, bite-sized chocolate coconut balls, and rich, creamy chocolate cake filled the table to overflowing. If Charlotte were here, she'd never want to leave.

Bailey laughed at Kylie's amazed expression. "It's unbelievable, isn't it?"

Ben's gaze traveled around the room. "Do Brooke and Megan cater for a lot of events?"

"Not really," Bailey said. "It's hard enough for them to keep Sweet Treats stocked with candy and cakes, let alone provide the catering for big events. As it was, they were working around the clock to make these desserts."

Bailey wasn't exaggerating. Each night this week, when Kylie finally headed upstairs to her apartment, the lights in Brooke and Megan's commercial kitchen were still blazing brightly. "They'll need a vacation soon. Otherwise, they'll never get one. I wouldn't be surprised if the Halloween and Christmas orders are already flooding into Sweet Treats."

Ben pulled his cell phone out of his pocket and read a text.

"Are Robyn and Charlotte all right?" Kylie asked.

"It's my lawyer. He wants me to call him right away."

Kylie checked her watch. "It's eight o'clock."

Ben's gaze shot around the room. "That's what's worrying me. I'll be back soon."

As Ben dodged the line of guests waiting for dessert, Kylie grew more worried. Something was wrong, and there was a high chance it involved Charlotte.

CHAPTER 14

*B*en strode into one of the church meeting rooms. He could still hear the band playing, but at least there was less noise from Zac and Willow's wedding guests.

His heart pounded as he thought of all the reasons why Roger might be calling him. Robyn hadn't said anything about contacting her own lawyer. She was happy with the visitation document Roger had put together, so that shouldn't be an issue. And even if it were, surely she would have said something when she flew into Sapphire Bay yesterday?

He called Roger's number and waited for him to answer.

"Hi, Ben," Roger said. "I'm glad you called me so quickly."

"That's okay. What's wrong?"

"The results from Charlotte's DNA test have come back earlier than I expected. Are you sitting down?"

"I couldn't sit if I tried. Just tell me about the results."

When Roger sighed, Ben's heart plummeted. "There isn't an easy way to say this. Charlotte isn't your biological daughter."

Ben closed his eyes and took a deep breath. "Are you sure?"

"The results prove you aren't her father. We also asked the company to confirm Robyn's relationship to Charlotte. She is her grandmother. Therefore, Heather was Charlotte's mother."

He leaned against the meeting room wall. "What does that mean for Charlotte?"

"Even after these results, you're still presumed to be her father. Charlotte can continue to live with you. You can still see her medical records, enroll her in school, and do everything else a parent would do. But the biggest question is whether you still want Charlotte to live with you."

Ben's heart ached. If Charlotte didn't stay with him, she'd end up in foster care. "I'd like her to stay in Sapphire Bay." The last two weeks had changed Ben's life. Charlotte had missed Robyn, but he hadn't expected anything less. She'd become part of his life, part of the reason he looked forward to waking up each morning. He saw traits of his own family in Charlotte's expressions, in the way her blue eyes absorbed everything around her.

In his mind, Charlotte was his daughter, and he was having a hard time thinking of her in any other way.

He held his phone tight against his ear. "What if Charlotte's biological father finds her? Can he take her away from me?"

"If he knows about Charlotte, then he could request supervised visitation." Roger rustled some paper. "You have a few options regarding Charlotte's guardianship. Do you want me to tell you now or email the options to you?"

Ben doubted he'd remember much, but he wasn't leaving the room until he knew Charlotte was safe. "Can we do both?"

"Sure. I know you wanted to add your name to Charlotte's birth certificate, but the easiest option is to do nothing. At the moment, you're considered Charlotte's presumptive father. As soon as you start the process of changing her birth certificate, you'll need to go in front of the courts. I don't think there'll be a problem, but it could take a while. The second option involves formally adopting Charlotte. Again, I don't think this is necessary. As far as shared custody with her biological father, if Robyn doesn't know who he is and we can't find him, the chance of his ever coming forward is not very high. He may not even know Heather was pregnant."

Ben felt sick to his stomach. "Heather and I were both unhappy, but we hadn't talked about getting a divorce. I don't even know when she would have seen anyone else. She worked as many hours as I did."

"If you want my advice, don't second-guess what happened. The best thing you can do for Charlotte is to work out what you're going to do next."

Ben wiped the tears from his eyes. "I'll try." He still couldn't believe Heather had slept with someone else. After everything they'd been through, to know that she couldn't trust him enough to talk about how she was feeling hurt deeper than her betrayal.

"I know this has come as a shock, but Charlotte is a delightful little girl. Keep that in mind if you decide to ask Robyn about Charlotte's biological father."

"I will."

Roger sighed. "I wish the news was different. I'll send you an email with what we've discussed. Call me after you've decided what you want to do."

"When do you need to know my answer?"

"Usually, there would be no rush. But with Robyn's health issues, it would be better to start any legal proceedings sooner rather than later. That's if you want to do anything."

Ben rubbed his hand across his eyes. Robyn would be devastated when he told her about the DNA results. "Thanks for everything you've done."

"You're welcome. Take care." Roger ended the call, leaving Ben to come to terms with what he'd heard. Before he'd met Charlotte, he thought there was only a slim chance he was her father. But she was so much like his mom and sister that it hadn't occurred to him they wouldn't be related.

And now…he tried to think rationally, to logically work out what he needed to do next. But all he could see were Charlotte's big blue eyes and her cheeky grin as she called him daddy.

He wasn't Charlotte's biological father, but he needed to know who was. And one of the few people who could help him was Robyn.

With more determination than he'd had a few minutes ago, he left the room. Before he did anything else, he needed to go home and speak to Charlotte's grandmother. Urgently.

As Ben made his way across the room, a prickle of unease slipped along Kylie's spine. He didn't stop to say hello to anyone or even smile at the people he knew.

She tapped Bailey on the shoulder. "I need to see Ben. He doesn't look happy."

"Do you want me to choose some dessert for each of you?"

"No, we'll be fine."

"If you need me to take you home, just ask."

Kylie gave her friend a quick hug. "I will. Thanks." She left the dessert line and met Ben in the middle of the room. "Is everything all right?"

Ben looked devastated. "I need to see Robyn."

Kylie didn't ask any more questions. "Come with me." She grabbed hold of his arm and headed toward the big double doors opposite them. Thankfully, the noise from the wedding wasn't as loud in the foyer. "What's happened?"

"Charlotte isn't my biological daughter."

Her mouth dropped open. Ben had shown her photos of his mom and sister. Charlotte looked exactly like them. "I'm sorry. Does your lawyer know her father's name?"

Ben shook his head. "Robyn is one of the few people who might know. Would you come to the farm so we can talk to her?"

"Of course, I will. I just need to get my bag. Do you want me to drive?"

He already had his keys in his hand. "I'll be all right. I'll park the truck in the front entrance and meet you there."

"See you soon." She kissed his cheek and rushed back into the wedding reception. Before he'd traveled to Los Angeles, he was concerned Charlotte wasn't his daughter. Now that his worst fears had come true, Kylie hoped Robyn, Ben, and his lawyer would do everything they could to keep Charlotte safe.

Whatever happened next would have to be in everyone's best interests. And knowing how the legal system worked, that might not be easy.

BEN PARKED his truck in the garage and took a deep breath.

"It will be okay," Kylie said reassuringly. "Robyn will probably be just as shocked as you are."

He stayed where he was, needing the extra time to come to terms with what lay ahead of them. "What if she's known all along that I'm not Charlotte's biological father?"

"Then we deal with the news and you decide what to do after that."

"You make it sound so easy."

Kylie turned toward him. "I know it's not easy, but you have to start somewhere."

He took another deep breath and undid his seatbelt. Charlotte deserved a lot more from him than his name. He wanted her to be able to trust him, to know that he would always look after her. If he didn't ask Robyn what she knew, it would be too late by the time Charlotte was old enough to ask the same questions. If nothing else, that gave him the courage to push aside the hurt he was feeling and focus on what was important.

Charlotte.

When he walked into the living room with Kylie, Robyn was sitting on the sofa, knitting.

"You're home early." Robyn looked over Ben's shoulder and smiled at Kylie. "Hi, I'm Robyn. Charlotte's grandmother."

Kylie held out her hand. "I'm Kylie Bryant, Ben's girlfriend. It's nice to meet you."

Robyn set her knitting aside and shook Kylie's hand. "It's nice to meet you, too. How was the wedding?"

"It was lovely." Kylie looked uncertainly at Ben.

When he was younger, he'd seen a photo of a bright yellow canary sitting in the middle of a gilded cage. He'd wondered how it felt to be stuck inside, unable to escape, even if you wanted to. Now he knew.

Robyn's gaze darted from Ben to Kylie and back again. "Is something wrong?"

He took a deep breath. "I think we should sit down."

Robyn frowned. "What is it?"

"I talked to my lawyer while we were at the wedding reception. Charlotte's DNA results have come back."

"That was quick." She studied his unsmiling face. "I'm assuming the news wasn't good."

"Charlotte isn't my biological daughter."

Robyn gasped. "There must be a mistake. Heather told us you were Charlotte's father."

"While we were married, did she ever mention a relationship with anyone else or even meeting anyone else?"

"Not that I remember."

Heather must have said something to her mom and dad. "If Charlotte was born around her due date, she would have been conceived a few weeks before I was attacked. Are you sure Heather didn't say anything about another man?"

Robyn shook her head. "I know I'm not being very helpful, but I honestly can't remember her talking about anyone. She was upset after you were attacked. Heather kept blaming herself and didn't know how she would cope if you had permanent injuries." Robyn rubbed her hand across her eyes. "We tried to reassure her, to tell her we would help, but she panicked."

She'd done more than that, Ben thought. In the space of ten days, she took all the money from their bank account and filed for divorce.

Robyn bit her bottom lip. "I can't believe this has happened. Do you want me to take Charlotte back to Los Angeles?"

In all this mess, that was the last thing he wanted. "No, I'd like her to stay here. As far as California law is concerned, I'm still Charlotte's dad."

Kylie held his hand.

He gave her fingers a light squeeze, letting her know he appreciated her support. Trying to identify Charlotte's biological father brought back memories he thought he'd forgotten. But, like mold growing in a leaky building, they were still there no matter how many patches you used to fill the holes.

Robyn's eyes filled with tears. "When we met Charlotte for the first time, Heather was scared we'd say something to you. She was drinking heavily and not looking after herself. If there was any question about who Charlotte's father was, she would have said something then."

"You couldn't trust anything Heather said, whether she was drunk or sober." Ben tried to keep the bitterness out of his voice, but it was hard. He could still remember the drunken blackouts, the times when Heather's behavior was so out of control that he had to call the police. Through all the violent outbursts and mood swings, Robyn and Garry made excuses for her behavior. They let her pass the responsibility for what she was doing onto someone else. And that someone was usually him.

"I still have Heather's belongings stored in my garage. I'll go through the boxes and look for an address book or something with her friends' contact details. If I find her cell phone, I'll try to recharge the battery and see what's there, too."

Hunting through her daughter's belongings must be the last thing Robyn wanted to do.

Ben looked closely at her face, at the dark circles under her eyes and her sunken cheeks. "Can I ask you a personal question, Robyn?"

She smiled sadly. "After what we've been through, you can ask me anything."

"Are you okay in Los Angeles?"

"I'm as okay as anyone else in the same situation. A group of friends drive me to my doctors' appointments and collect my groceries. I don't go away from the house too much— even less now that Charlotte is living here."

"And financially?"

"I have some insurance. You don't need to worry about me."

Even to Ben, Robyn's smile seemed forced. "If you need anything—"

"Don't be silly. I'll be fine." Robyn deliberately looked at Kylie. "While we were driving back from the airport, Charlotte told me you sprinkle fairy dust on your flowers."

"I own a flower shop. Sometimes I add glitter to an arrangement to make it look extra special."

"Well, it's certainly special to my granddaughter. She said she wants to sprinkle fairy dust on flowers when she grows up."

Kylie smiled. "Charlotte has a great imagination."

"She does." Robyn looked at her watch and sighed. "It's been a long day. I think I'll go to bed and think about anyone Heather might have mentioned. If I remember any names, I'll tell you in the morning, Ben."

"Thank you." He handed Robyn's knitting to her. "If you need anything, just ask."

"I will. It was lovely meeting you, Kylie."

"It was nice meeting you, too."

And with a small wave, Robyn left the living room.

Ben waited until he heard her bedroom door close before talking to Kylie. "What am I going to do?"

"I'm not sure, but what I do know is that your lawyer was right about Charlotte. She is a wonderful little girl. Whatever you decide to do, you have to keep her safe."

Ben sighed. "That doesn't help."

"It might be easier to think through your options when you aren't tired."

He held Kylie's hand. "Is it that obvious?"

"Only to someone who's known you for a while. Do you want me to call Bailey? She'll take me home."

"No. I can drive you into Sapphire Bay."

"Okay. And just in case you need to hear this, you're doing a great job of raising Charlotte."

His eyes filled with tears. "I thought she was my daughter."

"Just because you don't share any DNA doesn't mean you can't be her dad. All she needs is love."

Ben rubbed his hand across his face. He had a lot of important decisions to make in the next few days and a lot of questions that may never be answered.

Upstairs, a little girl was sleeping in her bedroom, cuddling her teddy bear, and totally unaware of what was happening. For Charlotte's sake, he wanted to make the right decisions.

By five o'clock the next morning, Ben was up and dressed and making himself a cup of coffee. He had tossed and turned for most of the night, worrying about Charlotte, upset with his ex-wife, and wondering what the future held for everyone.

"Good morning," Robyn said with a cautious smile. "You're awake early."

"I couldn't sleep."

She sat at the kitchen table and sighed. "Neither could I. I kept thinking about Heather and Charlotte, and how difficult it must have been to find out that Charlotte isn't your daughter."

"I thought... I guess it doesn't matter what I thought."

"It does matter. If Heather knew Charlotte had a different father, she let everyone down by not telling the truth." Robyn took a piece of paper out of her pocket. "I made a list of Heather's friends. Some of them may have moved away from Los Angeles and some are probably still living in San Diego.

When I get home, I'll see if Heather wrote anything down that would tell us how to contact them."

Ben read each of the names, trying to see if he recognized any of them. "Did Heather and Susan spend a lot of time together after our divorce?"

Robyn nodded. "They should have been sisters. Susan was a godsend while Heather was going through the withdrawal process. She made sure Heather had everything she needed and kept her away from any alcohol when we weren't there.

"Does Susan still live in Los Angeles?"

"I don't know. After Heather's funeral, we lost contact with most of her friends."

He picked up the coffeepot. "Would you like a cup of coffee?"

"No thanks. I'll stick to water. If I have too much caffeine, it gives me a headache."

While he poured Robyn a glass of water, he glanced at his watch. Charlotte wouldn't be awake for at least another hour.

During the night, he'd thought about Robyn and what was happening in her life. There was a solution that would make it easy for her to see Charlotte, but it would take a lot of work on both their parts.

He placed the glass of water in front of Robyn and sat at the table. "I was thinking about Los Angeles and how far it is from Montana. I know that's your home, but why don't you stay on the farm with us? It doesn't have to be a forever move. You could keep your home in Los Angeles and stay with us for a month or two at a time."

"I can't. My friends and doctors are in Los Angeles. Without their support, I wouldn't cope on my own."

"Charlotte and I could be your network. We have a good health center in Sapphire Bay. But if you need anything we don't have, we can drive you to Polson."

Robyn looked around the kitchen. "You have a beautiful home, but it wouldn't work. I'm happy in Los Angeles."

Ben wasn't convinced that Robyn wanted to stay in California. He knew how easy it was to become isolated when you were living in a big city, especially when you weren't in good health. It was one of the reasons he'd left the concrete jungle behind. "Before I take you to the airport, I'll show you the cabin the previous owners used for staff quarters. If you're worried about sharing the house with Charlotte and me, we could do a little remodeling and create the perfect cottage for you."

"That's very sweet, but I don't think it would work. I would have to change my oncologist and continue my treatment from another hospital. At the moment, it just seems too hard."

The last thing he wanted to do was to push Robyn into coming here if she didn't want to. Everyone had gone through a lot this weekend. And those changes were bound to get even more complicated as they discovered more about Heather's life. "I understand. But if you change your mind, just call me. It will only take a few days to tidy the cabin."

"I'll definitely call you if anything changes." Robyn took a sip of water. "Last week, I looked at The Christmas Tree Farm's website. It's wonderful."

Ben was proud of what they had achieved. "A friend designed it for me. It's bringing a lot of people into the store. We've already had orders for more than one hundred Christmas trees."

"Is that good?"

"Very good. Most of the time, people don't start thinking about their trees for another two or three weeks. It doesn't sound like much of a difference, but it will give us the extra cash flow I need at the moment."

"Will Charlotte's day care center be open through your busy season?"

He nodded. "The only day it's closed is Christmas Day. I don't know what I'd do without Little Sprouts. Charlotte loves spending time with the other children and I know she's safe."

A sad smile drifted across Robyn's face. "Make the most of your time with her. It's funny how your perspective on the world changes when you know how little time you have left."

He'd been down that road before and he couldn't agree more. It was also one of the reasons he'd asked Robyn if she wanted to live with them. Family was family, regardless of what had happened in the past.

"Before you go home, I'll take you on a guided tour of The Christmas Shop."

Robyn smiled. "I'd like that very much. There was so much traffic in your front yard yesterday, that I didn't dare go there with Charlotte. She's so quick on her feet that I was worried she would dart in front of a vehicle."

"We won't have to worry about that this morning. The shop doesn't open until ten o'clock. That will give us a few hours to enjoy the peace and quiet together."

"I can't wait."

Neither could Ben. Yesterday had been frantic, but he was hoping today would be a lot quieter. Especially if it was the last time Charlotte would see her grandma for a while.

CHAPTER 15

*A*s Kylie drove toward Bailey's house, she was glad she'd had an extra cup of coffee this morning. Santa's Secret Helpers were about to make another Christmas wish come true but, after last night, she was finding it hard to be enthusiastic about anything.

She parked the borrowed mobility van in front of Bailey's cottage. The house was cute, but desperately in need of a coat of paint. Unfortunately, Bailey hadn't had a lot of options when she was looking for somewhere to rent.

Although she couldn't do anything with the outside of the cottage, Bailey had made the most of the small garden. She'd planted colorful flowers and shrubs that would brighten the property in the summer, spring, and fall. For now, Mother Nature had lent a helping hand by camouflaging the faded, olive green walls in a blanket of snow, making them almost respectable.

The front door opened and Bailey stepped outside.

Her cheerful wave made Kylie smile. Two years ago, she would never have thought she'd find such a wonderful friend or be helping with projects that were changing people's lives.

Bailey opened the passenger door and pulled on her seatbelt. "Is everything ready?"

"As ready as it will ever be. I promised Mabel I'd take a photo for the community Facebook page."

Bailey looked over her shoulder. A shiny, red electric wheelchair sat in the middle of the van, waiting for its new owner. "I'm glad we're doing this. I can't wait to see Joshua's face when we show him his new wheels."

"Neither can I." Kylie pulled onto the street and checked her watch. They still had plenty of time.

Everyone who was part of Santa's Secret Helpers had worked with Joshua and his parents at The Welcome Center. Before Joshua was diagnosed with motor neuron disease, he had helped prepare meals in the kitchen, weed the vegetable garden, and mow the lawns. His diagnosis, when he was nineteen years old, had shocked everyone. But that wasn't the only heartache Joshua and his family had to bear.

In the last twelve months, his ability to move independently had taken a dramatic turn for the worse. No one had expected the disease to overtake his body so quickly. And that's why Bailey and Kylie were here today; to help Joshua enjoy a little more independence while he still could.

Bailey placed her wallet beside her feet. "You don't need to stop at the church. John's meeting us at Joshua's parents' house."

"That's good. I was worried we wouldn't get him back to the church in time for the next service."

"So was he. Have you spoken to Ben this morning?"

Kylie had texted Bailey after she arrived home last night. She'd told her Ben had some upsetting news, but not what it was about. "I talked to him. He's tired, but better than he was before he took me home."

"That's good. Is there anything I can do to help?"

"There's nothing anyone can do," Kylie said sadly. She

looked in the rearview mirror and turned right at the next intersection. "I couldn't tell you what was wrong because it was personal to Ben. If I'd said something, I would have betrayed—"

"It's okay." Bailey placed her hand on Kylie's arm. "You don't have to explain."

"I asked Ben this morning if I could tell you what had happened. He said yes."

"Are you sure you want me to know?"

"I'd like to talk to you about it. You might have a different way of looking at everything." Kylie's hands tightened on the steering wheel. "Charlotte's DNA results came back. Ben isn't her biological father."

Bailey frowned. "And Charlotte's mom never told him?"

"No. Even Robyn thought Ben was Charlotte's dad."

"How does that affect Charlotte?"

"It doesn't change anything at the moment. It's later, if her biological father contacts her or she wants to meet him, that there might be issues."

"So Ben can still look after her?"

Kylie nodded.

"How does that make you feel?"

"It's sad that Ben isn't her biological father. He's so proud of Charlotte. The connection they've formed is really sweet. But, above everything else, I'm glad that he's still looking after her."

"I didn't mean that," Bailey said softly. "You went through something similar with the man you thought was your dad."

"Except he didn't stay with Mom and me."

"Would you think any less of Ben if he didn't want to look after Charlotte?"

Kylie's heart pounded. She'd asked herself the same question, but couldn't face the answer.

"Kylie?"

She looked across the van at Bailey's worried frown.

"It's okay, you can be honest with me. I won't say anything."

"I know you won't. It's just…" Kylie took a deep breath. "There's something else you don't know. Robyn, Charlotte's grandmother, has terminal cancer. It makes the whole situation more tragic."

"That's terrible. She must be feeling incredibly overwhelmed."

"I can only imagine what she's going through."

Bailey frowned. "Apart from Robyn's health and wellbeing, it places Charlotte in a vulnerable situation."

"That's one of the things I'm worried about. I love Ben, but when he told me about the DNA results, I had flashbacks of what happened to me. But Ben isn't like my father. Part of the reason I care so much about him is because I know, deep down, that he wouldn't turn his back on Charlotte. It just took my brain a few minutes to listen to my heart."

"What if that changes and he can't look after Charlotte?"

"Then I'll consider being her foster parent."

Bailey's eyebrows rose. "That's a big commitment."

"I know what it's like to grow up on your own. Mom worked long hours and we hardly saw each other. But she did her best, and I love her for it." Kylie glanced at her friend, hoping she understood why this was such a big deal. "You've met Charlotte. She's happy, bright, and full of life. If she doesn't find someone who will love her, that spark could die. I don't want that to happen."

"What if looking after Charlotte makes it impossible to continue your relationship with Ben?"

Kylie sighed. This was the part that had left her in tears. The ending that she didn't want to happen. "If Ben doesn't want Charlotte to be part of his life, then he's not the man for me."

"I hope it doesn't come to that."

So did Kylie.

KYLIE PUSHED the green button on the remote control and held her breath. The man she'd borrowed the van from had given her a quick rundown on how to operate the Slide-Away lift, but that was an hour ago. After worrying herself silly about Charlotte for half the night, Kylie's brain wasn't exactly firing on all six cylinders.

"It's working," Bailey said excitedly. "Do you want me to tell you when to turn it off?"

Kylie unbuckled her seatbelt and looked over her shoulder. "It has a special sensor that tells it when to stop." She glanced at Joshua's parents' house, then opened her door. All she had to do now was make sure the tie-downs on the wheelchair were unlocked. Then it was just a matter of taking the wheelchair out of the van and getting it into the house.

Bailey stuck her head inside the van. "Someone's coming."

Kylie rushed to the front of the vehicle and breathed a sigh of relief. "It's okay. It's Simon, Joshua's dad." She deliberately parked outside their neighbor's house. That way, if Joshua looked through a window, he would think the people in the glossy, black van were visiting someone else.

Simon was in his mid-forties. He was tall and lean, and before Joshua's diagnosis, was a keen runner. But the last twelve months had changed everyone's life. Instead of being full of energy and ready for anything, he was tired and stressed, and it showed.

He met Kylie beside the van. "No one knows I'm here. I had to sneak out the back door so that Joshua wouldn't see me."

"Are you all set for the big reveal?"

Tears filled his eyes. "You don't know how much this means to us. It will make Joshua's life so much easier."

Bailey joined them. "The lift is ready."

Kylie smiled at Simon. "Do you want to drive the wheel-chair onto the platform?"

"I'd love to." Without hesitating, he pulled himself into the van and unclipped the wheelchair. Carefully, he drove the chair forward until both sets of wheels were in place. "I'm ready to come down whenever you are."

Kylie pushed another button and the lift began its descent.

"This is a lot easier than the ramp in our mobility van." Simon smiled when the lift came to a standstill. "It takes us five minutes to get everything ready. And that's before Joshua has moved his wheelchair."

"I'm just glad this wheelchair fits inside your vehicle." Kylie studied the front windows of Simon's house. "It doesn't look as though anyone has noticed us. Do you want to take the chair into the house, Simon?"

"I thought you'd never ask." He grinned. "I cleared the snow off the driveway, so it should be reasonably easy to get to the back door."

"We'll meet you there," Kylie said as another vehicle parked behind them.

"See you soon." Simon waved at John before swiftly moving up the driveway.

John jogged toward them. "Sorry I'm late. I had to answer a last-minute phone call."

"Don't worry about it," Bailey said. "All we have to do is lock the van and follow Simon."

"Does Joshua know what's happening?"

Kylie kept a close eye on the lift as it folded itself into the van. "Not yet. I don't know how his family kept it a secret but they have."

John closed the sliding door and smiled. "Are Santa's Secret Helpers ready to make another Christmas wish come true?"

Kylie handed John and Bailey their red Santa hats and straightened her favorite Christmas dress. "I'm ready, but don't be surprised if I cry. This wish is going to be heartbreaking."

Bailey took a deep breath. "We can do it."

"Of course, we can," John said softly. "Let's go and make Joshua happy."

IN THE PAST, when Ben felt lost and alone, he would retreat into his own world. Long walks helped him focus on what was important. He would count each step, listen to music, and stay away from anyone else. But since he'd met Kylie, his way of coping was to spend more time with her.

Today was no different. Right now, he would have traded everything he owned to have her beside him.

Saying goodbye to Robyn was worse than he imagined. Charlotte and Robyn were in tears and Ben wasn't far from joining them.

Unlike the first time she'd said goodbye, Charlotte knew exactly what was going on. As soon as they drove into the airport, she'd become quiet and clung to her grandma.

"Look after, Daddy," Robyn said to Charlotte. "I'll come for another visit as soon as I can."

"I don't want you to go," Charlotte wailed. "Please stay with me."

Robyn hugged her granddaughter tight. "I need to go

home, little one. But I will come back." She wiped her eyes and stood beside Ben. "Take care of each other."

Ben picked up Charlotte to stop her from wrapping herself around Robyn's legs again. "We will."

"I'm sorry this didn't turn out the way we wanted it to."

Ben sent Robyn what he hoped was a reassuring smile. "At least we know. If you need anything when you arrive home, call me. I can organize most things from Montana."

"Thank you, but I'll be okay." She checked her watch and took a deep breath. "I'd better head to my departure gate."

"Grandma, no," Charlotte cried. "Stay with me."

"I'll call you on Daddy's phone when I'm home." Through a fresh set of tears, she blew Charlotte a kiss, then walked away, pulling her carry-on behind her.

Ben didn't spend any more time in the terminal. Without speaking, he hightailed it back to his truck, needing to be out of the airport as much as Charlotte did.

As soon as they were driving toward Sapphire Bay, he took a deep breath and checked his rearview mirror. Charlotte was holding her teddy bear and sucking her two middle fingers. "It will be all right, Charlotte."

Her fingers made a popping sound as she took them out of her mouth. "I want Grandma."

"I know you do. Grandma loves you, but she needs to go back to Los Angeles."

Tears filled her big, blue eyes, and her bottom lip quivered.

"Do you want to stop for ice cream?" After mac 'n' cheese, chocolate ice cream was Charlotte's favorite. If that didn't give her something to look forward to, he didn't know what would.

She shook her head and lifted her teddy bear to her face, hiding behind his brown, furry body.

Ben didn't say anything. They both needed a chance to find their new kind of normal. His only hope was that Robyn would change her mind and move to Sapphire Bay. He had a feeling that in the coming months, she would need them as much as Charlotte needed her grandma.

LATER THAT NIGHT, Kylie carried an empty dish into the kitchen at The Welcome Center. "Do we have any more baked potatoes?" she asked Mabel.

"Coming right up. How are the green beans?"

"They're okay for now." Kylie made sure her oven mitts were firmly in place before picking up the hot dish Mabel placed on the counter. It had been a busy night at the center, with more than forty people arriving for a home-cooked meal.

As she walked toward the food tables, Kylie smiled at their regular guests and made sure the new arrivals were comfortable. The good thing about The Welcome Center was that anyone could come and enjoy a lovely meal. It didn't matter if you had a large home or no home. You could be driving through town or lived here for fifty years.

The Welcome Center's philosophy was simple. Everyone deserved a full belly of good food, a kind word, and a dry, warm, and safe roof over their heads.

Emma walked toward Kylie with another empty dish in her hands. "The spaghetti is a hit. We'll have to make that recipe again."

"Natalie is cooking some more. It should be ready soon."

"Thanks. Have you seen Jack and the twins?"

"They're helping John set up the story time. They should be back soon."

Kylie slid the potatoes onto the table. Before now, she hadn't considered telling Ben about Jack. But the more she thought about it, the more she realized Jack might be the best person to find Charlotte's biological father. If Ben wanted to find him.

As she walked back to the kitchen, she glanced at the entrance to the dining room.

Ben and Charlotte stood in the middle of the doorway, looking like lost souls.

She took off her oven mitts and hurried toward them. Charlotte's eyes were red and puffy, and Ben's weren't much better. "Hi. You're just in time for dinner."

Ben shook his head. "We'll be okay. I just thought I'd stop by and say hello."

"Did the flight leave on time?" Kylie deliberately left Robyn's name out of the question. If Charlotte had been as upset as she looked, reminding her that her grandma wasn't here would be like picking the scab off an old wound.

"It did. The ride back to Sapphire Bay was…interesting."

Kylie recognized the helplessness in Ben's eyes. She'd seen it too often in her mom's face and in the eyes of the people who came into The Welcome Center.

She might not be a mom and she had zero experience of looking after four-year-olds, but she did have one serious advantage. "Mr. Whiskers is pretending to be Santa Claus," Kylie whispered to Charlotte. "And he's wearing a special Christmas bow. Do you want to see him?"

Charlotte's eyes widened. With her fingers still in her mouth, she slowly nodded.

Kylie pointed through the door. "When I saw him before dinner, he was sitting in his favorite spot."

Charlotte's gaze swung toward the living room.

She remembered the sleigh. Kylie breathed a sigh of relief. At least they were closer to finding Charlotte's happy place.

On their way across the foyer, Kylie talked about Mr. Whiskers and his uncanny ability to know when they were cooking carrots and corn. Because, as she told Charlotte, Mr. Whiskers loved his vegetables.

By the time they reached the living room, Ben didn't look as though the end of the world was coming, and Charlotte was almost smiling. And the star of the night, Mr. Whiskers, was sitting on a red velvet cushion in the middle of his favorite sleigh. If Kylie didn't know better, she could have sworn the old gray cat actually smiled.

Ben lowered Charlotte to the floor. In less than a minute, she was patting Mr. Whiskers and admiring the red and gold bow attached to his collar.

Ben wrapped his arm around Kylie's waist. "Thank you."

"You're welcome. How are you feeling?"

"Like I've run six marathons and there's another one coming."

She relaxed against his body. "Take each day as it comes."

"That's easier said than done. How was your day?"

"It was happy and sad. We delivered the new electric wheelchair to Joshua." Kylie had already told Ben where she would be this morning. Because she'd known Joshua before he became sick, it was even harder to see how much his life had changed. "He couldn't stop smiling. His dad joked that he'd probably get a speeding ticket."

"It sounds as though the chair was exactly what he needs."

Kylie sighed. "Just before we left, Joshua said something that made me cry."

Ben kissed the side of her head. "What did he say?"

Kylie's eyes filled with tears. "He looked at his mom and dad, and said that, 'family is where life begins and love never ends.' Motor neuron disease has taken so much from them, but it can never take away their love for each other."

"That's a powerful message."

"They're a courageous family."

Ben's arm tightened around her waist. "On the way home, I was thinking about Charlotte and where we go to from here. I don't know what to do."

Kylie froze. "What do you mean?"

"Charlotte was devastated when Robyn went home. How do I help her understand why they can't be together?"

Slowly, Kylie relaxed. Ben wasn't sending Charlotte back to California. All he wanted was to make sure she was happy. "I'm probably not the right person to ask. Why don't you talk to Bailey? She helps children and their families through all kinds of issues."

"I suppose it wouldn't hurt."

"She'll be thrilled by your enthusiasm," Kylie joked. "You never know, she might have other ideas about making Sapphire Bay feel like Charlotte's home."

Ben nodded toward his daughter. Charlotte was quietly talking to Mr. Whiskers and rubbing his favorite spot between his ears. "Adopting a cat from the animal shelter might be a good place to start."

"You could be right. I know something else that might help."

"You do?"

Kylie laughed. "Don't look so hopeful. I meant having dinner here. Natalie has made a delicious spaghetti bolognese. I'm sure there'll be enough for us."

Ben kissed the sensitive spot under Kylie's ear. "I thought you wanted to have your wicked way with me."

Goose bumps skittered along her skin. "Wicked doesn't happen when we have a four-year-old with us."

"We could find some time when Charlotte is at daycare?"

Kylie sighed. "Are you trying to lead me astray?"

Ben wrapped his other arm around Kylie, holding her in a cocoon of heat. "Is it working?"

She wound her arms around his shoulders. "Maybe."

"That's better than no."

Kylie grinned. "And a long way from saying yes."

CHAPTER 16

*B*y the time they had dinner with Kylie and drove home, Ben and Charlotte were both overtired. It had been a long day, but neither of them was ready to go to bed. So Ben lit the fire and made sure there were plenty of blankets on the sofa.

"Would you like me to read you a story?" he asked Charlotte.

Her instant smile was much better than seeing tears in her eyes. "Can we read the mouse book?"

"Okay. I think it's beside your bed."

While Charlotte rushed upstairs, Ben made a large mug of hot chocolate for himself and a much smaller one for Charlotte.

By the time he returned to the living room, Charlotte was already waiting for him on the sofa.

She waved the book in the air. "Here it is."

Frederick was Charlotte's favorite book. It was about a poetic little mouse called Frederick who used words to help his family feel happy during the cold winter months on the farm. After reading the book at least a dozen times, Ben could have recited the story word-for-word. But Charlotte loved the simple illustrations and the way the book made her feel.

With a contented sigh, he sat on the sofa.

Charlotte snuggled beside him. "Do you think Frederick lives in our barn?"

"He might live here," Ben said softly. "But his family enjoys eating corn and wheat. We don't grow those on our land."

"They could visit Mr. and Mrs. Terry. They have corn in their store."

"That's true."

"Or they could live with Mr. Whiskers. He loves corn, but he might squish Frederick's family 'cos he's got such a big tummy."

Ben held back a smile as he opened the book. "You're right. That could definitely be a problem. Are you ready to hear Frederick's story?"

Charlotte's little hand held onto the soft wool of his sweater. "I'm ready."

Ben placed his finger below the first word so that Charlotte could read along with him. "All along the meadow where the cows grazed and the horses ran, there was an old stone wall."

"With mices!" Charlotte squealed.

Ben smiled and turned the page.

"There's Frederick and his family." Charlotte's hand shot to the picture. "Frederick has a mommy, and a daddy, and a brother, and a sister." She pointed to each of the mice. "One, two, three, four."

"That's awesome counting."

"Grandma showed me how to count. I can go all the way to ten. One, two, three, four, five, seven, nine, ten!"

"Wow, that's incredible. Do you think Frederick knows how to count to ten?"

Charlotte nodded. "He knows about everything. Daddy, where's mommy?"

Ben put down the book. "What did Grandma say about your mommy?"

"She said she's an angel in heaven. Can I go to heaven, too?"

"One day, but hopefully not for a long time. Even though your mommy isn't here, you can still talk to her."

"Like when I talk to Grandma?"

"Sort of, except we can't talk to mommy on the phone. You can talk to her in your prayers."

"Bethany says prayers are silly."

"Who's Bethany?"

"She goes to Little Sprouts. She said Frederick is silly, too, 'cos a mouse can't talk. But he talks in the story, so Bethany is wrong. And she's wrong about talking to mommy, 'cos Grandma talks to her and Granddad all the time and Grandma isn't silly."

Ben's eyes widened. "Your Grandma definitely isn't silly. What do you remember about your mom?"

Charlotte dropped her head onto his arm. "She read me stories and gave me cuddles. Granddad went to heaven, too."

Ben's heart ached. Losing the people you loved was hard, but it must be worse when you didn't understand what was happening. "Your mom and granddad would be very proud of you."

"That's what Grandma says. I wish she was here."

He kissed the top of her head. "So do I."

Charlotte rubbed her cheek against his sweater. "Can we read about Frederick now? He makes his family feel happy when they're sad."

Ben picked up the book and turned the page. Like Frederick, he wanted to hold on to this moment, keep it safe and warm, and remember it when times were hard. Because, no matter how much he wished their lives were different, the next twelve months could be some of the hardest each of them had ever faced.

ON MONDAY AFTERNOON, Kylie slowly drove along the driveway into Ben's Christmas tree farm. Snow had fallen for most of last night, coating everything in a thick, white blanket of ice. The snowplows had been out early this morning clearing the roads. And, thankfully, someone had done the same on Ben's farm.

When she saw the barn, Kylie smiled. A large snowman with a carrot nose and stick arms stood guard beside the doors to The Christmas Shop. In front of her, Charlotte and Ben were ducking and diving as they threw snowballs at each other.

Keeping a safe distance away, she parked her truck and walked across to them. "That looks like fun."

"We made a snowman." Charlotte grinned at Kylie. "He's looking after The Christmas Shop."

Ben jogged across the snow and kissed Kylie. "We thought we'd enjoy being outdoors before it gets too dark. Did you have a good day?"

"It was busy. I've got a few boxes of handmade gifts for your store. Do you want me to leave them in The Christmas Shop or take them into your house?"

"The Christmas Shop would be better. Jackie can update the stock spreadsheet tomorrow." Ben followed her to the truck. "Brooke brought us another five trays of fudge and a tray of marshmallow bars. We've been selling huge amounts of her candy over the last few days."

"It's because they all taste so good." Kylie opened the back door. "Mabel's craft group finished the hand-knitted Christmas elves and the church's sewing club has given me four dozen Christmas oven mitt and dishtowel sets. There are also more Christmas wreaths and some special pine cone creatures to replace the ones you've already sold."

Ben picked up the two closest boxes. "Everyone must be working day and night to restock our shelves."

"I wouldn't be surprised if they are. They want this to work as much as you do."

"Can I help?" Charlotte asked.

Kylie took one of the Christmas elves out of a box. "That would be wonderful. Could you take this into The Christmas Shop?"

Charlotte cradled the toy in her arms as if it were a precious jewel. "Like this?"

"That's perfect."

Ben turned sideways so that he could see Charlotte. "Follow me. We'll leave the toys and gifts in the storeroom."

"On the big wooden table?"

"That's the one." He waited for Kylie before heading to the barn. "Be careful. We plowed this area before The Christmas Shop opened, but it's getting a little icy."

"I'm glad I drove here when I did. It's getting dark so early." Even after living in Montana for two years, it was still taking her a long time to get used to the long winter evenings. "What time did you close The Christmas Shop?"

Ben pressed his back against the heavy wooden door to hold it open. "Three-thirty. The threat of fresh snow must have made everyone leave at a reasonable time. I thought Mondays would be quieter, but I was wrong."

Kylie turned on the pendant lights and smiled. "The Christmas Shop looks better each time I see it." With the shelves full of colorful crafts and sparkling toys, it was more like Santa's workshop than ever before.

Charlotte skipped toward the storeroom. "Nate showed me some of his special toys. Did you know he has a cat called Astro?"

"No, I didn't," Kylie said. "Is Astro like Mr. Whiskers?"

"No. Astro is black with white spots. He likes playing in the rain."

"It sounds like Astro is an adventurous cat."

Charlotte carefully placed the knitted toy on the counter. "Nate says he's silly sometimes, but he still loves him."

Ben slid the boxes he was holding onto the opposite end of the counter. "Charlotte, while I go back to Kylie's truck, can you show her one of the books Natalie gave us this afternoon?"

"Okay." With a happy smile, Charlotte rushed into the store.

Ben took Kylie's box out of her hands. "Natalie tutors a high-school art class. Her students worked with a creative writing class and made a series of illustrated books for children."

"That sounds like fun."

"It was fun and productive. They used a local printing company to make the books. Have a look while I'm getting the rest of the boxes."

After Ben had left, Charlotte showed Kylie the gorgeous books. From what she could see, the Christmas stories were funny, and the illustrations were adorable.

Charlotte opened another book. "Natalie read me this story. It's about Christmas fairies."

"It looks lovely. What's your favorite part?"

"When the pink fairy helps people." Charlotte carefully turned the pages until she found what she was searching for. "See. This is the pink fairy."

With a sparkly dress and big silver wings, Kylie could understand why Charlotte loved the pink fairy so much. "She is amazing."

"And she can fly. But she can't go to heaven because only angels can fly to heaven."

Kylie nodded. She wasn't entirely sure why Charlotte had heaven on her mind, but it seemed important to her. "What else can the pink fairy do?"

"She whispers in children's ears and makes wishes come true. Just like you."

Ben slid two more boxes onto the counter. "That's it. Do you want to come to the house for a drink, Kylie? Brooke gave me some samples of her new hot chocolate range."

She held out her hand to Charlotte. "I couldn't possibly refuse an invitation that involves Brooke's hot chocolate. Especially when I'll have such great company."

Ben laughed. "I'm glad the hot chocolate isn't the only incentive to stay."

Kylie looked into his eyes and smiled. She didn't need any reason to stay except to spend more time with the two special people in front of her.

KYLIE HAD NEVER IMAGINED that making three mugs of hot chocolate could be so much fun. While Ben fussed over the chocolate powder and made sure he was following Brooke's instructions, Charlotte told her what she had been doing at Little Sprouts.

"You're welcome to stay for dinner," Ben said as he waited for the milk to heat on the stove. "I made a casserole in the slow cooker."

"It's Grandma's recipe," Charlotte said proudly. "She makes it all the time at her house."

Ben tested the temperature of the milk. "Robyn sent it to me after I spoke to her this morning." He looked at Charlotte and grinned. "Tell Kylie what grandma is doing."

"She's going to live with us!"

Kylie's eyes widened. "That's wonderful, but I thought she wanted to stay in Los Angeles?"

"So did I," Ben said. "But as soon as she arrived home, she realized how much she misses Charlotte. So in four weeks' time, she's moving to Sapphire Bay."

"But grandma isn't living in this house. She's staying in the little house behind the barn."

Kylie had visited the two-bedroom cottage on her first tour of the farm. Built originally as staff quarters, the floor plan was surprisingly spacious. All it needed was a fresh coat of paint and it would be perfect.

"We're going to call it Grandma's Cottage. Daddy said we can make a sign for above the door."

Ben turned off the stove. "We'll see how it goes. If Robyn decides she wants to move into this house, we have plenty of spare bedrooms."

"I'm sure everything will work out fine. You must be super excited, Charlotte."

"Grandma can give me lots of real cuddles and she can pick me up from Little Sprouts and make cookies with me."

Kylie smiled. "It sounds like you'll be doing lots of wonderful things together."

Ben poured the milk into the mugs and sniffed the sweet aroma of the hot chocolate. "If this tastes as good as it smells, I'm ordering some for The Christmas Shop." He placed the mugs on a tray with a plate of cookies. "Let's sit in the living room. It's nice and warm with the fire going."

Charlotte raced ahead of them. "I'll get my book," she yelled from the bottom of the stairs.

Kylie made room for the tray on the coffee table. "I'm glad

Robyn's staying with you."

"So am I. I was worried about what would happen over the next twelve months. At least this way, Charlotte and I are close by if she needs us. Although, knowing her, she'll be fiercely independent and won't want our help."

"But you'll be together and that's the main thing."

"I have other news, too." Ben handed Kylie one of the mugs. "Be careful, it's hot. I heard from my specialist. I'm seeing him in three weeks' time for a preoperative consultation. A month from tomorrow, he'll fit the cochlear implant."

"That's fantastic." Kylie placed the mug on the table and gave Ben a hug. "I can't believe your specialist can do the operation so quickly."

"Neither can I, but I'm grateful. At least this way I don't have a lot of time to worry about what will happen."

Kylie held his hand. "Your specialist knows what he's doing. Nothing will go wrong."

"What if it's like the CROS hearing aid? I couldn't stand hearing strange sounds coming out of the implant."

"Has your specialist said there's any risk of that happening?"

Ben shook his head. "They've had a lot of success with the implants."

"There you go. I know it's hard, but listen to your doctor."

Charlotte ran into the room. "Here's my book. It's called *Frederick*. Have you read it, Kylie?"

She looked at the cover. "I don't think I have."

Ben's cell phone rang. He looked at the caller display and frowned. "It's Robyn. Would you mind if I took the call?"

Kylie shooed him away. "Charlotte and I will be fine."

"Tell Grandma I love her."

Ben smiled as he looked at his daughter and then at Kylie. "I won't be long." And before the call went to voicemail, he answered the phone and walked into the kitchen.

CHAPTER 17

*B*en listened intently as Robyn told him about the address book she'd found in Heather's belongings. She'd called half the numbers. Most were out of service, some messages had gone to voicemail, and others had led to a dead end.

Of the people Robyn had spoken to, no one could remember Heather mentioning anything about seeing another man.

"Have you spoken to Susan?" Ben asked. While he was married, Susan and Heather had been as close as any two friends could be.

"I tried the last number I had for her, but no one answered. I've left a message so, hopefully, she'll get in contact with me. Would you like me to scan the pages in the address book? You might recognize some names."

"That would be great. Do you have my email address?"

"I have. How's Charlotte?"

"Happier now we're home. We're looking forward to seeing you in a month's time."

"So am I. Thank you for caring about me. I'm not sure many people would have been as forgiving."

Ben ran his hand around the back of his neck. "I was hurt and angry, but there was no point holding onto those feelings. I can't change what's happened."

Robyn sighed. "But I could have, and for that I'm truly sorry. I'll do everything I can to help you look after Charlotte."

"Thanks, Robyn. That means a lot."

"I'll call you as soon as I've spoken to the rest of the people in Heather's address book."

"Sounds good." After they said goodbye, Ben stared through the kitchen window. The sun had set and the trees surrounding the house looked like dark, forbidding sentinels standing guard over a forgotten land.

He jumped when Kylie's hand landed on his arm.

"I didn't mean to startle you. Is everything okay?"

"As okay as it's going to get. Did Charlotte enjoy the story?"

"She did. It has a lovely message."

Ben wrapped his arms around Kylie's shoulders. "Have I told you how lucky I am to have you in my life?"

"Not in the last twenty-four hours."

He kissed her smiling lips. "I must be slipping."

"You just made up for it." She held him close. "Whatever's on your mind will be okay."

He rubbed Kylie's back. "I know that, in the eyes of the law, I'm presumed to be Charlotte's dad. But I want to make it official. I'd like to add my name to her birth certificate. But, before I fill out the forms, I need to know what you think."

"I think she would like that very much."

Ben sighed. Kylie didn't realize why he was asking her. It was hard at the best of times to explain how he was feeling, but this was worse. Even though he thought he knew how she would react, he might be wrong. And if he was wrong, he had to end their relationship.

He kissed the top of her head before stepping away. With her hands in his, he took a deep breath. "I couldn't imagine Charlotte not being part of my life. Adding my name to her birth certificate will only formalize what I feel for her in my heart. One day, I'd like to ask you to marry me and to be Charlotte's mom. I need to know if that's something you'd think about. If you can't see yourself being married to me, then tell me—"

Kylie silenced his words with a kiss. "I won't need to think about it. When the time is right and you ask me to marry you, I'll say yes. If there's one thing I know above everything else, it's that I love you. And Charlotte is such an amazing little girl that I can't help but love her, too."

"Are you sure?"

"I am. You make me happy."

Ben breathed a sigh of relief. "I thought you might have had second thoughts. With Robyn coming here and Charlotte never leaving, I have a completely different life than when we first met."

Kylie grinned. "That's not a bad thing."

Ben thought back to the first time he'd talked to her. "I didn't mean to be grumpy when we first met."

"I know, but you were so good at it."

Ben nudged her lips with his mouth. "I'm good at a lot of things."

"Lucky me." She groaned as his lips nibbled their way down her neck.

When Kylie's hands found the bottom of his shirt and yanked it out of his jeans, he nearly melted. "You're good at a lot of things, too."

Kylie's soft laugh made goose bumps race along his skin. As her hands traced the shape of his chest and the dips and curves of his ribs, all he could think about was finding somewhere warm, comfortable, and quiet to…

"Charlotte," he groaned.

Kylie's hands froze. With a sigh, she untangled herself from his body and rested her head on his shoulder. "Please tell me she isn't standing in the kitchen."

He looked over her shoulder and breathed a sigh of relief. "No, but I'd better check that she's okay."

"All right."

Ben ran his hand along her long, silky hair and smiled. "Are you okay?"

Kylie lifted her head and smiled. "Almost. Let's go and see Charlotte. Hopefully, she hasn't drunk all the hot chocolate."

"If she has, I won't be getting any sleep tonight." He held Kylie's hand as they walked into the living room. Charlotte wasn't there.

He looked at Kylie and frowned. "She must have gone to get something from her room."

"I'll check." Kylie left the living room and headed upstairs.

Ben searched the downstairs bathroom, the hall closet, and any other places she could have gone. "Charlotte! Where are you?"

Kylie ran into the living room. "She isn't upstairs."

He looked through the living room windows. It was cold and dark outside, and the worst place for a four-year-old. "I'll check the barn."

Kylie was already heading toward the hallway. As she opened the front door, she threw his jacket at him before grabbing her own. "I'll check the cottage and the backyard. I've got my phone."

They both tore out of the house.

Cold dread filled Ben with terror. It wasn't snowing, but it was close. If Charlotte stayed outside for more than half an hour, she'd die.

And no matter how hard he had to search, he wouldn't let that happen.

Kylie sprinted across the yard.

Ben made it to the barn before her, flicking on all the lights to make it easier to find Charlotte. Not that it made a lot of difference behind the massive building.

She pulled out her cell phone and turned on the flashlight. The beam of light cut through most of the darkness, but it was too narrow. Swinging her hand from left to right, she looked in every nook and cranny she could find.

"Charlotte!" Ben's voice filled the still night air.

Taking a woolly hat out of her pocket, Kylie pulled it over her head. Even though there was no wind, it was bitterly cold. If Charlotte was only wearing her sweatshirt and leggings, she'd have hypothermia within minutes.

The outline of the cottage loomed ahead. "Charlotte! Where are you?" she added her voice to the muffled words coming from the barn. No answer.

She checked the lock on the door, searched for any broken windows or small footsteps in the snow. Nothing.

As she rushed around the edge of the cottage, she collided with a low-hanging branch. The instant sting on her face made her breath catch, but she kept moving forward.

With her cell phone as the only source of light, she slowed down. Even though the trees were planted more than ten feet apart, their deep canopy made it impossible to see anything. "Charlotte!"

She waited, listening for a small voice, footsteps, anything that would tell her where Charlotte had gone. Still nothing.

After circling the cottage and searching as much of the yard as possible, she turned back to the barn. Charlotte couldn't have gone far. Kylie was only in the kitchen with Ben for five minutes, ten at the most.

She saw Ben as he was running up the driveway.

"Have you found her?" he asked.

"No."

He looked frantically around the yard. "I searched either side of the driveway, but she isn't there. Where could she be?"

Kylie's gaze locked onto her truck. It was a long shot, but worth checking. "I'll look in my truck. If she's not there, I think we should call the police."

"I've already tried. The storm that's coming is interfering with the signal. My cell phone isn't working."

Kylie checked hers. "Neither is mine. After I've checked my truck, I'll call the police from your landline."

"I'll call them. I want to check under the veranda and around the outside of the house, too."

"I'll meet you there." When Kylie arrived at her truck, she checked the doors. Ben must have locked them after he took the last box into the barn. She shone the flashlight under the truck, then threw the beam of light across the yard. "Charlotte!"

Quickly, she ran toward the house. The nearest stream was miles away, so that was one less thing to worry about. Ben had already checked the driveway, so she wouldn't be heading toward the main road. But if she wasn't in any of the places they'd looked, where was she?

AFTER BEN CALLED THE POLICE, he paced back and forth. They were only fifteen minutes away, but it felt like a lifetime. There must be somewhere he hadn't checked, some place Charlotte would have gone.

He needed to stop panicking and force himself to think like a four-year-old.

The last place he'd seen Charlotte was in the living room.

He stood in the doorway and deliberately focused on every square inch of the room. The three mugs of hot chocolate were still sitting on the coffee table beside an empty plate. The blankets were on the edge of the sofa and Charlotte's book was on the floor in front of the hearth gate.

His gaze shot back to the empty plate. He'd put half a dozen chocolate chip cookies on the plate. They were Charlotte's favorites, but she usually only ate one at a time. Before he'd gone into the kitchen, the plate was full. Even if Charlotte and Kylie had a cookie each, Charlotte wouldn't have eaten the rest in the time she was on her own.

A log crackled and hissed inside the fireplace. He walked across to Charlotte's book and stared at the page. Cookie crumbs sat on top of a picture of Frederick's mouse family. They were sitting inside a stone wall, listening to Frederick tell them about the sunshine.

Last night, Charlotte had told him that Frederick should have taken his family to the barn if they were cold. He stared at the page.

She couldn't be in the barn. He'd hunted everywhere, yelled her name at the top of his lungs. But what if she'd gone to find Frederick, to give him and his family some cookies?

He sprinted out the front door, rushed across the yard, and bolted into the barn. "Charlotte!"

He'd already looked everywhere in here. Where would a little girl hide? He glanced up at the lights and frowned.

There was one place he hadn't gone. The loft.

Gritting his teeth, he held onto the rickety old ladder that he'd told Kylie he would replace.

He didn't just hate heights; he was terrified of them. And since becoming deaf, his sense of balance was a whole lot worse. But if there was any chance Charlotte was in the loft, he needed to know.

Holding his breath, he scrambled up the first half of the ladder. *Don't look down. Keep your eyes on the rungs.*

Below him, a door banged and he looked down. *Bad move.*

The room spun, his foot slipped, and he pushed himself hard against the ladder. "Charlotte!"

"Ssh! You'll scare Frederick."

He sagged against the splintered wood.

"What are you doing on the ladder?"

Ben looked up and almost lost his footing again. "Get back from the edge," he yelled.

"It's okay, Daddy. The Christmas Shop looks pretty from here."

"Move back, Charlotte. Now!"

She looked shocked that he'd yelled at her, but he didn't care. All he wanted her to do was move away from the edge of the loft.

When she disappeared from sight, he took a deep breath and closed his eyes. He could do this. He could climb to the top of the ladder and sit with Charlotte.

With sweat dripping down his forehead, he slowly moved one foot onto the next rung, lifted one hand, and pulled himself up. He moved again, clinging to the ladder like a fish caught on a twelve-inch skewer.

When he could see over the edge of the loft, he searched for Charlotte. She was sitting on the floor with her knees curled up to her chest. Tears filled her eyes as she watched Ben cling to the last rungs.

He didn't say anything. He couldn't say anything. It was bad enough climbing the ladder, but he hadn't thought about stepping onto the loft floor.

"Ben? What are you doing up there?"

He didn't know whether to be relieved that Kylie was

here or worried that she'd try to help him. "Charlotte's in the loft."

"Is she all right?"

"Daddy isn't very nice. He yelled at me."

Ben wasn't going to have a conversation about life and death situations with a four-and-a-half-year-old. Especially when it was his life hanging in the balance. "She's fine."

"What about you?"

"I'm stuck."

"Stuck?"

He closed his eyes. "That's what I said."

"Hold on tight. I'll be there in a few seconds."

"No, don't. The ladder won't hold both our weights." The ladder wobbled and Ben gripped the rungs tighter. Kylie wasn't listening.

"Keep breathing," she said from below him. "You're doing great."

"I can't move."

"Yes, you can." She patted his leg. "You're nearly there. We're going to climb into the loft together. Are you ready?"

"I can't do it."

"You can and you will."

Was it just him or had he never noticed the steel in her voice?

"Ben? Are you listening to me?"

"You don't have to shout."

"At least you've still got a sense of humor. You have to go up another two rungs."

He slowly moved his feet and hands.

"That's it. Now we're ready to step onto the loft floor. Lift your right hand and put it on the top of the side rail."

Ben clenched his jaw and did as he was told.

"That's it. Now take your left leg off the ladder and step into the loft."

Sweat stung Ben's eyes as he stared at the last rung. "I'll fall."

"No, you won't. I'm right here."

"I'm a lot heavier than you are. If I slip, we'll both be in trouble."

"Do I look as though I'm going anywhere?"

"I don't know. I can't see you."

"You can do it, Daddy. I love you."

Ben took a deep breath. At least he would die a happy man knowing Charlotte had forgiven him.

"Come on, Ben. Left leg up. Crawl into the loft if it's easier. You can do it."

He said a final prayer, pushed off the rung, and hauled his body into the loft. When his knees hit the floor, he collapsed like a marooned starfish.

"Good job." Kylie patted him on the back. "I was worried you weren't going to move."

"So was I," Ben muttered into the dusty floor.

"You'll be okay."

"Tell that to my heart. It's pounding so hard that I can feel my pulse in my earlobes."

Charlotte's cold hand wrapped around his. "It's okay, Daddy. I'll look after you."

He lifted his head and stared into his daughter's big, worried eyes. "Did you find Frederick?"

Charlotte nodded and a huge, dimpled grin spread across her face. "I gave him some cookies and he said, 'thank you'."

Ben sighed. At least Frederick had good manners. When his muscles didn't feel like jelly, he hauled himself into a sitting position.

Kylie took off her jacket and wrapped it around Charlotte. "Let's sit by the wall so Daddy feels better."

Charlotte jumped to her feet and held onto Ben's arm. "Come on, Daddy. You can sit beside me and Kylie."

Ben wiped his forehead and crawled after his daughter. He'd never been so glad to feel a solid wall behind him. He held Kylie's hand. "Thank you."

"You're welcome. How are you feeling?"

"Better. How did you know I was here?"

"I walked around the edge of the house just as you were running toward the barn. When I went into the living room, I saw Charlotte's book and realized why you were coming here."

"I'm glad you did. I should let the police know Charlotte's safe."

Kylie squeezed his hand. "I'll do it."

"I should have listened to you."

As she pulled out her phone, Kylie smiled. "About buying a new ladder?"

Ben nodded. "If we ever get down, I'm building a hatch with a proper staircase."

Charlotte clapped her hands. "Then we can see Frederick every day."

He closed his eyes and sighed. He'd better add a child-proof gate at the bottom and a decent rail across the front. Otherwise, he wouldn't make it through the next few years without having a heart attack.

CHAPTER 18

*S*IX MONTHS LATER...

BEN CARRIED another box of Christmas lights across to John. "Are you sure we have enough?"

John climbed into the cherry picker. "It's May. You must be the only person who's putting Christmas tree lights up at the moment. If we need any more, I'll call Mabel and she'll organize another delivery."

Zac patted him on the back. "It will be okay. I was just as nervous when I asked Willow to marry me."

"But she said yes. Kylie might have changed her mind."

The cherry picker rose into the air, stopping halfway up one of the tallest trees on the farm. "If she was going to change her mind, she would have done it by now," John called down.

"Is that supposed to make me feel better?"

Zac laughed. "Believe me, nothing will make you feel better until she says yes."

Behind him, Charlotte giggled. Six months ago, he wouldn't have heard her but, after the cochlear implant, everything had changed. It took longer than he thought to get used to hearing sound from his left ear. But it felt good to be part of the conversations around him and hear the sounds he'd always taken for granted before he lost his hearing.

"I've been collecting pine cones with Grandma," Charlotte said proudly. "You can give one to Kylie, if you want."

"That's a great idea. Thank you." Ben chose a pine cone from the bag in Charlotte's hand.

"I could sprinkle glitter on the outside. Then it would become a special wishing pine cone, just like the flowers in Kylie's shop."

He brushed a stray lock of hair off Charlotte's face. The latest fundraising project Santa's Secret Helpers were organizing involved people buying a flower to support individual wishes. Charlotte had helped sprinkle glitter on the flowers and place them in special containers for delivery.

His daughter had a big heart and Kylie was showing her just how powerful a kind word and a helping hand could be.

Robyn left another bag of pine cones on the ground. So far, the doctors were encouraged by her test results. It didn't change her prognosis, but it meant the time she had with them was better than they could have imagined.

"I'll take Charlotte home for lunch. Do you want me to bring everyone some sandwiches?"

Ben shook his head. "Thank you, but we don't need any food. Mabel gave me a cooler full of sandwiches and cookies when I borrowed her Christmas lights this morning."

Zac grinned. "In return, she wants a photo of Ben and Kylie standing in front of the tree after Kylie says yes."

"That's if she says yes," Ben muttered.

Robyn patted his arm. "You don't have anything to worry about. Anyone can see how much she loves you."

Ben knew Kylie loved him, but that didn't help his nerves. Especially when their friends would be listening to everything they said.

KYLIE SAT at the kitchen table while Ben loaded the dishwasher. He wasn't usually this quiet, but they'd both had a busy week. "Is everything all right?"

Nervously, he looked toward the hallway.

Robyn had taken Charlotte to bed and was reading her a story. Although it was late, Ben had let her stay with them. With the lovely, long evenings and warmer weather, it was a shame not to make the most of each day.

Ben stacked another plate in one of the dishwasher racks. "Everything's fine. I was just thinking about Charlotte. She enjoyed going to school to meet her teacher."

Kylie smiled. "It's a shame she doesn't start for a few more months. She's really looking forward to being a schoolgirl."

"She's growing up so fast. I'm worried that one day I'll wake up and she'll be twenty years old."

"Charlotte still loves fairy tales and baking with Grandma, so I guess you're safe for a little while." She picked up her empty coffee cup to take across to the dishwasher.

"I can do that," Ben said quickly. "All you need to do is relax."

Something weird was definitely going on. "Are you sure everything is okay? You're acting a little strange."

"Because I want to put your coffee cup in the dishwasher?"

"Did something happen on the farm?"

Ben frowned. "A lot happened, but nothing out of the ordinary." He checked his watch. "There's something special I want to show you."

"Did Charlotte's new birth certificate arrive?"

"Not yet, but it can't be too far away." He closed the dishwasher and turned it on. "This is better than her certificate."

Kylie leaned forward. "Did you bring home a kitten from the animal shelter?"

"No kitten, but the shelter has an open day next weekend. I thought we could look for one, then." Ben held out his hand. "Come with me."

"Don't you want to wait for Robyn?"

"Robyn's happy to stay with Charlotte."

Kylie held his hand. She assumed he wanted to show her the new range of crafts that had arrived today. Even though it was a long time until next December, the Christmas gifts were still selling well, much to the delight of the people who created them.

As soon as they stepped off the veranda, she breathed in the fresh night air. "Look at the stars. They're so beautiful."

Ben looked up at the sky. "We live in an amazing part of the world." He cleared his throat and led her across to his truck. "I need to blindfold you."

"We aren't going to the barn?"

"Not tonight."

Kylie grinned. With Robyn and Charlotte now part of Ben's family, they didn't have a lot of time on their own. "Is this a date night?"

Ben frowned and her smile disappeared. "If we aren't going on a date, can you give me a clue about where we're going?"

"It's a surprise," he insisted. Pulling a scarf out of his pocket, he wrapped it around her head and over her eyes. "Is that comfortable?"

"Not really."

Ben ignored her less than enthusiastic reply. "I'm opening

the passenger door. Step forward. That's it. Now bend your head and sit in the seat."

Kylie lifted her hands and felt for the top of the door-frame. When she knew where that was, she turned sideways and sat down. "I hope the scarf belongs to Robyn and not someone else you need to tell me about."

The split second of deathly silence told her more about Ben's reaction than words could have.

"It's...it's Robyn's," he stammered. "You don't think I'd have someone else's scarf, do you?"

Kylie felt bad for teasing him. "Of course not. You're a one-woman man. Just the way I like it." She lifted her chin and tried to see below the scarf. "Where did you say we're going?"

"I didn't and I know what you're doing."

Slowly, she lowered her chin and turned toward Ben's shadowy outline. "I wouldn't peek."

"Yes, you would." He closed the door, stopping any further questions until he was sitting beside her.

Reaching for her seatbelt, Kylie clicked it into place and waited for the truck to start. "Does Robyn know where we're going?"

"Yes."

"She didn't say anything."

The truck moved forward and Ben turned on the radio. "I asked her not to."

A country ballad about love gone wrong filled the truck. Just as Kylie was beginning to enjoy the song, Ben changed the channel. "Why did you do that?"

Ben muttered something about poor radio reception. It had sounded all right to Kylie. Maybe she was the one who needed a hearing aid?

As they bumped and jolted their way to wherever they

were going, she became even more confused. "We aren't on the highway."

"Nope."

"If we're not on the highway, then we're still on the farm. Why can't I take off the blindfold?"

The truck slowed and she lifted her chin. Nothing but pitch-black darkness surrounded them.

"We're nearly there. Stop peeking."

"I wouldn't have to peek if you'd tell me what's happening."

Ben's door opened, then closed.

Kylie waited patiently while he took his time walking around the truck and opening her door. "I thought you were leaving me in here."

"Don't tempt me," he muttered.

She grinned. "I really do love you."

"I hope so."

Even to her half-covered ears, Ben's strained voice sounded worried.

He reached around her, unclipped the seatbelt, and held her hands. "I'll help you out. Keep your chin close to your chest or you'll bang your head."

Kylie did as she was told, mostly because she didn't have a choice.

Ben led her away from the truck and straight into goodness knows where. "Is this a confidence course where I have to trust that you won't throw me into a river?"

"We aren't going anywhere near the water."

If the crunch of dry pine needles wasn't a give-away as to where they were, the smell was. "Why are we walking through the trees?"

He took a few more steps before stopping. "I brought you here for a special reason. But before I tell you what it is, I need you to close your eyes."

Kylie closed her eyes. "Done."

"I'm taking off the scarf."

When the silky fabric fell away from her face, she breathed a sigh of relief.

"Are you ready to open your eyes?"

"Now?"

"Yes, now."

As she opened her eyes, she blinked a few times to make sure she wasn't imagining what was in front of them. "Oh, my goodness." Her mouth dropped open as she stared at the most magnificent Christmas tree she'd ever seen. "It's beautiful."

The tree must have been over thirty feet tall. From top to bottom, it was smothered in multi-colored fairy lights, twinkling against the endless night sky.

"When did you do this?"

"Today. I had a lot of help from John, Emma, Zac, and Bailey."

"I saw Bailey and Emma this morning. They didn't say anything..." Kylie sighed. "You told them not to, didn't you?"

"It was a surprise."

Kylie walked toward the tree. Up close, it was even more impressive. "There's no electricity out here. How did you turn on the lights?"

"Solar power. We needed to recharge the panels, but that wasn't difficult."

"This is the best surprise ever. Charlotte and Robyn will love—" She turned around and frowned. Ben had followed her and was kneeling on one knee. "What are you doing?"

"Something I've wanted to do for a while."

His gentle voice made her heart pound. It was difficult to breathe, difficult to do anything except drown in the longing in his eyes.

Tears filled her eyes as he held her trembling hands.

"I love you, Kylie. I've never met a woman who makes me feel so alive. You give me the best of who you are and ask nothing in return. You love my daughter and you care deeply about Robyn. I can't imagine my life without you."

Reaching into his pocket, he took out a small, black box and opened the lid.

Kylie gasped. Nestled on a satin lining was a sparkling solitaire diamond ring. "It's beautiful."

Ben pulled himself to his feet. "It reminds me of the snowflake you wore in your hair at the Christmas party." He let go of her hands to wipe the tears from his eyes. "After what happened in Los Angeles, I never thought I'd see the good in the world again. But spending time with you has changed my life. I asked if you would consider becoming my wife when the time was right, so…" He took a deep breath. "Kylie Bryant, will you marry me?"

She didn't need to think twice about her answer. Stepping forward, she gently kissed his lips. "I love you. You are gentle and kind, and want to make a difference in people's lives. When I'm with you, my life is complete. So, yes. I'll marry you."

Ben's arms crushed her to his chest. "I love you."

Kylie barely heard the whistles and cheers erupting around them. It wasn't until she turned around that she saw how many people were there.

She smiled through her tears as Charlotte and Robyn hurried toward them. "How did you get here?"

Charlotte hugged her tight. "We came with Willow and Zac and hid behind the trees. Bailey said we had to be quiet 'cos it was a surprise."

"Congratulations," Robyn said as she wrapped her arms around Kylie. "I know you'll be very happy."

"Thank you." Tears that had nothing to do with loving Ben filled Kylie's eyes.

"I know," Robyn said softly. "But this is what life is all about. Enjoy every moment."

"I will."

Bailey and Emma opened their arms and Kylie stepped into their warm embrace.

"Congratulations," Bailey said through her tears. "I can't believe Ben finally asked you to marry him."

"It was worth the wait."

Charlotte held Kylie's hand. "Where's your pretty ring?"

"Oops." Ben held up the black box. "Here it is." He knelt beside his daughter. "How about we both slide it onto Kylie's finger?"

Charlotte's dimpled smile made Kylie's heart melt.

As they wiggled the sparkling ring onto her finger, Kylie felt like the luckiest person alive. And when Ben lifted Charlotte into his arms and pulled Kylie close, she knew she'd found her happy-ever-after, right here in his embrace.

THE END

THANK YOU

Thank you for reading *Mistletoe Madness* I hope you enjoyed it! If you did…

1. Help other people find this book by **writing a review.**
2. Sign up for my **new releases e-mail**, so you can find out about the next book as soon as it's available.
3. Come like my **Facebook** page.
4. Visit my website: **leeannamorgan.com**

Keep reading to enjoy an excerpt from ***Silver Bells***, Bailey and Steven's story—the third book in the *Santa's Secret Helpers* series!

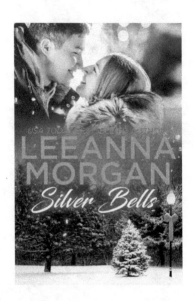

Silver Bells
Santa's Secret Helpers, Book 3

This Christmas, something magical is happening in Sapphire Bay.

Bailey Jones is a family therapist, not an event planner, but when her friends ask her to organize Sapphire Bay's first Christmas carol competition, she can't say no. Especially when the money raised will go toward another house in the tiny home village. When she meets eight-year-old Mila Butler at the local homeless shelter, her heart melts. When she hears her sing, she's in awe. Music could change Mila's life, but her father wants to keep her out of the spotlight.

Steven Butler spent seven years fighting a war no one could win. His time in Afghanistan cost him his wife and his sanity. With his spirit broken, the only thing that keeps him going is his daughter. And nothing, including the kindest woman he's ever met, will take Mila away from him.

When tragedy strikes, Steven and Bailey have to decide what's more important—being afraid of the past or building a future they never saw coming.

Silver Bells is the third novel in the *Santa's Secret Helpers* series and can easily be read as a standalone. Each of Leeanna's series are linked so you can find out what happens to your favorite characters in other books.

If you would like to know when Leeanna's next book is released, please visit leeannamorgan.com. Happy reading! For news of my latest releases, please visit leeannamorgan.com and sign up for my newsletter. Happy reading!

Turn the page to read the first chapter of
Silver Bells
Santa's Secret Helpers, Book 3

CHAPTER 1

ailey dropped her chin to her chest. For someone who taught people how to resolve conflict, she had to admit this afternoon's meeting was a disaster.

Even her former colleagues at the Mayo Clinic would run a mile if they had to deal with Margaret O'Brien. "I think we should all take a deep breath and consider our options."

Margaret's eyebrows rose. "The Archangel Choir does *not* sing 'Jingle Bells'."

"It's a Christmas carol competition," Duffy McBride muttered under his breath. "We don't need any of that hoity-toity stuff you learned in England."

Margaret sat ramrod straight in the plastic chair she'd commandeered. "I'll have you know that 'Hodie Christus Natus Est' is one of the finest examples of joyful carol music ever composed."

"Not in this century, it's not."

Bailey studied the faces of the other people at the meeting. Some were in a state of shock, others mildly amused by the not-so-friendly banter between Margaret and Duffy. But most looked bored beyond belief.

Mabel Terry cleared her throat. As the owner of the only general store in Sapphire Bay, Mabel was held in high regard. "We're part of a fundraising event for the tiny home village. It's not rocket science, people. All Bailey wants to do is make the evening enjoyable for everyone, whether they're children or adults. If the Archangel Choir wants to sing an old song, let them. After all, the audience will be choosing the winning choir."

Duffy snorted. "And I'd like to see anyone vote for them."

Margaret pushed her chair away from the table. "I have never been so insulted in my life." She slammed her meeting agenda on the table. "I should have known better than to waste my time traveling here. You have no appreciation for the finer things in life." And with the grace of a woman who knew how to walk in high heels, Margaret left the room.

Everyone started talking at once.

Everyone, that was, except Bailey. This meeting was supposed to bring the choirmasters together, not tear them apart. With less than four weeks until the competition, they still had to finalize the songs and the program. So far, they'd done nothing except disagree with each other.

Bailey tapped her pen on the edge of the table. "Excuse me. We need to make some decisions."

"I don't mind 'Jingle Bells' or 'We Wish You a Merry Christmas'," Duffy said. "It will give the children a night to remember."

A murmur of agreement went around the table.

At least it was a start. Bailey picked up the container of paper strips that had caused the latest disagreement. She'd thought writing down the names of songs and asking each choirmaster to select three titles was a fair way to organize the event. It turns out, it wasn't. Everyone had their own thoughts on what songs their choir should sing.

She handed Mabel the container. "Could you place these

song titles on the table? Everyone will have ten minutes to choose three slips of paper. If more than one person wants a song, you'll have to negotiate between you."

"What if Mabel puts all the songs she wants in one corner?"

Mabel sent Duffy a glacial stare. "We've known each other for more than fifty years. Do you really think I'd do that?"

For all his bluster, Duffy looked away. "Of course not, Mabel. Go ahead."

The door to the meeting room opened, and Bailey's friend, Kylie, slipped into the room.

After Mabel placed the song titles on the table, Bailey stood back. Lifting her arm, she checked the time. "Ten minutes, starting now!"

To save her sanity and the need to act as a referee, she headed toward Kylie.

"How's it going?" her friend whispered.

Bailey watched the drama unfolding on the other side of the room. "I've lost two choirs and a week of sleep worrying about the competition."

"Don't worry. It will all work out."

"I hope you're right."

Kylie smiled. "I know I am. Do you still want to come to the Christmas event at the elementary school? We'll understand if you have something else you need to do."

Bailey looked at the choirmasters. On the whole, everyone seemed reasonably happy with the choices they were making. "What time will you be there?"

"Four o'clock. Ben's meeting us there."

She rechecked her watch. "We should be finished before then."

"You'll come?"

"Charlotte loves spending time with the students. I can't wait to see what she's been doing."

"She'll enjoy seeing you there." Kylie pointed to the choirmasters. "It looks as though they've chosen their songs. Good luck."

"I don't need luck," Bailey insisted. "I need a megaphone and lots of patience. Goodness knows what everyone will be like over the next few weeks."

"You probably don't want to know," Kylie whispered. "I'll see you in an hour."

"Traitor."

The look Kylie sent her was pure mischief.

Bailey walked back to the choirmasters. With their song selections made, it was time to finalize the order in which the choirs would sing. She just hoped they were willing to leave their rivalry behind. Otherwise, Margaret wouldn't be the only person leaving the meeting early.

STEVEN RAN his four-inch putty knife along the wall. Within seconds, a thin coat of plaster covered the joint between two sheets of drywall.

For the last few months, he'd been working on the tiny home project, creating houses for people who couldn't find accommodation. After everything that had happened, he felt a deep sense of pride in being able to give something back to the community that had become his home.

Pastor John stepped into the half-finished house. "Hi, Steven. Have you seen Patrick?"

"He went into town to buy some supplies. Can I help?"

"No, it's okay. I'll call him. How are you feeling?"

Feelings were something Steven wasn't comfortable sharing, but John had become a close friend. As well as working at The Connect Church, John ran the only PTSD support group in town. Without his encouragement, Steven didn't know what would have happened to him or his daughter.

"This morning was difficult, but it's getting better. Tammy's mom called." Today was the anniversary of his wife's death. Five years ago, his heart was torn in two by the tragic loss of his soulmate. Tammy made his life complete. She filled his world with love and laughter, and made even the worst day bearable. After she died, nothing was the same.

John touched his arm, pulling Steven back to the here and now.

"Is your mother-in-law okay?"

He shook his head. "By the end of the call we were both crying. It doesn't get any easier."

"No, it doesn't. How's Mila?"

Steven's eight-year-old daughter meant everything to him. She was brave and kind and one of the most resilient people he'd ever met. "Last night, she drew a picture of her mom and placed a small vase of flowers beside it. Before she went to school, I told her some stories about Tammy. It helped both of us."

"That's a wonderful way to celebrate her life."

Steven swallowed the knot of grief in his throat. "I want to do the best I can for Mila."

He took a steadying breath. When they'd left Chicago, all he'd brought with them was a truck filled with boxes and the name of the local pastor. Steven's parents were horrified. Mila was upset about leaving, but had trusted him with her whole heart. And step-by-step, they were making a better life for themselves.

He glanced at his watch, nearly dropping the knife when he saw the time. "I have to go. Mila has a special event at her school and I told her I'd be there."

John pointed to the wall. "Do you want me to finish what you're doing?"

Steven's eyebrows rose. "You can plaster?"

With a grin, John took the knife out of Steven's hand. "I've got many hidden talents. Go to Mila. When I'm finished, I'll clean the knife and leave everything here."

"Thanks." After another glance at his watch, Steven made a hasty exit. Mila's school was ten minutes away. As long as the parking lot wasn't full, he should arrive on time.

As he changed out of his coveralls, he thought about the day he'd arrived in Sapphire Bay with Mila. They'd had nowhere to live and he'd had no job until John had taken them under his wing.

Pastor John had given them so much more than a warm place to stay. He'd helped Steven feel proud of who he was. Helped him realize he wasn't alone, that other people were doing their best to live good lives, too.

With his work clothes under his arm, he picked up his keys and ran toward his truck. By giving him a chance, John had changed their lives. And one day, Steven was determined to repay him.

BAILEY WALKED into the kindergarten classroom and waived at Kylie. Charlotte was sitting at a table, drawing on a large sheet of paper.

Once a week, the older children at Charlotte's daycare center spent a few hours with the students of the local elementary school. It was a wonderful way of helping them to feel more confident when they eventually started school.

When Charlotte saw her, she raced across the room. "Hi, Bailey. Do you want to see my picture?"

Bailey took her little friend's hand. "I'd love to." When she saw the colorful drawing, she smiled. "Wow. You've been busy."

"This is my dad's house and these are Christmas trees. And this," she said excitedly. "Is Frederick, the mouse who lives in our barn."

Charlotte's dad owned the only Christmas tree farm in Sapphire Bay. Last month he'd opened a Christmas shop. It was so popular that people came from across Montana to buy the locally made gifts and decorations.

"Frederick looks happy."

"Do you want to know why?"

Bailey nodded.

Charlotte slipped her hand inside her pocket. "I've got something special," she whispered. Opening her hand, she showed Bailey a little fabric mouse. "Grandma made this. It's not really Frederick, but it looks like him. Whenever I'm sad, all I have to do is hold my mouse and I feel happy again. That's why Frederick is smiling."

"That was a lovely thing for your grandma to do."

Charlotte nodded. "Are you staying here the whole time?"

"Just for a little while. I have to go back to the medical clinic to see some people."

"I'll make you a picture to take back to work."

"That sounds great," Bailey said. "I'll be sitting with Kylie."

"Okay."

Charlotte picked up a crayon, and Bailey found her friend. "Where's Ben?"

"He just texted me. There's an issue on the farm, but he'll be here as soon as he can. Do you want to find somewhere to sit?"

Bailey looked around the classroom. One side of the room was full of chairs. If that was any indication of how many adults the school was expecting, they should find some seats right away.

LEEANNA MORGAN

"That's a good idea." Bailey pointed to some chairs at the back of the room. "Would you mind if we sat over there? I need to leave in about twenty minutes."

"Sounds good to me. When Ben arrives, he can sit beside us without having to maneuver around too many parents."

Bailey sat down and slid her bag under the seat. "Ben's lucky to have you in his life."

Kylie sighed. "I'm the lucky one. If we hadn't needed Christmas trees and mistletoe for our last event, I wouldn't have met him."

It was easy to see how much Kylie loved Ben, and how much his daughter, Charlotte adored Kylie. No matter what issues came their way, Bailey was sure they would be happy.

At the front of the room, teachers were putting away the crayons and moving the tables and chairs.

Kylie frowned. "The choir must be getting ready to sing. I hope Ben makes it here in time."

"So do I." Bailey looked at the people coming through the door. She smiled when she saw Ben. "He's here."

Kylie waved. "Charlotte will be happy. This is a big deal for her."

Bailey studied the faces of the people around her. Charlotte wasn't the only excited person. For once, she was happy to be in a noisy, crowded room. Ninety percent of her day involved helping people through mental health issues, grief, and separation anxiety. It was nice to enjoy something positive.

Ben and another man walked toward them.

Although she'd only been living in Sapphire Bay for a few weeks, Bailey knew most of the people in the small Montana town. She'd seen the person who was with Ben but had never spoken to him. His daughter, on the other hand, was well known to her. Mila was a regular at their Friday youth nights. She loved buttered popcorn, pancakes, and Bailey's personal favorite, strawberry ice cream.

Kylie moved across one seat to give Mila's dad somewhere to sit. "Hi, Steven. It's good to see you."

"It's good to see you, too." Steven's gaze shifted to Bailey.

She held out her hand. With his intense blue eyes and short, dark hair, he looked like the type of person you could trust. "I'm Bailey Jones. I've seen you at The Welcome Center."

Steven's handshake was firm. "You help organize the youth group and have counseling sessions in the meeting rooms."

"That's right. I've spoken to Mila many times. It's nice to meet her dad."

A teacher standing at the front of the room blew into a microphone. Everyone winced as a high-pitched squeal shrieked through the speaker system. "Welcome to our special Christmas event. Our third-grade class has been learning lots of fun songs for today." The woman turned toward the students who were now standing in straight lines behind her. "Without further ado, I'd like to introduce Mrs. Birney's class who will sing, 'Santa Got Stuck Up the Chimney.'"

Charlotte was sitting on the floor in front of the students, smiling at the choir.

Bailey wondered if she recognized anyone. Halfway through the first song Charlotte waved at the choir, and Mila, Steven's daughter, waved back.

The children in Mrs. Birney's class put their heart and soul into the toe-tapping Christmas song. Cell phones flashed as proud parents recorded the performance, and more than one kindergarten student clapped along to the music.

By the time the second song began, Bailey had a big smile

on her face. She didn't know how long her happiness would last, but she was holding onto it for as long as possible—especially if her next two appointments turned out to be as emotionally draining as she imagined.

STEVEN PARKED outside The Welcome Center and looked at Mila. "We're home."

His daughter's happy smile pushed any worries about still living here to the back of his mind. "Do you think Mr. Whiskers is inside?"

Mr. Whiskers was the center's resident cat. When they'd first arrived in Sapphire Bay, Mila had been upset. She didn't understand why they had to leave Chicago. Why the life they were living would only lead to disaster. But when Mr. Whiskers started visiting their room, Mila's nightmares became less frequent. She started talking to the other children and, eventually, joining in with the center's weekly activities.

Steven looked at the snow-covered parking lot. "Mr. Whiskers will definitely be inside. Besides being too cold out here, it's nearly his dinner time."

"I'd better go to the kitchen. Mr. Whiskers likes it when I help make his dinner."

Before he knew it, Mila had the door open and her school bag in her hands.

"Be careful," he warned. "The ground will be slippery."

Mila threw a smile over her shoulder. It reminded him so much of her mom that his heart ached. "Don't worry. I'll be okay." After making sure no cars were coming, she rushed across the parking lot.

Steven took his lunch box out of the truck and grabbed

Mila's wooly hat and scarf. He didn't want to spend time hunting for them in the morning.

"You look happy."

Steven turned toward the deep voice. "Hi, John. Mila's on a mission to feed Mr. Whiskers."

John looked at Mila as she threw open the center's front door. "She won't be disappointed. Mabel's volunteering in the kitchen tonight."

They both knew that Mabel would make sure everyone who enjoyed feeding Mr. Whiskers was there.

Steven locked the truck. "How was your day?"

"It was great. We found another sponsor for a tiny home and we made another Christmas wish come true."

Steven didn't know how John did so much. Not only was he busy providing pastoral care to the community, but he was also creating a village of tiny houses for people who were homeless.

"When was the last time you had a few days to yourself?"

John buried his hands in his jacket pockets. "I can't remember. It's just as well I love what I do. Otherwise, you'd be telling me to book into a therapy session."

For the last four months, John had been trying to get Steven to go to one of the counseling sessions provided by the church. It was hard enough going to the PTSD support group, let alone telling a complete stranger how he was feeling.

"You don't need to screw your face into a ball. The sessions aren't that bad," John joked as they headed toward The Welcome Center.

"The support group is all I need."

John held open the door. "It's up to you. Thanks for all your help on the tiny homes. Patrick is impressed with your plastering."

"I enjoy working with him and the rest of the team."

Steven paused in the entranceway. "I don't think you realize how grateful I am. Without your support, I wouldn't be working on the tiny homes."

"As soon as Patrick met you, he would have realized what an asset you'd be. Besides, I didn't want you to leave Sapphire Bay. Who would have painted the bedrooms in The Welcome Center if you'd gone back to Chicago?"

"Someone else would have volunteered." When Steven first arrived in Sapphire Bay, he'd found a part-time job pumping gas. In his spare time, he helped other volunteers remodel six of the bedrooms in The Welcome Center.

Even then, he was humbled by the kindness of strangers and the warm welcome they'd received.

Mila rushed into the foyer. "Quick, Dad. Mr. Whiskers is having dinner."

John grinned. "It looks as though you're wanted in the kitchen." He looked down at his cell phone and sighed. "And I'm late for a meeting. I'll see you later."

Steven followed Mila into the kitchen. Four other children who lived at the center sat around Mr. Whiskers' food bowl.

Mabel smiled at Steven. "He's turned into quite the celebrity. Before you know it, he'll have his own fan club."

Each of the children was mesmerized as they watched Mr. Whiskers eat his kibble. The center's resident cat didn't need to start a fan club—he already had one.

AVAILABLE NOW!
Silver Bells
Santa's Secret Helpers, Book 3

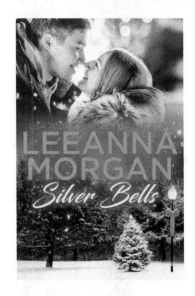

ENJOY MORE BOOKS BY LEEANNA MORGAN

Montana Brides:

Book 1: Forever Dreams (Gracie and Trent)

Book 2: Forever in Love (Amy and Nathan)

Book 3: Forever After (Nicky and Sam)

Book 4: Forever Wishes (Erin and Jake)

Book 5: Forever Santa (A Montana Brides Christmas Novella)

Book 6: Forever Cowboy (Emily and Alex)

Book 7: Forever Together (Kate and Dan)

Book 8: Forever and a Day (Sarah and Jordan)

Montana Brides Boxed Set: Books 1-3

Montana Brides Boxed Set: Books 4-6

The Bridesmaids Club:

Book 1: All of Me (Tess and Logan)

Book 2: Loving You (Annie and Dylan)

Book 3: Head Over Heels (Sally and Todd)

Book 4: Sweet on You (Molly and Jacob)

The Bridesmaids Club: Books 1-3

Emerald Lake Billionaires:

Book 1: Sealed with a Kiss (Rachel and John)

Book 2: Playing for Keeps (Sophie and Ryan)

Book 3: Crazy Love (Holly and Daniel)

Book 4: One And Only (Elizabeth and Blake)

Emerald Lake Billionaires: Books 1-3

The Protectors:

Book 1: Safe Haven (Hayley and Tank)

Book 2: Just Breathe (Kelly and Tanner)

Book 3: Always (Mallory and Grant)

Book 4: The Promise (Ashley and Matthew)

The Protectors Boxed Set: Books 1-3

Montana Promises:

Book 1: Coming Home (Mia and Stan)

Book 2: The Gift (Hannah and Brett)

Book 3: The Wish (Claire and Jason)

Book 4: Country Love (Becky and Sean)

Montana Promises Boxed Set: Books 1-3

Sapphire Bay:

Book 1: Falling For You (Natalie and Gabe)

Book 2: Once In A Lifetime (Sam and Caleb)

Book 3: A Christmas Wish (Megan and William)

Book 4: Before Today (Brooke and Levi)

Book 5: The Sweetest Thing (Cassie and Noah)

Book 6: Sweet Surrender (Willow and Zac)

Sapphire Bay Boxed Set: Books 1-3

Sapphire Bay Boxed Set: Books 4-6

Santa's Secret Helpers:

Book 1: Christmas On Main Street (Emma and Jack)

Book 2: Mistletoe Madness (Kylie and Ben)

Book 3: Silver Bells (Bailey and Steven)

Book 4: The Santa Express (Shelley and John)

Book 5: Endless Love (The Jones Family)

Santa's Secret Helpers Boxed Set: Books 1-3

Return To Sapphire Bay:

Book 1: The Lakeside Inn (Penny and Wyatt)

Book 2: Summer At Lakeside (Diana and Ethan)

Book 3: A Lakeside Thanksgiving (Barbara and Theo)

Book 4: Christmas At Lakeside (Katie and Peter)

Return to Sapphire Bay Boxed Set (Books 1-3)

The Cottages on Anchor Lane:

Book 1: The Flower Cottage (Paris and Richard)

Book 2: The Starlight Café (Andrea and David)

Book 3: The Cozy Quilt Shop (Shona and Joseph)

Book 4: A Stitch in Time (Jackie and Aidan)

CPSIA information can be obtained
at www.ICGtesting.com
Printed in the USA
BVHW050931230423
662871BV00028B/889